The Graft

KAREN WOODS

EMPIRE
PUBLICATIONS

First published in 2019

EMPIRE PUBLICATIONS
1 Newton Street, Manchester M1 1HW

ISBN: 978-1-909360-65-5

Printed in Great Britain.

ACKNOWLEDGEMENTS

Wow... 20 novels later!! Thanks to all my readers and the people who have supported me. Firstly, let me thank my lovely husband James for always being there and supporting me throughout my writing career. He is a special man and I love him now and forever; me and you forever kid! Thank you to Teenage Works and the staff and pupils there. Each of them has been inspirational to me during writing this book. Thanks to my children Ashley, Blake. Declan and Darcy and all my grandchildren.

I have already started my 21st novel called Hot Flush so watch out for that. Thanks to John and Ashley at Empire for nurturing my talent over the past 9 years and the ever-vigilant Caroline Burch for proofreading my work.

www.evolvemanchester.co.uk

www.karenwoods.net

Follow me on Facebook twitter and Instagram

My last thanks as always goes to my son in heaven Dale xxx

My brother Darren is never far from my thoughts when I'm writing you are my Angel always love and miss you every single day our kid... love you always xxx

Love,

Karen

The book is in memory of Darren Woods (Woody)
a legend always

CHAPTER ONE

Tony Clayton stood back from the rain-soaked windows scratching vigorously at his nuts. His greasy matted hair was stuck up all over the show like the eighties TV character "Worzel Gummidge". He could have done with a good scrub, sheep-dipping in fact.

Tony stretched his arms above his head as he looked out over his surroundings. His fingernails were long and discoloured with dark brown grit lodged deep underneath the nail bed. He smirked and scraped the crust from his dry cracked lips. "Another day in paradise," he whispered under his breath. The dark grey clouds hung low in the sky above him and it looked like it was going to hammer it down. Manchester's weather was crap and every day for the last few days it had been pissing it down; grey skies, dark nights, depressing weather.

Tony Clayton loved living on the tenth floor of a tower block and he always told everyone he could smell a rat a mile away living where he did. He was on the ball, always prepared for any prick who thought they were booming his front door down to stab him up. And many would, they'd do him in if he owed them money or they had a beef with him. These men would batter him within an inch of his life; scar him and stab him up, but Tony was smart. He never told anyone where he lived, and he always kept his head down when the shit hit the fan. He was a coward who would run a mile at the first sign of trouble. The life he lived was a colourful one. He was always ducking and diving and watching his back, but when he put his neck on the line every day and dabbled in the drug world, what could he expect?

Everything came with a price. A good arse-kicking was just one in a long list of occupational hazards for Tony Clayton. He was always rubbing somebody up the wrong way and it was only a matter of time before he would end up in a body bag. He was a shady character for sure, and no one could trust him as far as they could throw him. He'd have your eyes out and be back for the sockets given the chance. Tony was lucky to still be alive, truth be told. He'd had a fair few beatings over the years. He'd had his teeth knocked out, got several black eyes and had his nose broken many times, but it never deterred him from earning a few extra quid. He'd been stabbed up and even put in a boot of a car; yet he still carried on the life he was living. He was brain-dead and never learned his lesson. His best friend Mickey was just the same. He was another double-agent.

Tony had promised his family that he was going to sort his head out and get a job but that was just pure bullshit. He was a great liar – he'd just kept chatting shit to keep them off his case. He'd lied for so long that he wouldn't know the truth if it hit him full in the face. He lived in a fantasy world. It was the safe place in his mind where he could see a life without any problems; no crime, and no more drugs.

Tony had led a good life when he was younger but

that was so long ago that he'd forgotten what it felt like. Back when he was a young lad and wet behind his ears, he'd often tell his mates about how he could have been a professional footballer. It was true too; he was shit hot back in the day. His parents supported him and everyone who knew him thought he was set for stardom. What went wrong? Why wasn't he rolling in cash and living the high life? What happened to his dreams, his future, his football career?

Tony rubbed his knuckles into the corner of his eyes and scanned the area. He was knackered and ready for bed. This was the first time he'd been home in days. He had been on another drug binge, chilling with his mates, smoking crack, injecting heroin, popping pills. When he was in this mind-set he didn't give a flying fuck about anyone or anything except getting twisted and off his napper. They could all just fuck off pecking his head and leave him alone. He got wrecked and put all his problems to the back of his mind. Nothing mattered when he was spaced out. Tony had a head full of shit going on in his life and every now and then he just needed time on his own to chill-out and find peace and quiet away from his missus and his kids. Man-time he called it, with no nagging from her indoors. No pressure, no moaning, just him and his drugs. Tony scanned the area as he sucked in a large mouthful of crisp morning air. All was quiet for now and there was nothing for him to worry about. His beady eyes flicked one way then the other, he was safe, but it was still early, just after nine o'clock in the morning. The Post Office mob should be up soon, queuing at the doors waiting to cash their weekly benefits. The 'Monday Club' was well known to everyone who resided there. Fuck the bills and whoever else they owed money to; they were getting drunk on whatever money they had. Debtors could whistle; they weren't getting a carrot.

The Monsall Estate never really came to life until night time. Everybody was still getting some shut eye, recovering from the night before. There were few residents who worked on the estate and everyone thought they were stupid for getting up at the crack of dawn when they could have laid in their pit until all hours and still get paid for it. It was a no-brainer in their eyes. Riding the system was the way forward: disability benefits, universal credit, money for being sat on your arse all day doing nothing. Tony jerked his head back and spat out a great big ball of green phlegm from the back of his throat over the balcony. It spun for a few seconds before it dropped to the ground. He'd spent many an hour here bored, doing the exact same thing. It kept him entertained for hours. If he had a target to aim at it was even better. An old man, a dog, a kid, anything. They all made great targets. Tony dragged his bony body back inside the flat as he shivered, goose-bumps appearing over his pale grey flesh. Tony was full of spots and pimples. He had oily skin and hadn't had a good scrub in a long time. He was a soap dodger for sure. The doctor had told him he had scabies, but he'd never applied any of the cream that had been prescribed. He just kept thinking it would get better on its own.

He pushed the door open and went back inside his gaff. The place stank of stale cigarettes and wet dog. He was coughing and spluttering and looked like he was going to collapse. His chest was rattling like an old boiler. He plonked down on the sofa and sat with his head in his hands. "Fuck me," he mumbled under his breath. Small beads of sweat trickled down the side of his face. His body was rattling for drugs again; he was craving the heroin he'd been injecting into his veins for as long as he could remember. He was a silly bastard and he knew it; he could have kicked himself for ever letting himself get involved with the drug world. He only tried smack for a buzz at first. He was young and foolish and wanted to impress his mates. Everyone was doing it and he wanted to see what all the fuss about. Okay, he was young and naïve, but somebody should have warned him what he was getting into, but nobody did. Why would they when he was putting money into their pockets, helping them to get a new motor, and aiding them to live a nice cushy life with a few quid behind them. He had been young and foolish. It only took a few toots of the gear to get him interested in heroin and before he knew it the brown had got a firm grip of him and made him a prisoner.

Heroin was his master now and no matter how hard he tried, the drug still ruled his every breath, his every movement. As soon as Tony opened his eyes each morning it was there, calling his name, commanding him to feed the habit. He'd tried a million times to get clean, but it never happened. It was so hard, and he just couldn't do it. He always told his family that when he had enough money he was going to go into rehab and go cold turkey but to date it was just another dream that he had floating around his head, more bullshit even he believed.

Frank, the red-nosed pit-bull waddled over to his owner and placed his head next to his leg, nudging it, slapping its chops. He was craving affection just as his owner was. Tony lifted his eyes up slowly and swallowed hard as he looked directly into his pet's conker coloured brown eyes. His fingers ran over the deep cuts above Frank's eyes as he let out a laboured breath. "Messed up, again didn't I, son? I thought you could have taken that other dog down and earned us a few quid. What happened to you mate? I thought you were ruthless. I've seen you before ripping other dogs apart. You are a warrior," he smiled at his four-legged friend and raised his eyebrows high. "Look at the Jack Russell you savaged the other week in the park. You ragged it all over the fucking show. Threw it up in the air you did. Leathered it in fact." Frank looked at his owner and tilted its head slightly. Maybe it did understand what he was saying, maybe it didn't but for now Frank was the only one Tony could talk to about his problems, the only one he could pour his heart out to and the only one who wouldn't judge him. Tony swallowed hard, snivelling. His head shook slowly as a ball of emotion strangled his windpipe. Regrets about the choices he'd made during his life came flooding back. He picked up a medicine bottle off the table, popped a few more white tablets and threw the bottle behind him. "I can't do this shit anymore, Frank. Look at the state of this gaff. We've got nothing, not a pot to piss in," he gripped the dog's face closer to his own and rubbed his head along the animal's ears. His voice was low. "Go on, tell me where my next fix is going to come from, tell me where I'm going to get some money to make things better? The ball and chain will be up out of bed soon and fuck knows what I'm going to tell her. You know as well as me that she'll go ape when she's knows I've got no money left. She'll pack my stuff again and I'll be carted from here. My arse will be kicked right to the kerb."

Frank plonked down on the floor next to him and started to go to sleep. One quick lick of his ball bag and Frank was ready for shut-eye. No one was listening to Tony, not even his four-legged friend. Tony lay down on the sofa and looped his arms behind his sweaty head. He froze and held his ear towards the door. He could hear movement in the house and so quickly closed his eyes. The dragon was out of her pit and on the war path. If she saw him asleep maybe she would leave him to get a bit of kip before she kicked off and caused blue murder. He rolled on his side, hid his head underneath the pillow and made no movement whatsoever.

CHAPTER TWO

Elsie creaked open the living room door and stepped inside with her hands held firmly on her hips. Her temper was bubbling, and her cheeks were bright red, she was fuming. She stood looking at her husband lying on the sofa and snarled. What a waste of space! The moment he opened his eyes she'd one bomb him and make sure he was aware of what he'd done. The bullshit just rolled from this man's tongue and she didn't believe a word he said anymore. It was just one lie after the other; bullshit, bullshit and more bullshit. Elsie thought she could save Tony when she'd first met him, she thought they could help each other to have a half decent life. His family life at home was horrific when he was younger, and he had mental scars for sure, but it never worked out. He always had an excuse why he couldn't change but he'd never really tried to turn his life round. Her relationship with her husband was toxic and they rarely had a good word to say to one another anymore. He made her blood boil and she couldn't stand the sight of him half of the time. Her marriage was on the rocks, but she still stayed by her husband's side.

She knew that she should have left him years ago and found a life of peace and tranquillity. She knew she didn't need him and that she could get by on her own, she'd done it before and she could do it again. Yet here she was looking at her sorry excuse for a husband sleeping off yet another bender...

Yanking her black leggings up her waist she stormed over to where he was lying and prodded her fat finger deep into his rib-cage. "Oi, cheeky bollocks. You better wake up now and get your scruffy arse out of here. Do you think I'm some dickhead who will let you take the piss out of me?" She stood over him, waiting for any sign of life but he didn't move a muscle. Elsie hovered for a few seconds, her fists gathering into two rounded balls. She was ready to punch his lights out. Elsie was a scrapper, a rough bird who'd had her fair share of heartache. She'd had to fight all her life and she'd learned a long time ago that she had to toughen up if she was ever to survive in the world she lived in with Tony.

Taking a deep breath, she closed her eyes and shook her head. What was the point? It was just more extra stress that she didn't need in her life. Her nerves were shattered. He'd probably say it was all her fault, turn the tables on her and make her feel like shit again. The best form of defence was attack and Tony had this down to a tee. He knew how to make her feel guilty when she kicked off with him. He always played the victim. Elsie backed away and sat down in the chair facing him. She spoke in a clear voice and made sure he could hear every word she said. "I'm not arsed anymore Tony. I'll sit here all day until you wake up and then you'll be gone from here for good. You better have the money you owe me too, because if you haven't, I'll scratch your fucking eyes out. You're a cheeky bastard. A liberty taker." She froze for a few seconds and studied him, but there was nothing, no sign of life. "What kind of man are you? You left me with nothing; no money, no cigs, no fuck all. You're a selfish bastard who only thinks about himself. How do you expect me to feed the kids when I'm skint?" She sat back and gritted her teeth tightly together. She was getting angry. "No, this isn't happening anymore. I'm done with you Tony Clayton. It's the last straw. I'm better off on my jacks than with a wanker like you. You're sucking every bit of life out of me. I'm drained with you every bastard day." Elsie wiped a tear that was rolling down the side of her cheek. She was emotional and couldn't take much more of the life she was living.

Emily walked into the living room and sighed as she clocked her father sprawled on the sofa. She spoke in a sarcastic tone. "So, he's back then, is he? Where has he been this time?" Emily sat down on the ragged carpet and looked over at her mother for an answer.

Elsie growled as she looked over at Tony. "Oh, he's not said a bleeding word yet. I've just got up out of bed and found him here, asleep. He probably sneaked in early this morning. He's a rat, a low-life twat. I swear, I'll cut his fucking balls off when he wakes up. This is far from over."

Emily rolled her eyes and pulled her grey t-shirt over her chubby pink knees. "It's freezing in here mam. Is there any heating on or what?" Her mother let out a laboured breath and shook her head just like she always did when she'd let her daughter down. It was so unfair. She was trying her best to get on top of things but every time she thought she had things in order, Tony messed them up. It would take her weeks to get straight again. He was a selfish bastard, there was no other word for him. Elsie ragged her hands through her hair in desperation. She had to answer her, admit to her daughter that she'd messed up again.

"Don't you think I don't know it's cold. It's that cunts fault over there," she pointed her finger over at the body on the sofa. "He's spent the money again, just like he always does when he has a few quid in his pocket."

Emily opened her eyes wide. "So, we have no heating? Brilliant, just brilliant. I'll have to freeze, then won't I? What about having a bath, I stink?"

Elsie was losing the plot, she'd already told her the answer, was she thick or what? "No, we don't have any fucking heating. Emily, don't you start pecking my head too. Don't you think I've got enough going on with that prick over there without you adding to it? Just turn it in and shut up for five bleeding minutes and let me wake up properly."

Emily rested her chin on her knees and looked around the front room. The place was a shit-tip, clothes were all over the show and dirty dishes were left on every available surface. No wonder she wouldn't let any of her friends come round, it was a disgrace. Emily yawned and rubbed at her cold legs with her flat palm. "I'm going to Jane's," she said rolling her eyes. "At least I'll be warm there and she'll let me have a nice warm bath. I'm just as fed up as you are mother, so don't take your mood out on me. He's the one in the wrong, not me. Sort him out and tell him straight that you're not putting up with it anymore."

Elsie dipped her head. She was aware that she'd let her kids down. She was at the end of her tether and knew her husband was dragging her down with every day that passed. She replied to Emily in a softer tone. "I'm sorry. I'll sort it out later. I'll get a borrow from Tina or something. Just leave it with me for now. You know I always pull something out of the bag when we're up shit-street."

Emily stood and walked towards the door. "I'm going to get ready," she paused. "Mam, we need to sort him out. Every week he's like this. Why can't he just be normal and go to work like everyone else's dad? He's an embarrassment. Honest, I'm ashamed to even say I'm related to him." Elsie sat twisting the empty space on her fingers. The gold band was gone, and you could see she was missing the small piece of jewellery that used to be there. The wedding ring was in the pawn shop again. Twenty quid she'd pawned it for, enough to keep her family afloat for a couple of days. The living room door closed, and Elsie just sat staring at her other half. Her eyes clouded over, and she knew she would have to find a way to put some food on the table for her children. Maybe, if she got lucky down the shops, she could lift a few items to sell. Anything but sell her body, she'd never ever do that again. Then again most of the security guys knew her by face and she'd be watched like a hawk from the moment she stepped inside the store.

There was her family – before she'd always been able to tap them for a few quid, but they'd told her straight that while she was still married to Tony, they wanted nothing to do with her. They'd put the block on any hand-outs a long time ago. No more food parcels, no clothes, nothing. She was banished from ever returning to the family home. Elsie's parents were good people, they went to work and had a nice home. They were ashamed that their daughter had got herself hitched up with this dead-leg. Her father had pleaded with her not to marry Tony Clayton. He could see right through him and knew he was nothing but trouble. That scumbag could never give his daughter the life he wanted her to have and he knew without a shadow of doubt that it was him who got her dabbling in drugs too. He'd watched his daughter's downfall over the years, and he was heartbroken that his little princess, who'd he'd watched grow up, was disappearing with every day that passed. She was a shell of her former self. Where was the daughter he'd once known, the happy go lucky-girl who'd always told him that she would change the world one day and help people in need. Elsie had robbed from her family and done things to them that she wasn't proud of. The list was endless. Her father was the one who finally wiped his hands of her and carted her from the family home. He'd done everything to help her get clean, but she'd never once made him proud and turned her life around, she was a lost cause in his eyes, her life was set in stone now.

Elsie shifted in her chair. Something needed to give in her life and quickly. She reached over, got the medicine bottle from the table to the left of her and twisted the lid off. She held it in her hand for a few seconds and closed her eyes before she necked it. This was her methadone, her way out of the mess that was her life. For six months now she'd been trying to get clean, but it was him, that cunt lying over there who always made her fuck up every time she could see a light at the end of the tunnel. He dragged her back to square one every time she was getting better. He never actually said it, but she knew deep down that he didn't want her to get clean without him. She'd even told him they could do it together, go through it all as a team; the cold-turkey, the tremors, helping each other every step of the way, but he would never give it a go. He was weak. He always said he wasn't ready, but he would never be ready. It was always one excuse after another.

Elsie needed to make some big changes in her life if she was ever going to be normal again. She missed her family so much and she always dreamed of them being back in her life. Elsie often went and sat on the wall facing her parent's house reminiscing about the good old days, the days when she was a young girl and she had a bright future ahead of her. She could see the back garden from where she sat, the place she used to sit with her friends and practice her handstands and cart-wheels. Frank had woken up now and she spoke to the family pet to help ease her frustration. This animal was the family therapist, everyone spoke to Frank about their problems. The poor thing, no wonder he was tired all the time. It was Elsie's turn to bend his ear. She stroked the top of his head as she spoke. "Frank, you can see with your own two eyes what I have to put up with every single day. How can I help somebody who won't help themselves? God knows I've tried, but he just takes the piss out of me and he thinks he can talk me round when he's fucked up." Frank circled on the spot which was a sign that he needed to go out for a walk. It was either that or he would shit near the front door, like he always did when he was bursting for a crap. Elsie could see the signs and struggled to get up from her seat, she wobbled to her feet. If she didn't take the dog for a walk nobody would. She glanced over at her husband one last time and left the room with the dog following closely behind her. She would deal with him when she came back.

★

Emily sat on her bed, freezing. It was a scruffy room, but all her belongings were neat and tidy. Black mould crept along the ceiling, ripped wallpaper hung from the walls. The teenage girl lay on her bed and began texting on her phone, she was smiling as her fingers moved at speed. Her phone was her pride and joy and she never left it unattended. Her dad would have had it away without a shadow of doubt. He was like that; he'd nick anything to feed his habit when he was roasting for a fix. He'd done it before and he'd do it again given half the chance. He'd deny it, swear that black was blue to protest his innocence, but she knew deep inside he was the guilty party when anything went missing, he was never a good liar.

Something was making Emily smile, she was blushing and rolling about on her bed. A few weeks ago, she'd started talking to a new guy on Facebook. He was gorgeous and she never thought that in a million years he would be interested in her. Alright, she'd made herself out to have a fabulous life and a career and she'd even told him she was eighteen to keep him interested, but what harm was she doing? It was just a bit of fun. Nobody was getting hurt and it helped her escape the shit life she was living every single day at home with these bunch of half-wits. Her heart skipped a beat every time she got a message alert on her phone. It was constant messaging, all day long and well into night.

The guy had asked her to meet up a few times and she knew sooner or later she would have to tell him she wasn't the person she'd made out to be. But she didn't want this feeling to end, this fantasy world she was creating in her own head. It was perfect. The man complimented her all the time and he even called her "Babe". She'd never had anybody who treated her like this. She felt loved, cared for, pretty and attractive for the first time in her life. Everything he said to her made her heart skip a beat and made her feel better about her shit, stinking life. Mark had sent a few snaps of himself over the last few weeks and he was still waiting on Emily to send one back, a recent one of herself. He was always asking for rude photographs if truth be told; snaps of her tits and other body parts but she'd never sent him any. Her boobs were too small anyway and to show anyone her swollen pink nipples was never on the agenda. They looked like two fried eggs. Not now, not ever. Her body parts were private, and they were staying like that. Well, for now anyway. Emily sat back and took a deep breath. It was time to take a selfie. She leaned one way then another, changing her expression with each snap, puckering her lips tightly together. She looked at each picture, examined every inch of them and once she'd changed filters and backgrounds she smiled. At last she found a photograph that was half decent. She cringed as she sent it over to Mark in a text message with two red love heart emoji's at the side of it. Her mind was racing. What if he didn't like her anymore? What if there were no more messages from him? Fuck, fuck fuck, she'd messed it all up.

Her heart was racing and already she was regretting sending him a snap. She kept picking her phone up and checking it constantly. He was taking ages to reply, much longer than he normally did. It was over for sure; she had a gut feeling. Emily sat up on the bed and folded her arms tightly in front of her chest. She'd ruined it, she'd never hear from him again. Why did she ever send him the photograph? Her face said it all, she was gutted.

Just as she was giving up, the phone vibrated. Her eyes were dancing with excitement. Taking deep breaths, she prepared herself for the worse. Her eyes scanned the text message. "You are gorgeous," was the reply. She read the message over and over again and held her mobile phone close to her heart. Maybe Mark would be the man she would marry and have children with? The one who would take her away from this dump and give her the life she'd always wanted. Nice white fluffy bath towels, nice furniture and a home she could invite all her friends to and be proud of. No more threadbare carpets, no more ripped wallpaper hanging from the walls and no mouldy black fungus growing on the ceilings. No, she would have a lovely clean house that smelt fresh. There was no way her dad would be invited to her new home either, not while people were there anyway. He could come when she was alone, when nobody could see him.

Emily started humming a tune and flopped down

on the bed, she was staring at the ceiling, smiling. She was excited to tell Jane about Mark, she would be gobsmacked. Jane had been her best friend since they were babies and they were as thick as thieves. They were both in the circle of trust and knew each other inside out. Jane was a lot prettier than Emily and her family life was a million miles away from Emily's. Both Jane's parents worked, and her home was a palace compared with Emily's. Jane's mother loved to hear about the problems of her daughter's friend, and she couldn't wait to see her to get an update on her family life. She would sit on the edge of her seat, enthralled about the stories Emily told her. Her friend's life was a million miles away from her own. When she told her friend's mother about the loan sharks who knocked at their front door (every day for over a week) for the money her mother owed them, she was gobsmacked. She'd wondered how anyone could live like that. She'd asked why the family was borrowing money in the first place when they should have been managing the money they had. Jane's mother was organised, every bill was paid on time, nothing ever out of place, she was a bit OCD really. Emily lay looking at the photo of Mark, she slowly stroked her long fingernail along his chiselled jawbone and snuggled deep into her pillow. "I think I love you already," she whispered.

What the hell was she getting into?

CHAPTER THREE

Tony had been asleep for over an hour. He'd dozed off listening to his wife moaning. Gradually, one eye opened slightly and then the other one followed. Lying still, he listened carefully inside the room. Nobody was about, he was sure of it. Silence. Twisting his body round slowly he scanned the living room. He was alone. Phew, that was close. He whistled and shouted in a loud voice. "Frank, come on son. Come to daddy." Sitting up straight he whistled again. "Frank, come on lad." Nothing. Tony sat scratching his head with his legs spread wide apart. He was mumbling under his breath as he stood to his feet. This could be a trap. His missus could be lurking, hidden away, waiting to capture him before he went out. He tiptoed about the room, aware he could get whacked over the head at any second. Elsie was a head the ball when her cage was rattled. She was an evil bitch and a snapper. The scar on his head told you that. She'd whacked him with a baseball bat when they were at logger-heads. If it hadn't been for his son Jordan, she would have gone to town on him and finished him off. Tony had ended up with six stitches. Elsie had anger issues. Once she was in the zone and the red mist came down there was no going back. A proper nut-case she was.

Tony started to relax, he could see his wife's black padded jacket was missing from the peg in the hallway.

He headed into the kitchen and rubbed at his body to keep warm. "Fuck me, it's freezing in here," he mumbled. Yanking the fridge door open he bent down slightly and peered inside. The end of a cucumber, mouldy tomatoes and an empty bottle of milk was all that he could see. He stared in the fridge for a few seconds more and slammed the door shut. Yep, the penny had dropped, and he'd realised that he'd spent the shopping money again. No wonder Elsie was gunning for him. Tony walked back into the living room and headed toward the balcony. He rammed a dimp from the ashtray into his mouth and held the lighter to the end of it, sucking at it with all his might. Once it was lit, he stood looking out onto the estate. He needed to earn some money and fast. Alright, alright, he'd fucked up, but he could make things better and fix this mess if he was given the chance. Once he'd been down to the shops, he was sure to earn a few quid; if he lifted a few packets of razors and batteries it would be enough to buy some bread and milk at least. He pulled his jeans up over his scrawny waistline and flicked the cigarette butt over the balcony. He had to be quick and get his arse out of here before Elsie came back. He needed to let her calm down when she was like this - if she knew he was pot-less she would rip his head off. Turning around on the spot he headed back inside. It was probably warmer on the balcony than it was inside the house.

Tony froze and nearly jumped out of his skin. His eyes were wide open and he looked as if he'd seen a ghost. "Yes, you may as well look at me like that, dad. You're lucky my mam isn't here because you would be lay on your back by now. You've only got yourself to blame. And, don't expect me to stick up for you this time because you've caused it all yourself. Just like you always do."

Tony was defensive. "Come on Emily, don't be like that sweetheart. You know as much as me that she goes over the top. I went out for a few beers with the lads that's all. Where is the crime in that?"

"The crime is that you left us with no food or gas Dad. I can't even have a bath. That's just a basic thing that a child needs, and you can't even provide that. You should have put me in care or left me at nana's if you couldn't look after me. Given me a chance to live a decent life."

Tony was shocked. Where had all this come from? It wasn't as if he'd done something really bad, was it? "I'll make some money soon and everything will be back to normal. Don't I always come up trumps when we have fuck all?"

"No, dad. It's never normal in this house. You two do my head in arguing all the time and we never have nothing; no money, no decent food, and no family life. Go on, when have we ever done stuff like a normal family?"

Tony edged to the sofa and sat down. He never expected this. "We do loads of stuff. We go shopping together, we play cards, and we have a film night. That's family time. What more do you want?"

"Dad, when we go shopping and you and mam are shoplifting. As for film night, when was the last time we all sat down and watched a film together? You're either twisted or pissed out of your head. I want a dad, someone to take care of us all. You know," her eyes were wide open as she stressed her words. "A father who protects us all at any cost."

Tony swallowed hard; she'd hit a nerve. He choked up and dropped his head. "I would do anything for my family. Nobody will ever hurt us. I'd do any cunt in if they ever laid a single finger on any of you. Oh yes, don't underestimate me. I'm a nutter when I get going."

Emily sighed. Words needed to be said here today and she was holding nothing back. "Dad, you're a smackhead. We live in a shit-tip and me and our kid are lucky to still be alive. Don't you think it's time to grow up and kick the drugs in the head. Maybe take us on holiday?" Her eyes were wide open, and she was staring directly at him. "Go on Dad. Promise me now you will take us all on holiday. Put your kids before drugs for once in your life."

Tony was shocked. "Ay, you cheeky cow. Don't you dare speak to me like that otherwise you'll get a bleeding slap. I'm your old man, have some respect. You've been listening to the way your mother speaks to me; she's rubbed off on you."

Emily rolled her eyes and plonked down on the chair with her arms folded tightly in front of her. Okay, she'd over stepped the mark and hurt his feelings, but so what? He needed telling. "I'm just saying that's all. It's not a big thing to ask is it? I mean, how hard is it to get some money together for a holiday. I'm sixteen now. It would be a great present for us all to go on holiday. It's what we need. Imagine it, no drugs, no beer, no tablets. Just our family being normal for once."

Tony was on the spot, fidgeting about. He sucked hard on his gums and stuck his chest out. "Well, if that's what you want then I'll sort it out. You know I never let you down. Maybe, I needed a kick up the arse and you've just given it to me. Consider it done. If you want a holiday, then a family holiday it shall be."

Emily chuckled and shook her head. If she had a pound for every time he'd promised her something, she'd be a rich girl. "That's debatable isn't it, dad?"

Tony shrugged his shoulders. "Nar, when I say I'm doing something, I fucking well do it. Go on, tell me when I've let you down before. I always stick to my word."

Emily chuckled. Did she need to remind him of the past? "Dad, you said I could get a new pair of trainers for the school trip last month," she paused and held her head to the side. "What happened to them, ay?"

"Oi, come on now. I told you what happened. I had the money and got had over. Those dirty bastards down the boozer robbed me. I had the money safely stashed in my pocket and they must have seen me steaming drunk and dipped me when I fell asleep."

"Yeah, yeah, yeah. You have a story for everything don't you? In fact, you are the unluckiest man who walked this planet. Nothing is ever straightforward with you. Something always happens. You should write a book about it all, it would be a best seller."

Tony sniggered; he knew his daughter was onto him. She wasn't a baby anymore and he knew she was a wise-head, just like he was. Looking over at his daughter, a sadness filled his body and strangled around his heart. He'd let her down, he'd let them all down.

He swallowed hard and struggled to speak. It was time to have a heart to heart. "Things have just got on top of me lately love. You know with no work, no money, no fuck all really."

Emily couldn't believe what she was hearing. Did he think she'd come over on the banana boat? "Since when have you been looking for a job? You've never worked a day in your life. You said it yourself that you couldn't hold down a nine till five job, so stop lying."

Tony's eyes opened wide. "I'm always down at the jobcentre looking for work. I've told them I will do anything to earn some money. I'd clean shitters, mop floors, anything to get me out of this mess we're in. See what I mean? You don't know the half of it. You need to stop listening to your mother. All she does is bad mouth me. She's out of order."

Emily was pissing in the wind and just sat listening to him waffle. The lies just rolled from his tongue. One after the other, he just couldn't help himself. The front door slammed shut and Tony gasped. He kept his voice low. He was trembling, his hands were shaking. He dragged his daughter back by her arm. "Emily you stay in here with me. She won't be as bad if you're here. Tell her that I'm taking us all on holiday too, that should help her calm down."

She wriggled free from his grip and smirked over at him. "No way, Dad. You're on your own. I'm going to Jane's. This is your mess, so you can sort it out. Our Jordan should be here soon, so he can protect you. I'm getting off. It's your own fault for pissing the shopping money up the wall. Deal with it." Emily smiled over at him and walked to the door. "Good luck, I wouldn't want to be in your shoes when she gets hold of you. She's livid. I'm off out."

Tony sat cracking his fingers. *Fuck, fuck, fuck.* He never even said goodbye to Emily. It was like waiting on death row, his arse was twitching for sure. Frank came rushing into the room first. His tail was wagging at speed and he headed straight over to Tony. He quickly reached over for him. "Come here boy. Where have you been? Have you been out for a walk?" Frank was panting, and slaver was hanging from the side of his mouth. He shook his head and the warm wet clear liquid from his mouth went flying all over the sofa. "Fucking hell, Frank. Look at me now, you scruffy twat. Why do you always do that?" He pushed the animal away with a firm hand. "Go on, do one now. Go and lie down. You scruffy fucker." Frank had his marching orders and knew by his owner's tone of voice that he'd done something wrong. Tony was wiping his jeans when he felt the air change. A cold, eerie silence filled the room. Lifting his eyes slowly he could see her feet not far from him. He cringed and knew he'd have to face the music. His head lifted with caution. "Hello baby. I wondered where you were." He gulped and waited for a reply.

Elsie was ready for him, she was fuming. He was getting told without a shadow of doubt. She'd waited all morning for this, he was getting a mouthful. "Don't you fucking 'baby' me, you wanker. Get into that bedroom, get every stitch of clothing that you own and get out of this house. I told you last time that it was your last chance and you didn't listen. Are you thick or something? Is there something missing in that daft brain of yours?"

Tony held his hands up in the air. "For fuck's sake, love. Don't be bin-bagging me over this. I've done nothing wrong. Fuck me! Shoot me for having a few beers with some old pals. Johnny got out of the big-house after a four stretch and we just ended up getting on it. Nothing was planned, honest. I just got caught up in the moment."

"Fuck off out of my face. Every bastard time it's always another lie. Just tell the truth for once in your fucking worthless life. I might have a bit of respect for you then."

Tony knew he needed to pull something special out of the bag to get out of this one. He'd have to put an Oscar winning performance to wriggle out of this one. "Babe, may God strike me down right now if I'm lying. I'll get Mickey here to tell you himself, if you don't believe me. You know me, I'm as honest as the day is long." Elsie walked over to him and booted his foot. There was only so much bullshit anyone could listen to in one day.

"So, if it was a party then, you won't have spent the money you had. I mean, what party makes you pay for your beer?"

Tony's nose started to twitch, he rubbed his flat palm over it and licked his dry cracked lips rapidly. He had to think on his feet and stood up protesting his innocence. "Babes, I've got the money. I told Mickey to mind it, so I didn't spend it. That's where I'm going now. On my life. I'll have the hundred quid to you within the hour. Just let me get sorted and I'll burn around there and get it. I can't believe you think I'm lying. What do you take me for? Bang out of order you are."

Tony made to get up and grab his coat, but Elsie pushed him back down with force. She gripped him by the scruff of his neck and went nose to nose with him, her warm stale breath spraying into his face. "I don't believe a word you say. Get in there and pack your shit up. I told you I meant it last time, and you still think you can have me over! Did you really think you could just walk back in here and everything would be alright?"

Tony upped the ante. He knew she wasn't joking, "Baby just give me an hour or so and I'll show you I'm telling the truth. I know I've told you a few white lies in the past but not this time love. Honest, I'm telling you the truth. Just let me prove it to you."

Elsie growled and showed her crooked yellow teeth. "You left me with fuck all for days. We could have been dead for all you cared. We had no bread, no gas and the electric meter has two-pound fifty left on it. I've had one packet of pickled onion "Space Raiders" to last me since seven o'clock last night. You're a cheeky cunt and you know it! Don't try and smooth this over because I'm not listening. I'm throwing the towel in. Me and you are over."

Tony moved her hand from his neck and looked directly in her eyes. He always pulled this move when the shit hit the fan. "I love you more than anything. I'd never do anything to hurt you on purpose. I admit, I should have come home with the money, but you know what I'm like when I get a few beers down my neck. I was telling all the boys how much I love you.

Honest, I was singing your praises all night long. Telling them what a mint wife you are; understanding, caring."

Elsie backed off and let out a sarcastic laugh. "Go and tell someone who gives a fuck because I'm not listening to a word that comes out of your mouth. Bullshit. Every single last word you speak is bullshit." She twisted back around to face him. He wasn't getting off that easily. "I'll burn everything you own if you don't get it out of here before the day is out. I swear, I'll torch everything. You won't have a stitch of clothing left."

Tony was in a panic. He shoved his trainers on with speed. "You'll see baby. I'll be back in an hour with your money. I swear, you just wait and see. Tony Clayton is a man of his word." He grabbed his coat from the side and quickly put it on. He wanted out of this place before she started launching things at him. He watched her from the corner of his eye as he slithered out of the doorway. "I'll be back soon. And, I'm taking us all on holiday. Ask our Emily. Cross my heart and hope to die, we're going on holiday."

Elsie covered her ears with her hands. Did this man ever stop lying? "I wouldn't go to the toilet with you Tony Clayton. Now, fuck off out of here before I lose my rag and do something I might regret." She ran towards him and screamed at the top of her voice. "I'll burn everything! Mark my words, if your stuff is still here at the end of today then the lot is getting torched. And, you know I will, just you put me to the test."

The front door slammed shut and Tony was on his toes. Elsie sprinted to the balcony. She wasn't finished with him yet. She was having the final word. She yanked the door open and hung her head over the balcony, eyes flicking one way then another. There he was, she could see him. Quickly, she picked up an old tin of paint from the corner of the balcony and hurled it at him. She was screaming at the top of her voice. "You're a cheeky cunt Tony and everyone will know about you because I'll make sure I fucking well tell them. A waste of space you are. She sucked in a large mouthful of fresh crisp air and lowered her voice, deflated she was. "Just leave me alone to get on with my life. I'm better off without you."

Tony dodged the paint tin spinning towards him. He held his hands in the air and shouted up to his wife. "You're a crazy bitch. I'll be back with the money later. Get back inside instead of making a show of yourself. Bleeding hell, there's no need for this." Elsie stormed back into the flat and nearly fell over the dog. She booted him in his stomach and snapped. "And, you can fucking go with him too. I can't afford to feed myself, never mind a flea-bitten mutt." The poor animal cowered and crept under the table. It wasn't the first time she'd hit this animal. Frank was used to it. Poor animal.

★

Tony jogged down the road. He was always looking behind him dodging the traffic. He was aware that his mad wife could be behind him with a weapon in her hand ready to do him in. He was sweating and out of breath. His skin was grey, and his eyes seemed to change. He was rattling for drugs, it was obvious. He had no pills left on him to calm himself down either, he was shaking like a shitting dog. Tony's hands gripped his stomach as he winced in pain. He sprinted towards a door close by and hammered on the letterbox frantically. "Mickey, it's me Tony, open up mate. Hurry up. I'm going to shit my pants." Tony kept flicking the letterbox, booting at the bottom of the door. He was desperate. A face appeared at the top window. Tony stood back and cupped his hands around his mouth shouting. "Fucking hell, hurry up and open the door. I'm touching cloth here. Open the door before I fill my duds." Tony was walking around in a circle, face stressed, sweating, arse cheeks clenched together tightly. As soon as the front door opened, he barged passed the man stood there and headed straight to the toilet. "Fucking hell. I hope you've got some bog-roll in here. I'm going to burst. On my life, I've got seconds left before I explode."

Mickey sniggered and walked passed the toilet shaking his head. He could see Tony perched on the toilet and chuckled. "Close the door you smelly bastard. Ewww... the smell is knocking me sick. You need your arse raking out you do."

Tony kicked the bottom of the door shut with his foot and shouted back to him. "Start getting ready. I've got to earn and fast. It's a code red. Elsie is gunning for me and if I don't cough up what I owe her she'll be flinging me out. The bitch is mental. Honest, she was going sick at me."

Mickey went into the living room and sprawled across the sofa. There was no rush in his eyes, he was still knackered. This place stank like arse. Tony was still pulling his strides up as he walked into the living room.

Relief filled his face. "Another few seconds Mickey and I would have shed mud. On my life, I very nearly shit my pants."

"Hanging you are mate. What are you doing up so early anyway? I thought after the session we had; I wouldn't have seen you for a few days at least."

Tony sighed. "You're fucking joking pal. I've had about an hour's kip. The Mrs is going sick. I spent the shopping money, didn't I? Come on, get ready. I need to earn some money and fast." Mickey was falling asleep, his eyes closing slowly. Tony grabbed his big toe and yanked at it. "Come on. Stop messing around. I'm roasting my tits off. I need to score. Hook a brother up ay?"

Mickey was an addict too. His arms were bruised and full of track marks. Deep purple and blue veins bulged through his transparent flesh. Mickey rolled onto his side. "For fuck's sake. Let me open my eyes then. Stop stressing me out. I've had no sleep either you know?" Tony sat down and licked his lips. Reality was hitting home. "Mate, she's going mental. I've never seen her this bad before. Honest, I've fucked up big-time. I've dropped a right bollock. Why did you let me get in that state? You should have sent me home."

Mickey chuckled and started coughing. "Don't blame me pal. You're your own worst enemy. You'll have to man up and admit you are wrong. I did say to you last night that you needed to go home. But, oh no, you said Elsie could 'get to fuck'. I bet you wished you'd listened to me now, ay?"

Tony didn't remember a thing. He scratched his head and sighed. "Anyway, I've told Elsie you've got the money." Mickey's eyes were wide open, and he swallowed hard. "I had to mate, she was going to cut my balls off."

Mickey sat up straight. He was in shock. There was no way he wanted that mental cow hammering his front door down. He wanted his name kept out of it. "What the fuck have you said that for? If she comes here, I'm telling her the truth. Nar, fuck that, you're well out of order mate. Why would you do that when you know what she's like?"

"Oh, shut up you mard arse. She won't come here. And, if you move your arse, we can get the money sorted before end of play today. We can go to Asda. I've clocked some Smart TVs near the doorway. We can just run in and grab one. There's a quick two ton for us if we use our noggins, so move it. The early bird catches the worm and all that, remember?"

Mickey was a funny looking bloke and very ugly. He had shoulder length black hair and a massive conk on him. His facial hair seemed to be bald in parts and his teeth were rotten, like a row of Sugar Puffs. Mickey rubbed at his cold pale flesh. "I'll shove some clothes on. Ring Dean and see if we can tick some gear until later. He's sorted, and he knows we're good for it. I can't go out grafting when I'm roasting my nuts off can I?"

Tony shook his head. "No way. I owe him twenty quid already. Are you forgetting when we ticked some drugs from him last week? We told him we would pay him later that day and we never went back. He'll be on the lookout for us. Mark my word he'll be fuming."

Mickey held his head to the side and tried to

engage what was left of his brain. He didn't know what day of the week it was, the truth be told, and he was as thick as two planks of wood. "So, what the fuck are we going to do then? I can't think straight when I'm rattling mate."

Tony stood up scratching at his skin, picking at the scabs from the open wounds on his arms. "Join the fucking club. That's what I mean. We need to move our arses and get earning." Mickey left the room and Tony was rummaging in some newspapers that were lying about on a nearby chair. He opened one page and stared at the Page Three girl displayed there; black lacy underwear, perfect body, this was his dream woman. He held the newspaper closer to his eyes and sniggered to himself. "I'd lick them babies all night long given the chance darling." He tweaked his crotch and closed the newspaper shut. There was no time for filth. He had more important things on his mind now. He had to get some drugs into his system and quick. He couldn't function without them. Nothing made sense, he couldn't concentrate properly.

Mickey was dressed as he walked back into the room. Baggy clothes with a baseball cap pulled over his eyes. He rubbed his hands together. "Right, come on then. Let's go and earn a crust. We can have a butcher's at them TVs in Asda first. Let's see how the land lies and see if it's on top."

"Yep, time waits for no man" Tony replied and the pair of them hurried out the front door. They were both eager to find the money to fill their veins with drugs. Tony was living on borrowed time and if he didn't come up with some money fast, he knew he would be out on the streets tonight.

As they marched up Rochdale Road the lads huddled closely together to keep warm. The wind was bitter and cold, and leaves were blowing high in the air, swirling in perfect circles. The grey clouds hung low and it looked like another day of miserable weather. Tony was feeling a bit emotional as they walked along the path and he spoke to Mickey. "Am I a bad person Mickey? Our Emily said I was a shit dad and I never do anything with them. I thought my kids were happy. Granted, I fuck up a few times, but I do my best for them don't I?"

Mickey rolled his eyes. "Nar, you do more than most dads do round here. At least you're still with your family. Most kids on the estate don't even know who their dads are so she should count herself lucky you're still on the scene. Look at me, I've not seen my sprogs for years. I don't even know where they live anymore."

Tony straightened his jacket. "She wants me to take them on holiday. No drugs, no beer, no pills. Honest, that's what she's asked me for. I must be bad for her to say that, mustn't I?"

Mickey could see this was affecting his grafting partner. He'd never seen this side of him before. Usually he was the joker, the one cracking all the latest gags. He placed his sweaty arm around his mate's neck and pulled him closer. "So, take them on holiday. Prove them wrong. You earn a few quid all the time. Just bang it away and save some money up."

This was a no brainer, Mickey was right. He could earn - how much would it cost for a few weeks away in the sun with his loved ones? "It was just the way she looked at me Mickey. You know, like I'd let her down or something, she was genuinely upset."

"Fuck me mate. Sort your head out. Just take them away on holiday and put it to bed. Don't start all this soppy shit at this time of the morning, my head can't handle it. I've got enough problems of my own without you adding to them."

Mickey picked up speed when the shopping precinct came into view. Tony was the brains behind this operation, and he stopped them walking and started to clock his surroundings. He tickled the end of his chin as he spoke. "Right, here's the plan. No fucking about. We need to be straight in and out. The longer we stay in there, the more chance there is of it coming on top. The security guards know our faces and they'll be all over us like a cheap suit." Mickey was nervous, he stood fidgeting, itching at his face, scratching at it with force, ripping his skin to shreds causing it to bleed. "Right, come on then, let's get this done." Tony edged forward, and his eyes were all over the place. The local market was on today and the public was scattered about the area. This market was a landmark in Harpurhey, and it had been there for as long as he could remember. Tony had even had a Saturday job here when he was a young lad. That was in the good old days - he used to help the market traders unload their vans in the early hours of the morning. Five –thirty start. It was only a few quid but back then it was enough to buy him some luxuries like the "Beano" and "Buster" comics. He loved the characters inside them. Desperate Dan, Dennis the Menace and his dog Gnasher... He'd laugh his head off when he used to read them. Real belly laughs that had him screaming laughing. They really were the good old days. It was a time in his life when everything seemed simple and he didn't have a care in the world. His father was the one who had the problems, the one who made his life a nightmare every time he walked in through the front door. His dad was a bully, nothing less.

The market traders watched Tony and Mickey like hawks as they passed by. They knew them well and they were on their guard. These two were thieving bastards and the moment their backs were turned they would have anything away. An Asian man spoke loudly in his native tongue to another trader across the way from him. He must have been warning him that Tony and Mickey were about. The news spread like wildfire because in minutes the market traders were all stood at the front of their stalls protecting what they owned. Tony nudged Mickey and sniggered. "Muppets. If I wanted to nick something, they couldn't stop me. Clowns they are." He shouted over to them with a smirk on his face. "Take it easy lads. We're just passing through. No need to flap." Mickey kept his head low. There was no way he wanted any beef today, no way in this world. Tony was a right cheeky fucker and sometimes he just went over the top. Mickey had taken many a dig because of Tony and his uncontrollable mouth. Round the next corner Asda's entrance was ahead of them. Every time the sliding door opened Tony could see the boxes of TVs just to the left of the entrance. This mission was child's play.

"Mickey, you need to cover me. You go inside first and start looking at the clothes on the other side of the store. Once they clock you all their eyes will be on you and it should leave the coast clear for me to get in and out."

Mickey let out a deep breath. He hated the way he felt before he committed a crime and his heart was pumping inside his ribcage. "So, you're just going to run in and get a TV then?"

"Yes, well, I will if you get a move on."

Mickey was relieved. At least he didn't have to get his hands dirty. If this plan got foiled it would be Tony facing a charge and not him. There was no way he wanted to be banged up all day down the local police station. He'd been down this road before and knew if he got his collar felt the dibble would be here in seconds. They'd warned him to keep away from this shopping centre and if he was being honest, he had a life time ban from the store for all the crimes he'd committed in the past. Mickey flicked the collar on his coat up and pulled his hat down, it was show time.

Tony watched his partner enter the store. Within seconds of him entering Tony could see the security following him. They were like flies round shit, ducking and diving behind him. The plan was working. He had to keep his head and stay focused. Tony sucked hard on his gums and inhaled deeply. He rubbed the end of his nose with a flat palm and in he went. Sweat was pumping from every pore in his body, he was trembling from head to toe but he had to keep his cool, waste no time, straight in and out like he'd planned. Tony walked straight up to the TVs and picked one up. Fuck me, they were heavy. Maybe, this wasn't going to be plain sailing after all. Using all his strength he yanked the box from the shelf and held it closely to his chest. Here it was, the time when all this could go wrong. Mickey was watching eagerly from the other side of the store. He could see Tony ready to leave. This is where it could go tits up. Thinking on his feet he marched down to the bottom of the aisle. He picked up a couple of shirts and smiled at the two security guys who were positioned so they could see his every move. Right, he had to be fast. He folded the blue shirts over his arm and started to run to the other end of the store. It was a cat and mouse game now and people were starting to look at him. The coast was clear, Tony made his move.

He struggled at first to carry the box, but once he was near the exit, he seemed to find some inner strength. If he didn't get his arse into gear, he'd be spending his night in the local nick roasting his nuts off. Tony was out of the store and motoring as fast as he could through the market stalls, bumping into people, screaming at them at the top of his voice. A few members of the public were watching him but none of them dared approach him. This was none of their business and nothing they wanted any part of. If the police were looking for witnesses, then they were wasting their time here. There was a code of conduct around these parts and everybody kept their traps firmly shut. Nobody wanted to be labelled a grass, no way in this world. Names like that stuck and as soon as the cat was out of the bag and they found out who had blabbed, their houses would be torched, bricks launched through their windows and paint would be sprayed all over the brick walls outside, with a message that would never go away.

GRASS

Tony stumbled down the stairs that led to the estate. He never looked behind him once. His breathing was rapid and at one point it looked like he was going to have a heart attack. Running into a cul-de-sac he looked one way then the other. Resting his body on a fence he picked the TV up and placed it into a nearby garden. He had to sit down, his head was spinning, and he looked like he was going to keel over.

Mickey was still in the store. He smiled at the security guards as he walked back to the place where he'd picked up the shirts and placed them neatly back on the rail. There would be no arrest here today and the security guards knew it. What was this man playing at? They stood looking bewildered scratching their heads. Had they missed something? Mickey gripped his baseball cap from his head and flicked the balls of sweat from his forehead to the ground. He was dripping in it. He walked confidently passed the store detectives and smirked. "Just making sure you two are on the ball lads" and with a bounce in his step, Mickey left the store.

"Oi, over here," Tony whispered as he spotted Mickey speeding past. Tony reached over the garden fence and yanked the TV with his two hands. "Fuck me pal, this was heavy. I nearly dropped the fucker a few times. Honest, I was going to leave it at one stage. My back is in pieces."

Mickey patted the top of his shoulder as if he'd scored the winning goal in a cup final. "A job well done, Toe. I've had them wankers running up and down the aisle in there. Honest, they didn't know what fucking day it was."

Tony scanned the area. "We need to sell it now. One of us is going to have to wait here with it because like I said, it's a heavy fucker." Tony had already made his mind up that Mickey would be the one staying put with the stolen goods. He'd already put his neck on the line once today and now it was Mickey's turn. "I'll go and see Lance on the Two Hundred Estate. He has a few quid and he's always looking for a bargain."

Mickey wasn't sure. "Don't be selling it to him for peanuts. He's a tight fucker and the last time I went to him selling swag he took the piss. He had my eyes out for it. Fifty quid he gave me for a gold chain. I know it was worth a lot more than that and he knew it too."

Tony was agitated. "Just chill the fuck out will you. My head's going to explode in a minute. I know what I'm doing and if he thinks he's getting this for fuck all then he has another thing coming. I want one and a half ton for it. There's a ticket on the box and it says three hundred pounds. So, that's bang down the middle, half price."

Mickey nodded. His body was shaking more than ever now, and he needed to sort himself out. They both did. The gear was calling. "Hurry up then before it starts pissing down. If this box gets wet then it will be worth fuck all." Tony zipped his coat up and headed out of the cul-de-sac onto the estate.

CHAPTER FOUR

Elsie was at the kitchen table moaning about her husband to her best friend Tina. Her head was in her hands and she was stressed out. Nothing was going right and in her own words, life was shit and it couldn't get any worse. Tina shot a look over at her friend. She was well known for her openness and never held anything back. She folded her arms and began the usual lecture. "How many times have I told you that Tony brings you down? You never listen, and you carry on putting up with it all. What did you expect?"

Elsie lifted her head up slightly and sighed. "It's not what I need to hear right now, Tina. Fuck me, I've come here for a bit of support, not to hear you telling me what I already know. Do me a favour and shut up about Tony. I can't even stand to hear that man's name. My temper is boiling, and I just need to calm down before I bite someone's head off."

Tina flicked the invisible dust from the top of her shoulder and picked her cup of coffee up towards her mouth. She was only telling the truth here, what did Elsie expect? "I'm just saying what I see that's all. You know me love, I tell it like it is, don't blame me for being honest." Tina ran her index finger around the white mug and looked out of the window. She eased off the pressure slightly. "So, what are you going to do then? I'm not dictating what you should do, I'm just asking that's all."

Elsie rolled her eyes. "Fuck knows. I'm going to see if he comes back with the money today. If he doesn't, he's getting flung out. He knows I mean it too. If I'd have got my hands on the bastard this morning, I would have strangled him, on my life he would have been in a body bag."

"Good, he deserves it, the wanker."

Elsie blushed and pressed her lips tightly together. She looked uncomfortable as she spoke. "I need a borrow Tina, twenty quid if you've got it. I need gas and some bread and milk. It's only until Wednesday until I get my benefit."

Tina never flinched. She'd lent her friend money on more than one occasion and she knew she would return it as soon as she got paid. A lot of the residents lived from hand to mouth on the estate and they all helped each other to keep their heads above water when they were skint. "Yeah, no worries. I'll come down to the shops with you anyway. I need to pick a few bits up myself."

Elsie reached over and touched the top of Tina's hand. Her heart was low, and she was filling up. "I appreciate all that you do for me, you know. God knows where I would be if I didn't have you?"

Tina smiled and patted the top of Elsie's hand. "I care about you Elsie and I hate it when you get yourself into a fix. I've told you before. Just do a few nights with me a week and you'll always have money. Nobody needs to know. Just tell them at home that you have a cleaning job at night."

Elsie was alarmed and folded her arms tightly in front of her chest. "Fuck off Tina. I can't do that. Tony would go sick if he knew I was working in a brothel."

"You can just work on reception. It's not like you would be having sex with the punters. And, sometimes they ask you to watch, so you could earn a few extra quid there, stop being so prudish."Tina knew Elsie had pulled a few tricks in the past when she had no money, but it was all hush, hush and she hated ever admitting it. Tina had been doing it for years. She was a pretty woman and you could tell that in her day she'd been a right looker. "Thanks Tina but no, I have the kids to think about. It's alright for you. You don't answer to anybody. It would ruin the kids if they knew I was involved in anything like that."

Tina shrugged her shoulders and smirked. "Just think about it that's all. It's not like Tony is looking after you, is it? We all need a bit of extra money sometimes, don't we?"

Elsie nodded. "Thanks, but no thanks. If I change my mind, then you'll be the first to know. Our Jordan bungs me a few quid extra each week, so if I'm stuck, I can always ask him to help me out."

Tina melted at the mention of Elsie's son. "Oh, he's a good- looking lad. I can't believe he's Tony's son. He's bleeding gorgeous. If I was a few years younger, I'd ruin him."

Elsie chuckled, and her mood seemed to be lifting. "I know; he gets all the girls. He's never at home. He's always out at some bird's house. I've told him it will fall off if he carries on sleeping about. He's like a bleeding rabbit."

"You can't blame him love," Tina sniggered., "if there's a hole he'll fill it. He's like most men. They can't say no when it's offered on a plate."

Tina passed Elsie a cigarette and flicked the lighter underneath it. A large thick cloud of grey smoke filled the room as they carried on talking. "Are you still seeing that Henry who you met the other week?" Tina cringed and shuddered.

"You mean the guy I met at work?"

"Yeah, the one who was buying you all the flowers and chocolates."

Tina rolled her eyes and chugged hard on her fag. "He's a bit of a crank. You need to remember he's one of my punters too. I'd never have a man in my life who was into paying for sex. I bet he's got a wife at home and a few kids. He's not someone who'd make me happy. It would always be in the back of my mind that he was a punter."

"As long as he's treating you well, what does it matter? Get it while you can. Enjoy the ride while it lasts, take him for every penny he's got! Rinse him!"

Tina shook her head slowly and her voice was soft. "It matters a lot Elsie. Just because I'm a brass it doesn't mean that I don't want to have someone who loves me by my side each night. I want that too, you know," her eyes clouded over as she carried on speaking. This subject had really hit a nerve. "I've always wanted it, but I always fall for the wrong kind of bloke who treats me badly. I'm a good person, you know, and I deserve to be loved. I have a lot to offer a man."

Elsie was the one comforting her now. "I know you do love but your job is not the best place to meet a decent guy, is it? You need to get out of the area and meet someone decent. I know my Tony is a prick most of the time, but I know he loves me. He would go to hell and back to protect me."

Tina raised her eyebrows, "I never said he wouldn't. I just said he should realise how his actions affect his family life, that's all."

Elsie was reminiscing now as she sat back and folded her arms. "Tony was the boy everyone wanted to be with when he was younger. On my life, you wouldn't think it now, but he had it all going on back in the day. Sexy he was."

Tina's expression changed, and she was finding it hard to believe that Tony Clayton had ever been a good-looking man. He was ugly in her eyes. Elsie shot her eyes over at Tina and she could see she was having difficulty ever imagining her man to be a heart throb. She was excited as she carried on talking. This was her love story, the memory of times when her relationship was good. She continued and snuggled into her body. A nice warm red glow appeared on her cheeks. "Every girl on the estate wanted to be his girl and he picked me. I was no oil painting and I couldn't believe my luck when one night in the Queen's on the Monsall estate he asked to walk me home. Honest, all my mates couldn't believe it either. They actually told me straight that I was punching above my weight with him. I'd never been so nervous in my life. Everything about him made me tingle from head to toe. I knew then that he would always be the love of my life. Sometimes, I still have too pinch myself to believe I'm his wife," Elsie shot a look over at Tina. Her friend squirmed as a shiver passed through her body. She looked like she was going to puke. The man was disgusting, and never in a month of Sunday's would Elsie ever change her mind. She carried on reminiscing about the days gone by. "When we got back to my house we sat and talked all night long, we just clicked. It was such a strong connection, a bond that nobody would ever break. They say you can fall in love in the first few seconds of meeting somebody and that's what happened with me and my Tony. I was head over heels in love with him after just a few hours, I couldn't take my eyes off him. The first time he kissed me I knew I would never ever feel this way about another man. Honest, I fell in love there and then, hook line and sinker."

Tina pretended to gag into her hands and chuckled out loudly. "Oh my God. Stop it! Your making me feel sick. How could Tony Clayton ever make a woman weak at the knees?"

Elsie sat up straight. "He was the man Tina. Remind me the next time you come around to our house to get the old photographs out and then you'll see with your own eyes how sexy my husband was."

Tina sat back in her seat, she enjoyed a good love story, even if this one was about Tony Clayton. "So, what happened next, you kissed him and then what?"

Elsie started to blush, she opened the top button on her coat and blew a warm breath downwards towards her breasts. "We were inseparable. He used to come to our house every night after he'd finished work and we spent all our time together. His home life was shit and he hated going home. My dad hated him from day one though. He said there was something about him that he couldn't put his finger on. My dad didn't trust him as far as he could throw him."

"What about your mam and your sister? Did they like him?"

"Oh, our Gina was all over him like a rash. You know how jealous of me she used to be. Everything I had she always wanted, and she made no exception where men were concerned either. She used to flirt with Tony all the time. I knew her game from the off and nipped it in the bud. I got her by the scruff of the neck and told her if she carried on flirting with my man, I would rip every hair out of her bleeding head. I've never snapped like that before, but she could see it in my eyes that I meant business. Oh yes, I'd have scratched her bleeding eyes out if she thought I would take her flirting lying down."

"Bloody hell, was you that in love with him that you would fall out with your sister over him?"

"I was Tina. He was my world and I wasn't letting him slip through my fingers, for love nor money."

"So, did your mam like him?"

"Of course. Tony had the gift of the gab and he could win anybody over. My mother was putty in his hands. She thought he was the dog's bollocks. He would do anything for her. A proper brown-noser he was."

Tina sat in disbelief. "Well fuck a duck. Who'd have ever thought your mam had a heart. I'm glad you have those happy memories of him. It's nice to remember the good times."

Elsie was digging deep into her memory bank and she recalled another time when she was happy. "He was romantic too. He used to write me love letters and buy me flowers. I think he robbed the flowers if I'm being honest though, because on one bunch he gave me I found a small card saying, 'We'll miss you forever Sally. Rest in peace. From Natalie'."

Tina burst out laughing and covered her mouth with her hand. "Now, that's more like the Tony I know. What a cheeky bastard. I would have whacked him over the head with them."

Elsie nodded and smirked. "I know but I was in love and never saw the bad in him. His heart was always in the right place. The night he asked me to marry him went down in history as one of the most special times in my life. I'll never forget it as long as I live. He'd set it all up and everyone knew about it except me. Even our Gina was in on it. It was my birthday and my mam had planned a meal at the Indian restaurant on Rochdale Road for us all. I think it's still there now, but I think it's changed its name. Anyway, we were all having something to eat. I think we had just started with the first course when Tony started choking," her expression changed, and she became serious. "I shit my knickers I thought he was going to die. His face was turning blue and we were all trying to dislodge whatever it was he had stuck in his throat. He was lying on the floor and I had him held in my arms. I thought he was taking his last breath. Then he lifted his hand up to his mouth and pulled out a diamond ring. He smiled and looked directly into my eyes and then he said it. Those magic words."

Tina was on the edge of her seat and she was more than caught up in the story. "What did he say?"

Elsie fluttered her short black eyelashes and licked her lips before she got to the juicy bit. Taking a deep breath, she placed her flat palm on her heart and continued. "He asked me to marry him."

Tina gasped; this was better than any drama she'd watched on the box lately. This was real life. "And, what did you say?"

"After I'd strangled him half to death for scaring the life out of me, I finally said yes. Everybody was cheering, and it was the happiest day in my life. Honest, I'll never forget it as long as I live. My dad was the only one who wasn't celebrating. He just got up from the table and went home. He had a face like a smacked arse, he proper spat his dummy out."

"That's a bit over the top isn't it?" Tina added.

"No, not really because in the end he was right. I should have listened to him."

Tina was fighting Tony's corner now. "Well, that's out of order. He should have been happy for you. If Tony had gone to that much trouble to propose, then he should have been respectful instead of putting a dampener on it."

Elsie was opening- up. She'd never really told anyone her real story and it just seemed the right time to get it out in the open. "My dad never even came to the wedding. He said hell would freeze over before he stepped foot near that church. My Uncle Sam had to give me away, not my dad. Stubborn he is, very stubborn."

Tina was nibbling at her fingernails. She lit two more cigarettes and passed one over to Elsie. "I never knew he hated Tony that much. Why didn't he give the man a chance?"

"In his eyes I was still his little girl, and I suppose

he wanted more for me. I'd fucked myself up with drugs in the past and I think he was just scared of me getting involved in that kind of world again."

"Was Tony on drugs too then?"

"Yeah, but not like he is now. He just smoked weed and popped a few pills. He had trouble sleeping you see."

Tina flicked ash from her cigarette and shot her eyes over to the kitchen clock. She knew the rest of the story and was bored now. "Bloody hell, look at the time. I better get some slap on for work. My shift starts in an hour."

"I thought you was going to come down to the shops with me?"

"Sorry love, I've lost track of time. But here," she reached into her black leather handbag and pulled out her purse. "Here's twenty quid. Get what you need. You can sort me out when you get back on your feet."

Elsie rolled the money up tightly and shoved it into her bra. It was safe there and nobody would ever get to it. It was her secret stash. "Thanks love, like I said, once I get paid, I will be over with it to pay you back. Hopefully, that dead beat of a husband of mine will be back later with some money."

"No worries," Tina replied.

★

Emily sat in Jane's bedroom and looked around. Why couldn't she have a bedroom like this? She fanned her fingers out and ran them along the fresh cotton bedding. It was crisp white and not a single crease was visible on it. The décor was pink and silver and everything seemed to match. Bright pink curtains hung down gracefully from the window and everything about them said luxury. Emily let out a deflated breath as she waited for Jane to come back into the room. Lying down on the bed she dug her nose deep into the pillow and inhaled the fresh clean bedding. It smelt like summer meadows; fresh, sweet aromas, tickled her nose. Emily jumped up quickly when the bedroom door opened unexpectedly. She stuttered. "Did you get a biscuit, I'm starving?"

Jane juggled the packets in her hands and bent down slightly at the edge of the bed. "Quick then, grab the cans of coke. I brought us some crisps and chocolate up too. But be careful, if any crumbs go on the bed my mam will be up in arms, she hates me eating in my bedroom. You know what she's like."

Emily used her index finger to flick the sugary drink open and gulped a large mouthful of Coke. Within seconds she was scoffing a creamy bar of milk chocolate and anything else she could ram into her mouth, the greedy cow never stopped for a breath. "Careful, you nearly bit your finger off then," Jane chuckled.

"I'm starving. My dad spent the money again, so we've had no shopping in. The gas has gone too, so if it's alright with you can I get a bath here tonight because I stink of BO?"

"Yes, my mam has even bought you your own towel. It's in the cupboard on the landing."

Emily growled over at Jane. "Why has she done that? I don't have scabies or anything."

"Oh, you know what she's like. I have my own

towel too if that's any consolation. She's over the top with stuff like that. I only used her toothbrush once and she had the house up. She's OCD."

Emily wiped her mouth with the corner of her sleeve and plonked down on the bed. She sniggered and rubbed her palms together. She had hot gossip for sure. Jane opened her eyes wide. "What's up with you?"

Here it was, the secret she'd had bubbling inside her for what seemed like a lifetime. "I've met a guy on Facebook. He's older than me."

Jane sat back on the bed and held her head to the side. "Since when have you been talking to someone online? Why haven't you told me about this before? How long has this been going on?"

Emily snuggled her head deep into a pillow and played with her fingers. "Only for a few weeks. There was nothing to tell you really. Well, up until now. He's asked to meet me up with me."

Jane's eyes were wide open. "And, are you going to meet him?"

She hesitated slightly. "I'm a bit nervous. I've told a few porkies to him. He thinks I'm older than I really am. In fact, I've told a whole bunch of whoppers. He thinks I work too."

Jane was intrigued. "Show me his profile photograph then, let's have a butcher's at him."

Emily scrolled through her chats and clicked on Mark's profile, she smiled as she saw his face pop up. She looked at him for a few more seconds then passed the phone over to Jane. There was silence as she examined his profile in more detail. "He's gorgeous. Has he seen a photo of you?"

Emily bolted up from the bed. "Yes, he has why? Are you saying he's too good looking for me or what, you better not be?"

Jane realised what she'd just said and tried to back track but Emily was right in her thinking. Jane did think that Mark was too good for her friend. "No, I just mean, what's he said about you?" Emily flicked her hair back over her shoulder and sat with her back against the bedroom wall. She was in a mood and angry with Jane. Emily licked her lips slowly and watched Jane's reaction as she answered her. She bigged herself up. "He thinks I'm gorgeous. So, shove that in your pipe and smoke it. He's really into me."

Jane was jealous, you could see it in her eyes. She was the pretty one and up to now she'd never had any interest from someone this attractive. So why was her friend getting male attention when she wasn't?

"How old is he?" Jane said breaking the tension.

Emily stroked her fingernail along her red cherry lips. "He's not that old. Just a few years older than me." Emily was holding her cards close to her chest and not giving anything away. "I think I'll go and meet him. I mean, what do I have to lose?"

Jane was excited, this was hot gossip and the most exciting thing that had happened to either of them in a long time. "Right, I'll come with you. Has he got a mate for me? We can have a double date and that way you will be safe."

Emily sat thinking. This idea could work. "Yes, I think he has. I can try and arrange it but I'm telling you now, don't think you can make a move on my man. He's mine, so keep your mitts off him."

Jane held a cunning look in her eye and kept her cool. "As if I would ever nick your guy. I can get me own."

If this was completely true Emily would have had nothing to worry about but Jane was a flirt and she knew if she wanted her friend's man, she would only have to flutter her eyes at him, and he would be putty in her hands. This was getting interesting. Emily started to run her fingers through her hair, lifting it up high and dropping it back down. "Should I wear my hair up or down? I think I look sexier with it up, what do you think?"

Jane studied Emily as she held her hair up and looked at her. "I'm thinking if I just pull a few strands of hair down here and there it will look sexy."

"It depends. What are you thinking of wearing? Are you thinking a casual look, or are you going to go all out and wear a dress with a nice pair of heels?"

Emily shrugged her shoulders. She didn't have a clue. Jane was the fashion guru here and she needed her help. "I'll have a look in my wardrobe and see if we can put something together. I'll do that while you ask your new man if his friend can make it too. Get him to send a photograph, he better not be ugly otherwise I'm not going."

Jane jumped from the bed and headed to her wardrobe. She cunningly watched Emily send a text message. This was going to be interesting, very interesting indeed.

CHAPTER FIVE

Tony had sold the TV and the money was split two ways as agreed. He knew it was more than his life was worth to spend a single penny from what he'd earned. No way, he valued his life too much and he knew his wife would have cut his balls off if he let her down again. As soon as Tony walked in through the front door his wife was there to greet him. She stood with her hands on her hips snarling at him. Oh, this woman was ready to attack alright, her face was bright red as she growled over at him. "So, come on then, cough it up. Where's the money you promised me?"

Tony peeled his grey jacket off and kicked his muddy trainers off his feet across the floor. "Bleeding hell, give me a bit of time to get inside then. I've told you before that I'm a man of my word. Tony Clayton never lets anyone down. Especially not his beautiful wife." He edged past her and headed into the front room. Frank came to greet him, and he reached down and patted the top of his head. "You believed me, didn't you son? It's the missus who doubts me, not you. I know she should trust me, but, ay, what can I do if she doesn't?" Frank looked at his owner and tilted his head one way then another. He didn't have a clue what was going on.

Elsie was in no mood for games. She stood above Tony as he sat down and booted his foot. "Hand it over.

Go on, show me the money."

Tony was smiling, for once he'd come up trumps and had the cash for her. He lay back and reached inside his jeans pocket and dug deep. He was playing with her and he could see she was losing her rag. "Bleeding hell, have you got it or what?"

Tony had the money in his hand and counted each note out onto the arm of the chair. "There you go, babes. It's all there just like I said it would be."

Elsie was shocked, she wasn't sure what to do. She backed off and plonked down in an armchair. This was a turn up for the books and one she never expected. "I still detest you. You still pissed off and left me, so you're not out of the dog house yet."

Tony knew he was out of the danger zone and started to relax. "I'm sorry. For fuck's sake. How many times do I have to tell you that I'm sorry? That's the trouble with you Elsie, you never put anything to bed. You drag the arse out of everything, all the bloody time. For once in your life, just admit you're wrong."

Here he was again, doing what he always did best when he'd had his collar felt. He was turning the tables on his missus and making her think it was her fault. "Oh, be quiet Tony. You know as well as me that there is something more to this story. I don't know how you pulled it out of the bag, but I don't believe you. I'm not green you know."

He needed to change the subject, get things back to normal. "Do you fancy an hour in bed, love. I could do with a bit of tender loving care. After all, I did bring you the money back when I could have gone down the boozer with it and pissed it up the wall."

Elsie squirmed. Was he having a laugh or what? "Are you for real Tony? Do you really think I would have sex with you after what you've done?"

His expression changed, and his face dropped. "What's wrong with asking for a bit of slap and tickle with my beautiful wife. I'm a red-blooded male. I need some sex. That's what a man and woman do when they love each other. Or have you forgotten? It's been ages since we had a bit. I feel like a bleeding monk."

Elsie smirked and shot a look over towards him. "Well you'll just have to a have a wank then because I'm not in a mood for you today. You make my blood boil," she paused and held her head high. "And, just for the record you're still only here by the skin of your teeth. You mark my words I will find out the truth about the money and when I do, God help you."

Tony knew he was still in the bad books but at least he had a roof over his head for now. He plonked down on the sofa and looped his hands behind his head. "I'm taking us all on holiday. Our Emily had a right go at me this morning and she really got to me. She said we never do anything as a family. I thought I was a top dad?"

Elsie nearly choked. What planet was this man on? "She's right, you do nothing with any of us. It's all about you and where you're getting your next fix from."

Tony was alarmed. "No, that's a complete lie. You and the kids have always come before anything in my life."

Elsie's voice softened; these words were straight from the heart. She had to tell him how she felt, she couldn't go on living a lie. "We used to Tony but not anymore, the gear always comes first. I want my Tony back, the man I fell in love with, not the one I can see lying there. Have you had a good look at yourself lately?"

Tony sat up, where was all this coming from, he was a good man. A guy who bent over backwards for his family. "Whoa, just you hang fire there. I provide for this family the best I can. Yes, I go a bit nutty sometimes but that's not often. You're out of order love. You and the kids are my world."

Elsie sighed. "You need to sort your shit out. We can't go on like this. I've told you I'm here to support you, but you need to want to get clean. We can have a good life and put all this shit behind us."

Tony cringed as he prepared to listen to the latest lecture on how brighter his life would be without drugs in it and how much more money they would have in their pockets. "I want to help you. We can go through this together. I'm going through it just like you. We can do it as a team." Tony didn't say a word. She knew he was listening and continued. "Our Emily would love it Tony. She'd be so proud of you, of us both. Can you at least think about it?"

Tony's hands were trembling, there was fear in his eyes. Panic seemed to attack every organ in his body. "I'm too weak love. You know I have mad shit going on in my head. Maybe in a few weeks when I get my head together."

Elsie stood her ground and she wasn't standing for any more of his excuses. She smashed her fist against the arm of the chair sending dust flying into the air.

"No! It's now or never. I've heard the same story for months and if you're not going to get clean then I want you gone from here. I want a better life for me and the kids and I'm doing it with or without you." She meant every word; she'd had enough of his crap to last a lifetime.

Tony was on the spot now and just stared at her. For once he was stuck for words. "You can't just say that. I need time to do it, to get myself ready. Rome wasn't built in a day."

She was right back at him, snapping. "It would have been built if I was running the job. Anyway, I need an answer right now. It's a simple yes or no? You're either in or you're out?"

The front door slammed shut and in bounced Jordan. This lad had it all going on, he was gorgeous. Tony was relieved, he was off the hook for now and smiled as he looked at his boy. "Oi, oi Mr Loverman. Whose bed have you just crawled out of?"

Jordan ran his fingers through his thick dark brown hair and smirked over at his old man. He flicked the invisible dust from the top of his shoulder and sniggered. "You know me so well dad. It was just someone I met in town last night. A right filthy cow she was, she took advantage of me. Honest, my back is full of scratches, a right dirty bitch."

Tony was engrossed in the story; he rubbed his hands together and invited his son to sit down next to him. Once his boy was by his side, he rubbed his hands over the top of his head and playfully punched him in the ribs. "You're a chip off the old block you are son. I remember the days when the ladies were around me like flies round shit. I was the man back in the day, let me tell you."

Before he could continue Elsie flung a pillow over at his head. "Oi, I am sat here you know."

Tony rolled his eyes. "I know love, I mean before I met the love of my life." Jordan gave his father a shifty look and knew to change the subject before his dad got a bunch of fives. Elsie was a jealous woman and he often wound her up about his previous girlfriends. "So, have you been earning a few quid then son?"

Jordan licked the end of his fingertip and bent down to wipe a spot of dirt from his new white Nike trainers. He hated not being clean and everything about him had to be on point. You wouldn't have thought he belonged to this family, he was different to them; neat and tidy. "You know me dad. I've always got my finger in more than one pie. Wheeling and dealing, ducking and diving, you know how I roll."

Elsie jumped into the conversation and cracked a joke. "You have your finger stuck in anything son. You're a dirty bleeder. Ay, don't you be having no girls turning up here pregnant. I'm too young to be a granny," she added laughing out loud. Jordan swallowed hard and he looked like he was going to say something but stopped dead in his tracks. Elsie stood up. "I'm just going down to the shop to get some food and some gas. Do you want anything, son?"

Tony held his hands up in the air. "What about me? You know, your husband, the one who puts money on the table each week. I am here you know. I'm not the invisible man?"

Elsie smirked as she grabbed her jacket from the

sofa. "You can suck a fart right out of my arse! I'm doing nothing for you until you've sorted yourself out." That was him told, he shook his head and kept a low profile.

"Can you get me a can of Dr Pepper mam? I've got a craving for it lately. I'm drinking gallons of it."

"Do you want anything else? I'm getting some pickled onion Space Raiders if you want a bag."

"No way. They make your breath stink. I've got a date later, and I'm not going on it with pickled onion breath."

Elsie was addicted to the crisps; she ate bags of them each day. Dragging her coat over her body, she edged towards the door. "Please yourself. Right, I'll be back soon. Tony, you can straighten up in here and hoover round. It's a shit-tip in here."

Tony mumbled under his breath and rammed two fingers up at her. Elsie didn't see him otherwise she would have smacked him one. Once the front door slammed shut Tony started to speak. This was man time, his time to let off some steam. "That woman does my head in. I swear to you son, don't ever get married. You just carry on banging all those birds while you can. Because, mark my words, once you've walked them down the aisle it all changes. No sex, no TLC, no fuck all. Just moan, moan and moan."

Jordan chuckled. "Well, you must have done something to her. It's your own fault. How many times have I told you that women are sensitive? I treat my ladies like princesses; I give them flowers, chocolates, perfumes, they love it."

"Oi, you don't have to tell me about how to treat a

woman. I've had my fair share of them to last a lifetime, but don't be telling your mother that. Some things are best left unsaid."

Jordan nodded. "She'd cut your bollocks off if she heard you, so if I was you, I'd keep it schtum." These were wise words, he had his head screwed on for sure. He reached deep into his pocket and pulled out a roll of twenty- pound notes. Tony's eyes were wide open as he licked his lips slowly. "You're doing alright son. Look at that lot, how much have you got there?"

"About four ton. I've got to pick some more money up later too."

Tony was starting to sweat, he had to be quick before his wife come back home. He turned his head away and started to talk in a low voice. "I'm glad you're doing well mate. I wish we could get a bit of something to help us on our feet. I try my best, but fuck me, something always comes up. Sometimes I just feel like running away from it all. What does a man have to do in this world to get a break?"

Jordan knew his old man of old. He was on the scrounge again. He cut the sob story short and handed him two twenty-pound notes. "Here, that should help you both out. Make sure you tell my mam about it too, don't be keeping it to yourself."

He peeled another note from the pile and placed it on the table. "Give that to Emily. She could always do with a few extra quid to help her out." This was a turn up for the books, just what the family needed.

Tony patted the top of his son's shoulder. "You're a good lad, helping us like this. I'm so proud of the way you turned out."

Jordan put his money back in his pocket and sat back on the sofa. "I'm taking Emily and your mam on holiday," Tony blurted out. "They think I won't do it but I'm going to give it my best shot."

Jordan was gobsmacked. The family had never been away on holiday. He was twenty-two now, it was a bit late for his dad to start taking him on holiday. He should have done this years ago when he was growing up. "That's great dad. I bet my mam is buzzing. She deserves a break, she's had a lot to put up with lately."

Tony stared at the floor. He knew what his son meant. He hung his head with shame. "I'm going to get clean son. I know I've said it before, but this it's the truth this time. You just watch your old man in a few weeks. I'll be as fit as a fiddle and all these women around here won't be able to keep their hands from me."

Jordan pulled a sour expression. "Dad, if you really mean that, then great but don't make promises you can't keep. I want you to get clean, of course I do but, I don't want you doing it for a day and then giving up like you always do. Sort your head out and go on that holiday. I'll bung you a few quid for spending money. There's nothing I would like more than to see you get your head sorted out. It's been shit for us dad. Do you know how much beef I had growing up about you being on drugs? It's not nice let me tell you."

Tony had said it now, there was no going back. Maybe he'd just got caught up in the moment or maybe not. But he'd pledged to get off drugs and he'd have to do it.

★

Elsie screamed as she came back into the house. She was hopping about, jumping, dancing, covering her nose, gagging. "Fucking hell Tony. The dog has shit again near the front door. Did you not hear him scratching at the door to get out? Bleeding hell, what the hell has he been eating, it's rancid. Am I the only one who takes that animal out for a walk or what?"

Tony appeared at the side of her and knew this was his chance to earn some brownie points. "Go and take your shoes off and I'll clear this lot up. Fuck me, it stinks." He shot his eyes to the dog muck on the floor and squirmed. "Frank, you dirty bastard. You'll end up in the dog's home if you carry on like this. Bleeding hell, how much food have you scranned? There's mountains of dollop here?" Frank was nowhere to be seen. He was hidden away underneath the dining table in the living room, shaking.

Elsie walked into the front room and shot her eyes one way then the other. "Where's Jordan gone?"

"He had to get off. He got a phone call and just upped and left. He said he will call back later in the week," Tony replied from the hallway.

"Bleeding hell. I've got him his drink too. He could have waited for me. I've hardly spoken a few words to him in days."

★

Emily stood looking in the full-length silver mirror in Jane's bedroom. She twisted one way then the other. "Do I look alright, I mean older?"

Jane was behind her and looked at her reflection in

the mirror. "Yes, honest, you don't even look like you."

Emily edged closer to the mirror and examined her eye make-up. "Do you think I should wipe some of this off. I'm caked in it."

"No, that's how you wear your make-up these days. I've had a look on YouTube and followed the instructions. It looks mint, relax." Jane held a cunning smirk and carried on brushing her hair. "I hope his mate is good looking. Don't expect me to stay with you for long if he's hanging."

"I don't know what he looks like. Mark said he's nice so you will have to play it by ear."

Jane slipped a black mini-skirt on and a small white t-shirt. Her legs were long and tanned and she looked stunning. Emily was wearing a red dress. It was a bit clingy for her body shape, but Jane had worked on her telling her how sexy she looked in it. Jane was a liar and if the truth be told she just didn't want to lend her any of her other clothes. This red dress was old, something she hadn't worn in ages. Emily stood, tugging at the red lycra dress, it was stuck to every inch of her body and left no room for movement. Jane sat on the edge of the bed and slipped her silver shoes on. "So, are you going to sleep with Mark?"

Emily swallowed hard and her cheeks were on fire with embarrassment. She was a virgin and just the thought of a man touching her young supple flesh sent a wave of fear down her spine. She thought of Mark as a nice man, a kind caring soul who would want to date her, take things easy and have sex when the time was right. Surely, he wasn't going to want anything other than friendship to start with. "No, I'm not. God, this is the first date. He'll be lucky to get a kiss. Stop giving me a heart attack Jane, I'm nervous enough without you adding to it."

"Are you on this planet or what? He'll be wanting a leg-over. I was seeing Andy who was seventeen and he was always after sex. On my life, every night he was trying to get into my knickers. Why do you think I finished with him? Anyway, why are you being so prudish? You're supposed to be eighteen years old, remember?"

Emily was having a panic attack. This was going to be a date like she'd never had before. There would be no milkshakes and a snog in the cinema, this was the real thing. "Jane, I'm going on my first proper date, just help me calm down, stop making me nervous."

Jane smirked and stood up to look at her full outfit in the mirror, she nudged Emily out of the way. This was a date night for her too and she wanted to look her best. "Right, I've told my mam we are going to Jennifer's party. If she asks, we don't know what time it will be finished, and we are making our own way home. We can say we have a lift from one of the girl's parents. You know she will be stressed out otherwise."

Jane reached over and grabbed the bottle of perfume from her dressing table. She sprayed the Marc Jacob Daisy fragrance all over her body, with a cheeky grin she parted her legs and squirted the scent up her skirt. Emily playfully punched Jane in the arm. "You dirty cow," she giggled. The clock was ticking, and it was nearly time to go.

CHAPTER SIX

Tony was nibbling at his fingernails, itching at his skin and scratching his scalp as if something was crawling about in it. What the hell was up with him? His nostrils flared as he fell back onto the sofa. He was thinking. He stood up, sat back down, stood up again and plonked back down into his seat as if his head was going to explode. He was going cold turkey and rattling already. Elsie opened the living room door holding a cup of coffee in her hand. "There you go my darling. I've made nice brew for you." He never replied. Elsie sat down facing him and she could see he was agitated; small balls of sweat rolled down the side of his cheeks and his eyes were rolling. She knew what the problem was now, of course she did, she'd been through this herself. Taking a deep breath, she spoke. "It's day one Tony. It does get better, trust me, I know. You need to keep busy, keep your mind off the drugs."

Tony sat cracking his knuckles, he was weak, his bottom lip was trembling. He had to say something, he was struggling to get his words out. You could see it in his eyes. He finally blurted it out in a panic. "I'm not ready. I thought I was but I'm going crazy here. Look at my nerves," he held his flat palm out and he was right, he was shaking like a leaf.

Elsie jumped from the chair and came to his side, cradling him in her arms. "No one said this was going to be easy. I went to hell and back for the first few days when I started coming off drugs. I never slept a wink, soaking wet I was, shaking, spewing. But it passes."

Tony snapped and gritted his teeth tightly together. "I said I'm not fucking ready, are you deaf or what?" he pushed her arm away as if it was diseased. "You think I can just do everything overnight. I need medication, sleeping tablets, nerve tablets. I need the fucking lot. You're stronger than me. I'm not good with stuff like this."

"You're talking out of your arse Tony. You're the strongest man I know. You just don't know it. Please, look at me," she gripped his arm again, desperate for him to listen. "I'll go to Tina's and see if she's got a few sleepers for you. Tony, I said look at me," she needed him to look in her eyes. Maybe then he would see her pain, her heartache and the need for change. "You're my world. We need you, please don't bail on us all again. This is your last chance to fix it, to fix us. To change our family." His eyes clouded over, and he swallowed hard. The tears were there, and the floodgates were ready to open. No words needed to be spoken. His head fell onto her shoulder and she firmly pressed her dry crusty lips against his head. "It will be alright love. Me and you will have a fresh start, a new life. You know, the one we have spoken about for years?" Elsie choked up and sobbed her heart out. "Do you want me to carry on the way I have been doing? Do you want me to go out robbing?" Tony's eyes squeezed tightly together. He couldn't talk about this. He knew what his wife did when she was skint but he'd never admit that it was happening. It was easier that way. "Emily wants her dad back, Tony. And, I want my husband back too. Remember, the happy go lucky person you used to be?"

His heart was low, he was fed up, ready to throw the towel in. "You don't know what shit I've got going on in my head. I've been on the smack too long now to change. Just go and find someone who can give you the life you want. I'm washed up. You deserve better."

She pushed him away with force. "I won't listen to your bleeding sob story. We've all had problems in the past, but we've had to deal with them. Look at me, who'd have thought I would ever sort my head out?"

"You've had help from the doctor. You can't expect me to do a roast without fuck all to help me."

"So, I'll book you in the doctors and get you some meds. I can ring them now and see if there are any appointments left for today."

Tony was ragging his fingers through his hair, stressed, green looking. "Hurry up then, because I need something now. Move out of my way. I need the toilet I feel like my insides are falling out." He sprung to his feet and rushed out of the living room holding the back of his pants. It was touch and go whether or not he would make it. Elsie dropped her head into her hands. This was going to be a long day for sure, very long indeed.

★

Emily opened her eyes and looked about the bedroom. Jane was next to her and still sound asleep. Rubbing her knuckles into the corner of her eyes Emily stretched her arms above her head and yawned. She reached for her mobile and lay reading the messages with a smile across her face. She nudged Jane and poked her slender finger into her waist. "Come on sleepy head. Rise and shine. You need to fill me in on everything that happened last night."

Jane moaned and dragged the duvet over her head. Her voice was croaky. "Go back to sleep, I'm still tired. Wow, just leave me alone."

Emily was giddy and started to tickle Jane. She wasn't giving up. "Wakey, wakey. Come on. I want to tell you about Mark. After I left you, things got very heated. If you don't wake up now, then I'm not telling you."

Jane slowly peeped her head over the duvet. Suddenly she was awake and wanted to know every detail. She sat up and folded the pillow behind her head to make herself comfortable. "What do you mean, did you have sex?"

Emily snuggled her head into the pillow, rolling from side to side. "No, did I eck. But we kissed for ages, tongues too. He's a really sexy kisser. He made me go weak at the knees. I'm in love, I can feel it in my heart. Honest, I've heard people talk about being in love before and this is the real deal. He said he really likes me too."

Jane pulled a sour expression. Her date wasn't anywhere as exciting as her friend's, but there was no way she was telling her that. Anyway, she saw the way Mark had been looking at her and she knew it was only a matter of time before Emily's new boyfriend made a play for her. Would she really cheat on her best friend though? "So, when are you seeing Mark again?

Tell him not to bother bringing his mate again. He was knocking me sick; his hands were all over me from the start. I told him straight that if he touched me again, I was going home. He was a minger."

Emily chuckled; her cheeks blushed with a lovely pink glow. "I thought he was alright. He wasn't as sexy as my boy though."

Jane squirmed, *my boy*, what the hell was she going on about? She'd had one date with this bloke. Nothing was set in stone, he wasn't *her boy*, he was just a man who she'd kissed. "So, are you taking him home to meet your mam and dad then?" Jane asked knowing that this would strike fear into her friend.

"No way, don't even suggest that. Mark is my secret, and no one must know about him. Jane, you better swear down to me now that you won't say a word about this to anyone. This is the best thing that has ever happened to me and I don't want you spoiling it."

Jane sighed and raised her eyes towards the ceiling. "Relax, I won't say a word, but I'll have to come with you when you meet him again otherwise your mam and dad will be suspicious. I mean, you don't go anywhere without me, do you?"

Emily nodded and her heart was pounding inside her ribcage just at the thought of this love affair being uncovered. Her dad would go ape, he'd smash Mark's head all over the estate. She was his baby, his princess. A text message alert sounded, and Emily gripped her phone frantically. Jane was on the edge of the bed trying to get a butcher's at the message. Emily took a deep breath and looked at Jane. "He wants to meet me again tonight, he said he can't stop thinking about me."

Jane shoved her fingers down her throat and mimicked vomiting. "He needs to play it cool. It's a right turn off when a guy is all over me like that."

"Oh, shut up. It's usually you who's getting all the attention. It's about time someone took an interest in me."

Jane snarled. Who did she think she was now that she had a boyfriend? "Oi, don't speak to me like that. I'm entitled to an opinion. I'm just saying it's a bit too much too soon that's all."

Emily was staring into space as she spoke. "He might have fallen head over heels in love with me, have you ever thought about that? They say you can fall in love within minutes of meeting someone. I've read it in the magazines. So, why can't he be in love with me already?"

Jane knew she was wasting her breath; Emily was so far up her own arse it was untrue. Jane's mother walked into the bedroom and quickly clocked Emily's feet sprawled all over her crisp white bed sheets. They were crusty and her toe nails needed a cut. "Jane, can you take that duvet off when you get up? I'll bring a fresh one to put on later." She pulled a sour expression that let them know that she wasn't happy. Emily curled her feet under the cover and her face went red. This woman always made her feel so scruffy and she didn't even try to hide it.

"Right mam, I'll do it later. Can you make us some breakfast?" Emily licked her lips, she was starving.

"I'll make some breakfast but you're not eating it upstairs. You'll have to come down and eat at the dining table like everybody else does. I don't know, sometimes Jane I wonder where you get your dirty habits from."

"Mother, I never said I was eating food up here. I just asked for some breakfast, that's all."

Emily sat chewing her finger nails, she was anxious and knew her friend's mother thought all her daughter's bad habits came from her. She dipped her eyes as Jane's mother left the bedroom. Jane let out a laboured breath. "She's a right moaning cow lately. She's always nit picking about daft shit. When I get my own house, I'm going to leave the pots in the sink for days. I'm not doing any housework either. I've had years of her ruling my life with her OCD. Honest, it's not healthy to be obsessed with cleaning like she is."

Emily sniggered. "I wish my mam had the cleaning bug. Our flat is lucky if it's cleaned once a week. Nobody does a tap to keep it clean. I'm embarrassed, you know. I know you come to our house. But I'd never let anyone else step within a mile of it. Imagine the girls from the estate coming to my bedroom to chill for a bit?"

Jane smirked. "I know, they'd need a tetanus jab before they came into your gaff, it's rotten. You're right, your mam is a scruffy cow. You can tell that just by looking at her. She takes no pride in the way she looks either. Those black leggings she wears must be glued to her; she never has them off her back. Everybody can see her camel toe in them, it's disgusting"

Emily was annoyed. Okay, she could call her mam but she never expected it from her best friend. "Oi, leave it out. She's still my mother and she's had a lot to deal with over the last few months."

"It's no excuse, she should still brush her hair and have a wash." Emily sucked hard on her gums. What was wrong with Jane today? She was being so argumentative.

CHAPTER SEVEN

Elsie came sprinting into the front room. She bent down slightly and gripped her knees as she tried to catch her breath. Her cheeks were blood red. Tony rolled on his side and dug his hand down the front of his tracksuit bottoms scratching his nuts. "What's up with you?" Elsie fanned her hand in front of her face, she was still struggling to breathe. The cigarettes she'd smoked over the years were catching up with her. Maybe she should start getting some serious exercise and salvage what was left of her lungs. Sucking in another mouthful of air she replied.

"I've ran all the way home from the shops. Sit up, I've got some brilliant news to tell you. Go on, sit up straight so I can tell you."

Tony shook his head. He was in no mood for drama today. She was always like this when she had a bit of gossip. "Nar, I'm not sitting up. Just tell me. I can't be arsed moving. My bones are creaking."

Elsie plonked down on the sofa next to him and flicked her hand quickly across his legs. "Nudge up then. I want to get comfortable before I speak."

"For fuck's sake. You know how much my body is in pain. Why do you need to be next to me to tell me something?"

Elsie sucked in a large mouthful of air and blew it from her mouth slowly. She was calming down. "I was just talking to that posh woman who lives on that smart street in Moston. You know the one where I've always said I want to live? And, anyway, we got talking whilst we were in the Post Office queue and she told me she's looking for a gardener. Just a few days a week, that's all. To do some weeding and cutting the grass."

Tony ragged his fingers through his hair and held a blank expression, he shrugged his shoulders. "And what? What's the big fuss about?"

Elsie gripped his knees and closed her eyes as she got ready to deliver the news. "She said you can call around for a chat and if you fit the bill for what she's looking for she will give you the job. Tony, this is a Godsend. It's cash in hand and it won't affect your benefits. It's right up your street."

After a second to take in this earth-shattering news, Tony burst out laughing and shook his head. "Fuck off, I'm not doing any gardening. My back is fucked, I can hardly move some days. I'm not ready for work. Tell her to piss-off" he just shook his head and carried on laughing. At least it was taking his mind off his pain.

Elsie shot a look over at him, she was ready to kick off. "Your back is fine when that Mickey wants you to call around to his house though, isn't it? I've never seen you move so bleeding fast. Listen, this is a chance for you to get sorted out. You've done nothing but lie on that sofa for weeks, so it's time to sort your napper out and take the job."

"I'm no Alan Titchmarsh. These fingers are light, they're not green."

"Just go and see what you think. You need money to take us on that holiday, don't you? You know, the one you promised our Emily. How are you supposed to do that when you don't have a pot to piss in?"

Tony sat up and started to straighten his pillows. "I've been off drugs now for nearly two weeks and your telling me to get a job. Do I look like I'm ready to work? I've not slept properly for days and look at my nerves. My stomach is off too, it's non-stop shitting every day." He held his hand out and he was right, his hands were trembling.

"Just stop being negative and go and see her. That's all I'm asking. Please, for me. I've told her you would call later today. Don't be making me look like a fool. You're lucky she's even agreed to see you."

"Fucking hell Elsie, why would you do that without speaking to me first?"

"Because, it's a good earner for us! Unless, we have a money tree growing out on the veranda then I don't see what else we can do to earn a few extra quid." Elsie dropped her head and her voice changed. She knew what she was doing, she was playing the hard done to card. "I just want us to be happy. Maybe we could have a few nice things in this place. We're both guilty of neglecting the kids Tony. If we weren't on drugs imagine the stuff we could have bought them over the years. We owe our Emily a nice home, some new clothes, something to show we care. Jordan is too old now to make amends, but we can treat Emily, can't we?"

She was pulling on Tony's heartstrings and watched him from the corner of her eye. He shook his head from side to side. "I'll go. Okay. But don't be expect fucking miracles. I'm not a well man. Are you forgetting that?"

Elsie jumped over towards him and flung her

chunky arms around his scrawny neck. "Thank you, thank you. I knew you would see sense in the end. Just you wait until I tell Emily that her dad has got a job. She'll shit a brick. She won't believe it in a million years. She'll be so proud of you."

Tony wriggled free. "Turn it in now. I said I'll go and have a chat with her, that's all. So, don't get your hopes up." Elsie reached over and grabbed a packet of pickled onion "Space Raiders" from the white carrier bag at the side of her legs. She shoved a mouthful in her gob and sat munching. She sounded like a horse chewing an apple. "Where is Emily anyway?" Tony asked as he walked about the living room searching for his clothes.

"She's at Jane's. Emily said she was feeling down so she was spending a bit of time with her."

Tony screwed his face up and walked back towards his wife. "What does that girl have to be fed up about? She wants for fuck all."

"I'm only telling you what Emily told me. Jane's a bit of a drama queen anyway, you know what she's like. She's probably been told no for something that she wants from her parents. She's a right mard arse when it comes to things like that."

Tony paused. "It's just a bit weird that's all. Emily seems to be away from home a lot lately. When was the last time she even slept here?"

"Last week," Elsie said as she scoffed some more crisp into her mouth. "But, can you blame her not coming home to this shit-tip? She's probably being treated like royalty at Jane's house. You know they are wadded, don't you?"

Tony scratched at his face and still something seemed to be bothering him. He took a few steps forward and spoke. "Well, just keep a close eye on her anyway. I don't like it when I don't see her."

Elsie reached for the remote control and flicked the TV on as she curled her legs underneath her. "Go and get a wash and a shave. I've told Sue that you will be there at twelve o'clock. Stop worrying about Emily, she's not daft you know?" Tony bit down hard on his bottom lip. Whatever he was going say he changed his mind at the last second. He left the room in a strop. Elsie fed Frank a crisp and patted the space beside her on the sofa. "Come on son, let's get ready to watch Jezzar." Frank was in good books for a change and didn't hesitate to jump onto the sofa, this was a prime location and it was very rare he was invited to lie here. He sprung feet first onto the sofa and snuggled down next to his owner. Today was a good day for him.

★

Tony squeezed his eyes together as he tried to read the address Elsie had scribbled down. Her handwriting was shocking and his eye sight had gone right downhill in the last few years which didn't help. It was cold and he was shivering as he walked along the busy main road. Nothing much was happening around him and he just plodded along in a world of his own. His head was tucked down his jacket for two reason; it was freezing, but more importantly because he didn't know who might be on his case for any crimes he'd committed lately. The last thing he needed was some beef. Okay, there were a few questions hanging over him regarding a house burglary in the estate and of course his name had been flung into the mix as always, but he was innocent of course, or at least that was what he told everyone.

Tony looked over at a house to the left of him and looked down at the piece of paper again, his eyes squeezed tightly together as he tried to read the words. This was the right address; he'd checked it three times. The house was set back on a winding road and inside its own grounds, what a top gaff. The Fairway was an area he'd walked past a few times when he was on his travels. It was a nice place to live and he'd often thought that one day he would live here. Yes, he could see himself being part of this neighbourhood. Maybe he would be liked by all the residents here, perhaps he could even run the neighbourhood watch and make sure all the grafters knew he was the one in charge. He was the best of the best and he'd stop them in their tracks before they knew what day it was. There would be no crime here if he was running the show. Tony was daydreaming again, visualising himself being part of this nice community. He swallowed hard as he yanked the black metal gates wide open, this was hard work, he was getting a sweat on. His eyes shot one way, then another. His heart was racing and since being off the drugs it seemed like all his old self-confidence had left him. He was a nervous wreck and hated talking to anyone, he just wanted to be left alone. This gaff was top-notch. It was like something he'd seen on TV. He felt honoured even to be here. As he walked down the long grey gravel path, he clocked the large white bay windows. The smell from the flowers at the side of him made him choke slightly. He'd already self-diagnosed himself with hay-fever and he might have been right. His eyes were starting to itch, his nasal passage was burning inside. Tony edged nervously towards the front door and looked up at the windows above his head. No one was watching him yet. The CCTV on the side of the building might not be working, otherwise surely someone would have come to see what he was doing in the grounds. He was making a mental note of this, just in case things didn't work out...

Tony stepped forward and rapped on the letterbox. He was flustered and trying to stop his heart from racing. He muttered under his breath. "Calm down lad, for fuck's sake, what's up with you?" In his head he was hoping he wouldn't get the job. He was only here to keep the missus off his back. He could hear a female voice from inside and a dog yapping loudly. The front door opened, and a middle-aged woman stood there looking him up and down. "Can I help you?" she said in a high-pitched tone. Her eyes were glued to him, waiting on an answer.

Tony gulped and played with the cuff from his coat; this woman was sexy, she had shoulder length honey blonde hair and a great set of knockers. For crying out loud, why hadn't Elsie told him that this was a MILF's house? The least he could have done was have a good wash and spruce himself up. He started to speak. "Hiya love, Elsie, my wife, said you was looking for a gardener?"

Sue looked him up and down and elegantly flicked her hair over her shoulders. She bent down and scooped the little white fluffy dog into her arms.

Oh my God, he got a right glimpse of her breasts. The low-cut chiffon blouse she was wearing was leaving nothing to the imagination. He quickly tweaked his crotch and took a few deep breaths. This image was most definitely going into the wank bank. This bitch was hot and sexy, she was everything he wanted in a woman. His cheeks were beetroot and he didn't know what to say next. Sue fluttered her eyelashes and spoke in a gentle tone. "Would you like to come in and have a chat then? If you just let me put Savanna into the kitchen, we can have a good chat. She's friendly enough but gets excited when we have visitors," she chuckled and held the front door wide open, "she's a bit like me. I get excited when I have visitors too."

Had he just heard her, right? What was going on here, was she flirting with him? Tony had been out of the game for years now, but he still knew when a woman was interested in him. He gave her a cheeky wink. Tony walked into the house behind Sue. His eyes scanned up and down her body. Her arse was amazing and given half the chance he would have licked every inch of her bum cheeks, every single nook and cranny of it. He inhaled deeply as the smell of vanilla hit him. His house smelt nothing like this, and he looked around trying to find out where the aroma was coming from. This house had class. White marble floors in the hallway, crystal chandeliers hanging from the high ceiling, this house smelt of money. Sue invited him into the front room. "Can I ask you to take your shoes off? I've recently had new carpets fitted and I'm trying to keep them clean." Tony bent down and tugged at his mucky trainers. As his shoe slid from his foot he nearly died of embarrassment, there was a great big hole in his socks. Quickly, he yanked the sock over his toe. Sue walked into the front room and sat down on a cream leather sofa facing him. That must have been new too because he could smell the leather. Sue twiddled her hair around her finger and licked her bottom lip slowly. "So, tell me a bit about yourself. Your wife told me you can turn your hand to anything."

Tony blushed. What the fuck had Elsie told her? She was always telling people he could do stuff when in fact, he was clueless. He just went along with it, what else could he do? "Yes, that's correct. I'm well educated in a lot of areas. I used to play a lot of football too when I was younger. I just missed out on the big-time. I could have been as big as Wayne Rooney." Tony was talking pure bullshit again. Alright, he might have had a chance at being a professional football player but what areas was he educated in? He was a thick as fuck, he was just a blagger who lied his way out of anything. He was showing off, winging it.

"Oh, that's great news. You see my husband works away a lot and well," she paused as she ran her index finger slowly along her collar-bone. "The garden has got out of hand. I used to love tending to the flowers and planting new ones, but my social life is far too busy for me to find the time to keep them looking nice anymore."

Tony rubbed his hands together. "Well, worry no more. I'm your knight in shining armour. I can ease your burden. I'll have the garden looking mint in no time at all."

Sue looked over at Tony and she held a mischievous

look in her eye. "I'm sure we can work something out. You scratch my back and I'll scratch yours."

Tony's jaw dropped. He wasn't imagining it; this was the real McCoy. This woman was coming on to him. What a turn up for the books! He'd read about these rich women wanting a bit of rough and it seemed like this was his lucky day. Oh, come to daddy, you sexy beast! He was ready for ripping the back out of her given half the chance. He was confident now, breathing under control. "So, does that mean that I've got the job?"

Sue smiled over at him and nodded. "Yes, you seem like a nice man and just what I'm looking for. Shall we have a look at the garden, and I'll show you what I want you to do?" "Yeah, of course."

Tony watched as she dragged her black fur coat from a nearby cupboard. She snuggled deep into the fur and smirked over at Tony. "I love the feel of fur on my face, it makes me feel so…" she never finished her sentence, she left him stood there and walked towards the back door. Tony's tongue was hanging out. This wasn't happening, was it? How could this woman be attracted to him?

"I want you to trim the bushes on a regular basis, I also need the leaves removing every week. I don't mind what you do, as long as it looks clean and tidy. In the summer time you can plant some new flowers but it's too cold at this time of the year for anything to grow."

Tony could have disagreed with her there, something was growing in his groin area, something that was getting bigger every second that passed. He made sure his erect penis was covered as he carried on walking. "I'll look after everything for you love, don't you worry about that. It's a bit of a mess but I will have it ship shape in no time at all. I've always been good with my hands."

Sue giggled and slid a long slender fingernail over her cheek. "That's good to know. I'll keep that in mind."

Tony was hot and sweaty and didn't know where to look. They carried on walking around the garden and she pointed out some more jobs that needed doing. "I'll pay you fifty pounds a week. That will be paid in cash if that's alright. Or, would you like me to pay you in some other way?"

Tony's eyes were stretched wide open and a hot flush filled his face. What did she mean? Pay him with sex, a blow-job? His mind was racing and he had to pinch himself to make sure this was really happening. "Cash will be fine," he said as casually as he could manage.

Sue looked at him. "Can you start as soon as possible? Maybe, tomorrow?"

"Yeah that's sweet. I mean, that's fine."

She smiled and started to walk back into the house. "Would you like something to eat before you leave. I was just going to make a sandwich if you want one too?"

Tony refused. He needed to get out of here and start working on his body. This woman was well up for it and if she would have seen his thin scrawny body naked, she would have changed her mind in an instant. No, this job was a God send in more ways than one and he wasn't going to mess it up. If he played his cards right, he could be Lord of the Manor here, the governor. "No thanks. I'll be getting on my way, if that's alright. I'll be here bright and early in the morning. Do you have gardening tools, or do you want me to bring my own?" Tony was talking out of his arse as per usual. He didn't own a single spade, never mind any gardening tools.

Sue paused, "No, I have everything you need right here." She was looking at him again in a way that told him she was up for a lot more than just gardening. Mickey would never believe this story in a million years, no way in this world. Tony made his way to the door and turned around one last time before he left. "Thank you for the job. I'll see you tomorrow Sue."

"I'm looking forward to it," she said in husky voice.

Tony waited until he was out of the garden and punched his fist into the air and spoke to himself. "You've still got it Tony lad. Get in there. She's gagging for it. Give it a few weeks and she'll be begging for it." Tony had a spring in his step and the dark cloud that had been hanging over his head lately seemed to be lifting.

★

Tony hammered on Mickey's door with both hands. He was just going to walk past his mate's house but he needed a piss. Was this a really good idea coming here? Temptation would be right in front of him; drugs and tablets, were all there for the taking if he wanted them. Mickey opened the door as Tony pushed passed him. "Fuck me. Hello stranger. I thought you'd passed away. Where have you been hiding?"

Tony ran into the toilet and shouted from behind

the door. "I've been sorting my head out pal. It's been hard I can tell you" he said above the noise of the toilet flushing. Tony opened the door and followed Mickey into the front room. "Fuck me, this place looks like a bomb has hit it," Tony stressed.

Mickey shot a look over at him and raised his eyebrows high. "Fuck off. It never bothered you before. Don't start all this shit now you're off the gear, Mr Fucking Perfect."

"Nar, I'm just saying that's all."

There was an awkward silence. Mickey studied his mate and you could tell by the look in his eye that he was up to something. "So, how's it been, being off the drugs?"

Up until now Tony had been looking like death warmed up, but today he seemed to have a lovely pink glow in his cheeks. "It's different. Life doesn't make sense anymore. I just seem to be sat in the house staring at four walls. I mean, before I was out grafting, wasn't I?"

Mickey snarled over at him. "Yes, you were with me, but now you have just sold me out."

"No, it's not like that Mickey. I needed to sort my napper out. Elsie was throwing me out and our Emily turned snide on me too. They're all I've got mate. Without them I'd curl up in a ball and die. I need to at least give it a go. I can't be a junkie forever, can I?"

Mickey pulled out a small bag from his jeans. His eyes were wide open, and he was giggling. "So, you won't want a smoke of this then, will you? One last toot with your old pal?"

Tony lost all the colour from his cheeks. He was

white. What the hell was Mickey playing at? He should have been praising his friend and wishing him all the luck in the world with his new life without drugs, not tempting him to fail, like he was doing.

Tony fixed his eyes on the brown powder and hugged his body with both arms. He licked his dry cracked lips and closed his eyes. Suddenly, he opened them and marched towards the door. "I've got to go Mickey. I'll see you around. I can't be around this shit anymore. I'm weak mate, very weak."

Mickey shouted after him. "You'll be back. Trust me. It won't be long before your back on the gear. Once a smackhead, always a smackhead. Remember that pal."

What a horrible bastard Mickey was; selfish and jealous. Tony stood with his back pinned up against the wall outside. His windpipe was tightening, and he was struggling to breathe. His mind was racing, and he was having a full-blown panic attack. He was talking to himself. "No, Tony. Get your arse home. Don't fuck this up, just go home."

★

Elsie twisted her body on the sofa as Tony walked into the living room. Frank jumped up from the tattered carpet and barked as he spotted his master returning home. "Bleeding hell Frank, shut the fuck up and go and lie back down. You act like I've been away for weeks not hours. Go on, do one." The dog circled a few times on the spot and knew he wasn't getting any attention.

Elsie sat up straight and yawned with her arms

stretched high above her head. "How did you get on? Did you go and see Sue?" She was watching his every move, watching his facial expressions to see if he was lying.

Tony plonked down on the sofa and the corners of his mouth began to rise. "I nailed it. I start tomorrow."

"Fuck off lying to me. What really happened?"

Tony pulled a sour expression. "I've just told you. I start tomorrow. So, you need to make sure I have some decent clothes to wear. Why didn't you tell me she was posh? Fucking hell, I felt like a right scruffy twat when I was stood next to her. I stank of BO."

Elsie didn't know if he was playing with her. Had he got the job or what? She repeated herself. "Seriously, did you get the job?"

Tony spoke slowly and looked her directly in the eyes. "Yes. Sue loved me."

Elsie squirmed and sat forward in her seat. "What do you fucking mean, she loved you?"

He was giggling now and loved that his wife was feeling a little insecure. He was having her at it. "She said I was just what she's looking for. She's a lovely looking woman, isn't she?"

A pillow was launched across the room and smashed Tony in the face. Elsie snapped. "Don't start winding me up, Tony. If you fancy her then go and ask her if you can live there. She'll soon kick your arse to the kerb when she knows what a lazy bastard you are. Go on, off you go, if that's what you want?"

Tony knew he'd over-stepped the mark. He plonked down next to his wife and started to tickle her. "Come on. You know I only have eyes for you, my big chubby beauty."

She was on one. "You'd better only have eyes for me Tony because if I ever find out your playing away from home then I'll cut your balls off and make a necklace out of them." He was raging. He needed more than words to calm her down. His lips touched hers and he looked deep into her eyes. "You're the only woman for me baby. Don't worry." He kissed his wife and moved back onto the sofa. "Who'd have thought it ay? Me, Tony Clayton, with a job! A real fucking job!"

★

Emily walked into the front room and smiled at her father. She could see he wasn't twisted or off his napper and congratulated him. "You look really well, dad. Honest, you don't look as old anymore. You have colour in your cheeks. I'm so proud of you. Keep it up."

Tony could have burst out crying. A ball of emotion crept up his throat and he was finding it hard to hold the tears back. "Thanks princess. And, guess who's only gone and got a job?"

Emily looked over at her mother and then back at her father. She shrugged her shoulders. "Who?"

Elsie smiled from cheek to cheek and pointed her finger over at her husband. "Your dad," she said with excitement in her voice.

Emily sat down next to Tony and looked at him in more detail. These two were always lying to her and she didn't have a clue if this was just another one of their windups. The front door banged shut and in walked Jordan. Emily shot a look over at him and spoke. "Oi, our kid. My mam has just said my dad has got a job."

Jordan burst out laughing and sat down on the sofa. "Nar, has he fuck. They're having you over. Go on dad, tell her you are lying."

Tony had a face on him now and he was losing his rag. "Wow, I've got a job. What's the big deal and why don't any of you believe me?"

Jordan was the spokesman for the siblings and told his old man straight. "We don't believe you because you never tell the truth. Don't make me go into it dad, but you're a born liar."

Elsie had to say something. "He might have been a liar in the past but he's being honest for a change. I got him the job from a woman I know."

Tony protested. "I got the job, you just told me who wanted a gardener. Don't you be trophy hunting again and stealing the limelight."

Elsie folded her arms across her breasts. She growled over at him. "I was the one who got you the interview, you dickhead, so wind your neck in and stop being a tosser."

Emily and Jordan looked at each other in disbelief. Was this the truth or what? Had their feckless father finally got himself a job. Emily threw her arms around her father's neck and squeezed him with all her might. It was the truth; she could tell by the way he was acting. "Dad, I'm lost for words. Honest, I'm so, so, proud of you."

"And, so you should be. I'm going to make a difference to this family, like I promised. Emily, I made a promise that we would go on holiday and that's what will be happening. My word is my bond."

Jordan shook hands with his dad. "Well done. It's good news that you're working and even better news that you're off the drugs."

Tony's lips quivered. What the fuck was up with him lately, he was an emotional wreck. "I even turned down drugs today" he said.

Elsie quickly turned to face him. This was news to her. "Who offered you drugs?"

"It was Mickey. I called for a piss at his gaff and he asked if I fancied a smoke."

"He's a cheeky twat! Why would he offer you smack when he knows you've been sorting your head out? I've never trusted that one, shady he is, don't ever trust him."

Jordan held his flat palm up and nodded at his mother. "Mam, just chill will you. Temptation is always going to be there. My dad has just been open and honest and told you that he refused. Don't give him a hard time, he did well."

Tony was flavour of the month for sure in this house. He was the hero of the hour and everybody was praising him. Elsie was jealous, you could see it in her eye. She'd been off drugs now for months. Where was her praise? Where was her well done? Nobody flinched when she went cold turkey, bleeding nobody.

"I start tomorrow morning. It's only a bit of gardening but it's a start. Maybe I can get a few more clients and before long I will have my own business. Jordan, you could even start working for me."

"Dad, just take each day as it comes and don't fuck it up. This is a golden ticket for you and like you said it could turn into something much more if you use your napper."

"Yes son. I'm going to make it work. I just need to get some new clobber. I need some boots, gloves, and a few other bits. I'll have to look the part, won't I?"

Jordan pulled out some money and passed it to his father. "There you go. There's enough there to sort yourself out. Go and get kitted out."

Elsie was spitting feathers. She was potless and struggling to feed everyone and here was her husband being given money left, right and fucking centre. Tony quickly shoved the cash into his sock. He smiled at Elsie and smirked. "It's all gravy, baby. I'll nip on the market soon and get sorted out with some clobber. If there is anything left, I might get you some of them chocolates you like." Elsie had a face like a smacked arse and ignored him.

Jordan sat next to his sister and nudged her. "So, where have you been hiding. Every time I've been here you've been out. What have you been up to?"

Her eyes were wide open now, she could never lie, she stuttered. "I've just been at Jane's. It's boring just sat in here all the time so I just chill at my friend's house, listening to tunes and that."

Jordan sucked on his teeth. He could tell something wasn't right. "It's not like you to be away from home for long. Have you got a boyfriend or something?"

Emily's cheeks were on fire. Her mouth was dry, and she started nibbling on her fingernails. The family were waiting on an answer, all eyes were on her now. "No, why are you saying that? I'm not interested in boys. I'm living my life before I settle down."

Elsie was wide-eyed, "you better not be a lesbian!

What do you mean you're not interested in boys? All girls are interested in lads at your age."

"I mean, I'm single. When and if I get a boyfriend then you'll be the first to know mother. But, until then, get off my back and stop asking questions."

Jordan sniggered. "Wow, chill out will you. I was only asking. No need to bite my head off you moody bitch."

Emily stood up and marched to the living room door. Before she left, she shouted over her shoulder. "No wonder I stay at Jane's all the time. You lot are stupid." The door banged shut and she was gone. She nearly took the door from its hinges.

Tony looked at his family and rolled his eyes. "Is she on the blob or what?"

Elsie shrugged her shoulders. "Fuck knows, something is wrong with her though. Give it ten minutes and I'll go up and see if she's alright. You might be right, she's probably hormonal."

CHAPTER EIGHT

Emily had spent ages getting ready for her date. Her hair was done and her make-up was perfect. She was edgy as she walked up the dimly lit pathway. Tonight she was meeting him alone. Jane knew nothing about this date, she'd arranged this meeting behind her best friend's back. Emily wanted some quality time with Mark, time to get to know him properly. How could she do that when Jane was always there demanding his attention? When they were out her friend was always flirting with Mark; she laughed at everything he said and was always touching him whenever they spoke. No, Mark was her man and her friend could take a backseat for now.

Mark parked over the road from where she was. The cars headlights turned off. Emily's heels clipped along the pavement and she smiled when she saw him for the first time. She flicked her hair over her shoulder and picked up speed. This man made her heart beat faster than normal and something was happening between her legs too, a warm rush circling over her groin. A feeling she had never experienced before in her life. It happened every time she was near him. Emily opened the car door and leaned over and pecked Mark on the cheek. He smiled and looked her directly in the eyes. "You smell beautiful babes," he whispered into her ear.

"Thank you," she replied as she clipped her seat belt across her body. "Where are we going? Why won't you tell me. What's the big surprise?"

Mark placed his hand on her cold knee and turned the engine over. "It's a surprise. So, stop asking, because I'm not telling you. All you need to know is that I'm taking you to meet a few people that's all."

"Who? Who are we going to see?" Mark pulled out of the lay-by and never replied. He turned the music up and nodded his head to the beat of the music as they hit the main road. He was always checking his phone, texting and answering calls. Emily couldn't take her eyes off him; she was completed infatuated. She studied every inch of him, his skin, his hair, his firm thighs. Would it really be that bad if she had sex with him after knowing him such a short time? Most of her mates were sexually active so why should she be any different? At least then when the girls sat telling their stories about the guys they were dating; she would be able to join in too. She never had anything interesting to tell the group, absolutely nothing at all. Not even a grope of her breasts, her love life was non-existent, well, up until now.

Mark hit the motorway and picked up speed. Eighty miles an hour he clocked, he was in a rush as he bobbed and weaved through the traffic. "Where's Jane tonight? I thought you two were joined at the hip?"

Why was he asking about her? This date should have been about her, nobody else. "Oh, she's met a new lad and she's going out with him tonight," Emily lied.

"That's a shame, because she's a nice girl isn't, she? Bright, and bubbly and full of self-confidence. Who's this new guy anyway? She told me she was single."

Emily fidgeted about and looked out of the

window. She was never a good liar. "Jane's a bit messed up in the head if I'm being honest. She has loads of male interest but never stays with the same boy for long. She told me herself that she hasn't got time for a relationship. Her parents are strict with her and she has to study hard." What a liar she was turning out to be, Jane was single and ready to mingle, she was alone tonight, sat in her bedroom probably bored to tears.

Mark digested what she'd just said and tickled the end of his chin with a single finger. "Are you ready for a relationship? I don't want to put all my time and energy into someone who's going to cart me after a few dates?"

Emily was alarmed. "Of course I'm ready. I'm more than ready to be in a relationship. What makes you think that I'm not?"

Mark held a cunning look in his eye as he replied. "So, what do you think of me, do you love me?"

Her heart was racing, her mouth suddenly became dry, she was having a hot flush. Emily was lost for words; she took a few seconds to think about her answer. There was no way she was throwing her hands in to loving him, she was playing it cool, there was no way she wanted to come across as a bunny boiler. "I don't really know you enough yet to love you, do I? But I do like you a lot. Let's see how things go before we start talking about love."

Mark sneered over at her and his tone changed. "Oh, right. Well at least I know now. I'll hold back if you don't feel the same as I do. I'm not wasting time on someone who's playing mind games."

Emily was in a panic; she'd upset him, she could

tell by his body language. He turned the music up and picked up speed. Ninety miles per hour and now the car was shaking. They sat in an awkward silence. Emily felt the air change; he hardly spoke a word to her for the rest of the journey. Once he pulled off the motorway, he spoke for the first time in what seemed like hours. "Alex is a top guy and a close friend. He'd do anything for me, and he's helped me out a lot in the past, so be nice to him."

Emily was sheepish, like a scolded child. "I will. Are you alright Mark, you seem to have gone all quiet? Have I upset you or something?"

He let out a sarcastic laugh and patted her knee. "No, not really. I'm just a bit gutted that you don't feel the same about me as I do for you. But I'll get over it, don't you worry. I'll move on, if that's what you want?"

Was he saying he loved her or what, she wasn't sure? She tickled the back of his neck and tried to make amends. "Are you saying that you love me? What do you mean you will move on?"

Mark kept his eyes on the road and nodded his head. "I've been talking to you for ages online Emily. I would never have agreed to meet you if I wasn't getting feelings for you. You're just the type of girl I want to marry. I feel at ease with you and it's like I've known you forever. I don't like time wasters. I want someone who is genuine and not playing games with me. I don't fall in love every day you know. I wear my heart on my sleeve, that's all. It's not a crime is it?"

Emily was gobsmacked. This was her dream too and she wasn't holding her cards to her chest any longer. She just blurted it out. If she didn't tell him she would regret it for the rest of her life. If he did move on, she would be heartbroken, sat in her bedroom back to her lonely boring life. "I do have feelings for you too. Jane told me that I had to play it cool, so I wasn't sure if I should open up or not. I didn't want you to think I was clingy or anything. I just wanted you to like me."

Mark squeezed her hand and lifted it up to his mouth and kissed her fingers softly. "I would do anything for you already. I think about you all day long. From the moment I wake up to the second I go to sleep; you are constantly on my mind. You're like a drug that I'm addicted to, you've just got right under my skin." Emily was filled with love. His dream was hers too. This was her prince charming, her happy ever after.

Mark pulled up at a pub. He opened the door of the boozer and let Emily walk inside first. The pub was lively, and the music was booming. Mark stretched his neck and waved his hand above his head to a man sat in the corner of the room. "What are you drinking babes," he asked.

"Can I have a diet coke?"

Mark pulled a sour face and asked her again. "What, you want to drink coke?" Emily realised she'd dropped a bollock and quickly changed her mind. "Sorry, I meant can I have a Vodka and coke please." Mark spoke to the busty barmaid and ordered her a double vodka and coke. Emily was never a big drinker and knew she would have to take her time with her drinks otherwise she would be on her back within the hour. Mark led her to a table at the other side of the room. There were girls dancing around, grinding, twerking. They all seemed to know Mark and she was sure he let on to a few of them. She'd have to keep her eye on these tarts, they looked like they would shag anything with a wallet. Once she sat down, Mark sat next to her. Was it her imagination or was the blonde girl facing them trying to get Mark's attention? This girl was looking straight at Mark as she slut-dropped on the dance floor. Emily quickly looked at Mark and she could see his eyes were looking her way. Right, this was going too far she had to say something. "Do you know that girl?"

Mark turned his head quickly and faced her. "Yes, she's been trying to get a date with me for ages. Every time I see her, she's all over me. Honest, she's offered to suck me off and everything."

Emily clenched her fist tightly together. What a cheeky bitch this girl was trying to come on to her man. Emily growled over at the female and sucked hard on her gums. What on earth was happening to her, she was usually shy and timid and would run a mile from any kind of trouble, she was no fighter. Mark was loving it; she could see him smirking. He twisted his head when he heard his name being called from the other side of the room. He stood up and raised his hand over his head. "I'll be there in a minute, pal." Emily could see a fat balding man smiling at her from the other side of the room. He stood up and squeezed passed the gap in the table. "I won't be long. Just let me sort something out with Alex and then I'll introduce him to you."

Emily was still raging inside and kept looking

over at the blonde. She wanted to scratch her eyes out, rag her hair all over the show. Who did she think she was with her big tits and slim-line figure? "Yeah, no worries," she replied.

Mark left her side and Emily lifted her drink up slowly and sipped at it. As soon as he was gone Emily stood up to go to the toilet. She made her way towards the dance-floor and turned her head to see where Mark was. Once she could see he was busy she nudged into the girl who was making a play for her man. "Oi, can I have a quick word with you?"

The girl looked confused. "Me? You want to talk with me?"

The music was loud and Emily was struggling to be heard. "Come to the toilet and I'll explain." The youngish girl shrugged her shoulders at her dancing partner and plodded behind Emily. The restroom was hammered, one girl was looking into the mirror applying her candy pink lip-gloss while her mate sat with the toilet door open talking to her. Emily had to be quick and get her point across. She took a deep breath and went nose to nose with the girl. "Mark is my boyfriend so if you don't want any trouble, keep well away from him. Do you hear me? Back off?"

The girl looked her up and down and held a cocky look. "Listen sweetheart, if I wanted Mark then I would take him. Take a chill-pill and relax. He's not your man, he never will be. It's obvious you don't know him if you think he's yours."

Emily was bright red and didn't know what to say. Obviously, she'd not thought about this properly. Another girl joined them now and stared directly at

Emily. "What's going on? Is there a problem?"

"Yes, this tramp has told me to keep away from Mark because it's her boyfriend. Do me a favour Anne and word her up before I knock her block off."

Anne gripped Emily by the scruff of the neck and pushed her into a cubicle. Once she was inside, she growled in her face, her hot stale breath hitting the end of her nose. "I don't know what planet you're on love but trust me, Kelly is not interested in Mark. We all know what he is and wouldn't touch him with a barge pole." She rammed her index finger into the side of Emily's head. "Do you hear me or are you thick?"

Emily had to stand up for herself, she was the underdog and backed into a corner. Jane would never let anyone speak to her like this, she'd fight back. The colour drained from her face and her knuckles turned white as she squeezed her fingers into two tight balls. She'd seen her mother fight lots of time and she knew she would have to strike the first blow to stand a chance. She was weighing her up, looking for the right moment to make her move. Anne turned to walk away. Emily saw her chance and smashed a fist into her head. She twisted her fingers into her long dark locks and swung Anne about like a rag doll. Where had her strength come from? She was like a raging bull. "Don't ever speak to me like that. And, what do mean about Mark? Go on, spit it out, say what you have to before I finish you off." Emily was in the zone, she had her mother's temper for sure, she just didn't know it. Anne was screaming and trying to wriggle free. She managed to open the toilet door and get out before Emily swung another blow. "The man is a wanker, you'll see.

Trust me, he'll have you with them before you know what day it. Good luck with that."

Anne sprinted off and before Emily could get another grip of her she was gone out of the toilets. Emily licked the trickle of red blood dripping down her knuckles. As she stepped out of the toilet the room seemed to go silent. All eyes were on her and she didn't know where to look. She slowly made her way to the sink and stuck her hand under the cold tap. She looked into the mirror and raised her eyes at the woman stood next to her. "What are you gawping at? Do you want some?" You could see the girl didn't want any beef and she quickly washed her hands and left the toilets. Emily closed her eyes slowly and tried to calm down. Rage was pumping through her veins; she closed her eyes to snap out of the zone she was in. Once her breathing had returned to normal, she took one last look in the mirror and left the toilets. Anne and Kelly were nowhere to be seen. She twisted her head left then right to see if she could spot them, but they were gone. Emily made her way back to her seat and the corners of her mouth began to rise. She was her mother's daughter for sure. A fighter.

Taking a large mouthful from her glass she sat back in her chair. The words that Anne had screamed at her were still lying heavy on her mind. What did she mean? She was sat thinking and in a world of her own. "Emily, this is my friend Alex."

Alex stretched his arms over and hugged her. He kissed the side of her cheek too. "Mark has told me so much about you Emily. I'm glad we have finally met. Where is your friend Jane? Mark, did you say she had a friend?"

Mark whispered something into Alex's ear and he nodded. Emily looked uncomfortable as Alex examined her, he was just staring at her, licking his lips slowly. "Drink up Emily we are going to Alex's pad. We can relax there and have a few beers. A few of the others are coming too. Is that right Alex?"

"Yeah, yes I mean," he replied. Emily wasn't sure of where Mark was taking her, but she didn't have a care in the world if she was with her Mr Right. Tonight, was about enjoying herself, letting her hair down and throwing caution to the wind. Life was for living and she was living it alright. Bring on the party!

CHAPTER NINE

Tony looked in the mirror as he slapped aftershave over his cheeks with his palms. His mouth was wide open as the cold fragrance connected with his cheeks. It was only some cheap shit, something he'd nicked from a store donkey's years ago. He stood back from the mirror and shouted out in a loud voice, his eyes never leaving the mirror. "Elsie, have you ironed my clobber or what? Fuck me, I'm going to be late if you don't make a move. Make sure you iron them right too, don't leave creases in them like you normally do."

Elsie yelled back from the other room. "Why are you wearing your best clothes to go gardening. It's dirty work, you'll get filthy. You should be wearing your scruffs."

Tony smiled at his reflection in the mirror and mumbled under his breath. "I'm going to get dirty alright. I'm going to rip the back out of that woman given half the chance." Tony flexed his bony arms in the mirror and chuckled to himself. He edged closer to the mirror and pulled his lips apart, examining his teeth. "Elsie, have we got any whitening toothpaste. My teeth are minging. I need something to brighten my smile up now I'm a working man. I've never noticed how bad my teeth were until now. Bleeding hell I'm a right gummy fucker."

There were a lot of things that he'd neglected over

the years and his body image was top of the list. Tony's head smashed against the bathroom wall as his wife slung his clothes at him with force. She was fuming. "Oi, cheeky bollocks. If you carry on winding me up, you won't need any fucking toothpaste because I'll knock the fuckers out. I'm warning you Tony, stop now, before I lose my rag with you."

Tony stumbled and tried to steady his feet. "You idiot, I nearly fell over then. What's up with you now?"

She growled at him, ready to snap his jaw if he dared press her buttons again. "Well, stop winding me up then. You know how I feel about you with other women. You're planting seeds in my head; you know exactly what you're playing at. It's a dangerous game and someone will get hurt. And, more than likely, it will be you." He smirked.

He knew exactly what he was doing. "I've not said anything you weirdo. I only asked for some whitening toothpaste, where is the harm in that? God, shoot me for trying to look half decent."

She placed one hand on her hip and tilted her head slightly. It was her time to have a go at him. "You have no bleeding teeth Tony; you have one pickle–stabber of a tooth and the rest are brown stumps. So, what the hell are you trying to brighten up? You look like a gummy-bear. You have for years."

Tony investigated his gnashers. His wife was right, he was gummy and the one tooth he had was on its way out, it was wobbly and discoloured. With one last glance at himself, Tony started to get ready. "Elsie, sort me some tablets out before I go. Something to get rid of these shakes. How long is it before my body feels normal again? I hardly sleep anymore and I'm still shitting like a new born baby."

"Tony, it takes ages to feel normal again. I'm on twenty mils of methadone now and I can just about feel the difference in my body. I'm sleeping alright too. You're on sixty mils so you should feel alright. Plus, you've been necking diazepam like nobody's business, so you shouldn't be shaking like you are. It might be time to man up and just roll with it."

"It's nearly three weeks now that I've been clean. I never thought I would see the day if I'm being honest with you. Hard work it is, hard fucking work."

Elsie smiled over at her husband and spoke in a gentle voice. "I'm proud of you, we all are. I can see the light at the end of the tunnel. I feel calm and not on edge all the time. I'm starting to feel like me again. The person who I was years ago."

Tony held the tears back as his eyes clouded over. He was an emotional wreck. He cried at anything, sobbed his heart out. His emotions were well and truly out of control. Elsie sat down on the edge of the bed and kicked her legs slowly. She watched him come back into the bedroom. "I'm thinking of going to see my dad. He's been on my mind a lot lately. I've sorted myself out so I can't see there being a problem. What do you think?"

Tony let out a sarcastic laugh. "I think you need your head feeling. That old cunt will never change. I can't see why you are bothering with him after the way he's treated you over the years. He turned his back on you when you needed him most. Fuck him off, you don't need him."

"I was the one in the wrong, not him," Elsie snapped, "he gave me chance after chance and I just let him down. I'm ashamed of the things I've done to my family and what I put them through. I think it's time to make amends. They are good people, it was us who hurt them, not the other way around."

Tony could see she was getting upset and tried his best to support her. He hated her old man with a passion and he never lost any sleep over him not being in their lives anymore. "It's up to you love but don't let me say I told you so when he carts you again. You'll be heartbroken again. You know I'm right."

"I'm willing to risk that. I just have to try. Maybe you should take a leaf out of my book and try to sort your shit out with your dad. I heard he's been very ill."

A cup smashed against the bedroom wall and Elsie covered her head with her arms to protect herself from the shards of glass. His voice bounced against the walls. "Don't you mention that cunt's name in this house again! How many times have I told you that he's dead in my eyes, fucking dead? You go and do what you're doing but leave me alone. You know how I feel about him."

"Oh my God. Is there any need to be smashing things against the wall? Relax, will you! I'm just saying a lot of water has gone under the bridge since you were younger so maybe you could sort things out with him."

Tony shook his head, his ears pinned back, and she could see the hatred in his eyes. "He fucked us all up. Look at my mam because of him, he beat her black and blue for years and you expect me to forgive him for that. It was his fault I never made it in football. He broke my leg when he threw me down the stairs. Do you think I could ever forgive him for that? He ruined my dreams, my chance of making the big time. If anything, it should be him who's knocking my door down begging for forgiveness, not the other way around. Nah, the guy's a waste of space. A dickhead."

"Bloody hell, I'm sorry I even mentioned it. Just go to work and forget about it. I was only trying to help, that's all."

Tony left the bedroom with his jacket slung over his shoulder. He was on point today and the best he'd looked in a long time. Frank ran under his feet and made him trip up. Elsie sniggered and covered her mouth with her hand. "You silly mutt, get out of my way," he moaned as he wobbled about. "I'm off! See you later," he shouted behind him.

Elsie heard the front door bang shut and sighed with relief. In the back of her mind she thought Tony would have changed his mind about the job and let her down at the last minute. He'd surprised her really. Emily stood at her bedroom door and just stared at her mother. Elsie was surprised to see her there. "God, blimey. I nearly shit my knickers then. When did you come in?"

"Just now. I saw my dad leaving as I pulled up in the taxi, but he never seen me, he's as blind as a bat. He needs glasses."

"Taxi? Where did you get your money from to pay for a taxi?"

"Jane's dad paid for it. He was going to drop me off but changed his mind at the last minute."

Elsie looked at her daughter with love in her eyes. "Come and get on the bed with me. We've not had any bonding time in ages. Let's have a girly day." Emily used to love lying on her mother's bed with her. Usually she'd just watch Elsie sleep all day, off her head, but today her mother was wide awake for a change. Elsie patted the side of the bed with her hand. "Come on then before I change my mind and have a kip. You can fill me in about life at the Royals." She sniggered and shuffled her bum-cheeks across the bed slightly. Emily yawned and stretched her arms over her head.

"Mam, I'm not really in the mood to chat. To tell you the truth I'm tired. Jane was gabbing until late and to tell you the truth, I just want to go to sleep."
"Cheeky cow, here's me ready to shower you with love and affection and you turn it down. You'll be moaning soon saying nobody cares about you."

"I don't need any love mother, you're a bit late for that. I've grown up now or have you not noticed?"

Elsie squirmed and lifted her head up from the stained pillow. Where was this coming from? Emily always loved a few cuddles. "Bleeding hell, what's up with you lately. Your dad has started work today and both of us have sorted our heads out, so what's your problem? It's all you've ever wanted isn't it?"

Emily plodded to the side of the bed and sat down. She looked knackered. "It was mam, but I suppose when you've waited so long for something and it doesn't happen, well, you give up hope, don't you?"

Elsie dragged her daughter back onto the bed and kissed her on the cheek. "Orr, does nobody care about my little baby then? Come here while mummy loves you."

Emily wriggled free. She was in no mood for fun and games. Maybe a few months ago she would have welcomed this but not now, not now that she had someone special to love. Emily's mobile phone was ringing and Jane's name was flashing across the screen. Elsie clocked it. "Bloody hell, you've only just left her and she's ringing you. Are you sure she's not a lesbian or something? I mean, you're never away from her house lately."

"Eww mam, why would you say something like that? I'm not a rug-muncher and neither is Jane. We're just good friends, that's all. Stop saying we're lesbians when we are clearly not." Elsie watched closely as her daughter left the room and looked puzzled. Something was wrong with Emily, something she just couldn't put her finger on at this moment in time. Elsie lay on the bed thinking, pondering her thoughts.

★

Tony had a bounce in his step as he approached Sue's house. He was like Jack the Lad as he walked up the pathway. In his imagination he'd already gone over every scenario. She was going to open the door wearing only her fur coat and heels and suddenly she was going to open the coat and reveal her curvy sexy body. He was ready for that. His cock was clean and he'd even had a quick trim of his pubic hair to give him that extra inch of penis to show when the time was right. Okay, he wasn't at his best, but he was ready for whatever she had to throw at him. Fuck Elsie and her fat blubbery body, if he had a chance of a woman like this then he was taking it, no matter what. All the blood from his brain had run to his penis and he wasn't thinking straight. Imagine all the lads' faces in the boozer when he had this hotty on his arm. He could see their boat-races now, sick with jealousy. Tony knocked on the front door and stood back. He quickly straightened up and ran his fingers through his hair. He was ready to see her again, more than ready. He could hear her voice from behind the door. He cupped his hands together and blew his warm breath inside them.

Sue answered the door in a cream silk dressing gown. "Good morning," she said in a sexy voice before she quickly looked at her wristwatch. "You're here early, honey. I didn't expect you for at least another hour. Oh, what must you think of me? I've just got up out of bed. I bet I look terrible."

Tony smirked as he replied. "You look lovely, you have nothing to worry about. I wish I looked like you when I get out of bed in the morning. I look like I've been dragged through a hedge backwards. You should see the state of my hair, it's like a big afro. Anyway, I thought I'd get here early and get a good start on things. I reckon I can sort all the weeds out today if the rain holds off."

Sue held the door open. Her cream silk dressing gown was opened slightly, and he got a good look at her long, tanned legs. "You must have a coffee with me first before you start work. I can make you some breakfast too. I mean, you will need your strength today won't you? You can't work on an empty stomach."

If she could have read his mind she would have been shocked. You could see by the way that he was tugging at his groin area that he was already excited. "If you don't mind I will. I rushed out this morning without a bite to eat and her indoors won't make me anything to eat, she's a lazy cow. Bone idle."

Sue chuckled. "Have you been married long?" Sue asked as she led Tony to the kitchen table.

"Too long if I'm being honest. Our marriage has been stale for years. I only stay for the kids. Elsie is a nice enough person, but the spark has gone. It went years ago." What a lying bastard. His poor wife had got up early out of bed this morning to make him something to eat and iron his clothes. He was a blatant liar. Elsie lived and breathed her husband and if anything, she did too much for him.

Sue flicked her hair over her shoulder and sat twisting the gold band on her long slender finger. "My marriage is something like that too. It's lifeless, he never shows me he cares anymore," she covered her mouth quickly with her hand and opened her eyes wide. "Whoops, I shouldn't be telling you about my private life, should I? It's just so hard sometimes to hold it all in. I just pretend to everyone I'm happy but I'm far from it. Yes, I have a nice home and money has never been a problem but that's not enough for me. I want affection. I want to be kissed. To be the most important person in his life." Sue dipped her head, she was sad. Years of frustration reaching the surface.

Tony reached over and touched her knee softly. "Tell me about it Sue. It looks like we are two lost souls, unhappy in our marriages. Fate always finds a way and one day you will find someone who makes you happy. Happiness might not be where you expect to find it, it may just sneak up on you." Tony studied her, watching her body language. Maybe, he should kiss her now, grope her tits, stick his tongue down the back of her neck? He watched her leave the room and head into the kitchen. His blood pressure was sky high, he blew a laboured breath and closed his eyes slowly. Maybe, the time wasn't right after all.

Tony and Sue sat at the dining table in the conservatory. It was lovely here. The morning light seeping inside, the calming colours, everything about it making him relax. He visualised himself living here, looking out each morning onto the green lawns, sipping tea, reading the newspaper. Yes, he could live here given the chance. Tony looked over at his employer. Just the way she was eating was sexy. She was teasing him for sure. She nibbled at the end of the long thin juicy sausage. It was driving him wild, he so wished it was his penis she was nibbling. He was drooling with every mouthful she ate. Sue crossed her legs and flicked her silken locks over her shoulder. She finished her mouthful of food and smiled over at him. "So, tell me more about yourself Tony. I've heard a bit from your wife, but it would be nice if you told me some things too."

He gulped and emptied his mouth as quickly as he could. Nobody had given a flying fuck about him in years and here he was with this beautiful woman eager to know about his depressing, sad life. But what was there to tell her? He couldn't tell her the truth that he was a smack head, a thief, a liar and a piss-head, could he? He took his time before he answered. He had to think about this first before he messed it up.

Tony licked his lips slowly and sat back in his seat. "I've been a little bit ill lately as you can see by looking at me," he stuttered and hung his head low. "I had cancer, but I've had Chemo now and I've been alright for the last year. It took it out of me it did. I shit myself if I'm being honest. I thought my number was up. I just knew I had to be strong and fight the disease. I wasn't giving up for love nor money. I'm a survivor."

Sue covered her mouth with her hand. She was shocked. "You poor soul. You're such a brave man. I'm so glad you're alright now though. Your family must have been worried to death. I could only imagine what your wife was going though, bless her soul."

His voice was low and he choked up. He was pretending to wipe his eyes with the cuff from his jumper. "My children were devastated. They were brilliant, honest, they did everything they could to look after me. I'll never forget that. It broke my heart. I suppose you take a lot of things for granted don't you, until something like illness happens."

"You never know the day, do you? Like I said, you're one of the lucky ones who pulled through. I've lost a lot of family and friends to cancer. It's a wicked disease. It doesn't care who you are it just takes you and there is nothing you can do about it." Tony wriggled about in his seat. It was the way she was looking at him again. Sue leaned over and patted his thigh. "I love finding out about people. Do you have any hobbies Tony?"

He nearly choked. His hobbies were shoplifting, popping pills, taking drugs, and watching porn but he couldn't tell her that. He lied again. "I like playing football and snooker. I love DIY too. I like to create things. I'm good with my hands." Oh, you had to hand it to Tony, he was a class act, the lies were just rolling from his tongue. What a lying bastard he was. "I could help you around the house if you wanted me to. Bang a few nails in here and there, put some shelves up. You know, basic stuff."

Sue liked that, she opened her eyes wide. "That would be great. There are lots of little jobs that need doing. I'll pay you for them too. I'm not a charity case. I don't expect anything for nothing." She giggled and reached over for her cigarettes. She didn't really look like a smoker, but there she was popping a fag into her mouth. She raised her eyes. "My husband thinks I quit two years ago, but what he doesn't know won't harm him… will it? I only smoke a few a day anyway. I just can't stop. God knows I've tried."

She was talking to the right person here regarding addiction. Tony could have talked all day long about the struggles he'd faced in every day life, but he kept schtum. She hesitated as she passed him a cigarette. "Sorry, how rude of me, do you smoke?"

Tony was gagging for a bifta and quickly took her up on her offer. "Yes please. I'm like you. I've tried to knock it on the head, lots of times, but I'm struggling. Like you said it's so hard and after me having cancer I feel like a hypocrite. It's like I don't care about my health." Sue flicked the lighter under his cigarette and watched as he sucked his cheeks together. The two of them had a quiet few seconds before they spoke again.

Today was going to be interesting, very interesting indeed.

★

Emily lay on her bed and closed her eyes. Last night was amazing and one of the best nights she'd ever had in her life. Okay she loved the "Take That" concert she'd been too last year but this was so much better. This was real life. Emily had stayed with Mark all night. Alex offered them both a bed for the night and it just made sense to stay there rather than getting a taxi home. What a nice man Alex was, he let most of the guests stay at his pad. Mark was steaming anyway and way over the limit to dive, so it was a good choice to stay. Today Emily was a woman, she'd lay in the arms of her true love all night long. He never pressurised her to have sex with him. It was what she wanted to do. He was tender with her, never rushed anything, it was magical. Even his kiss was gentle and sweet. Her mobile phone started to ring. It was Jane's name flashing across the screen again. Emily answered the call and rolled on her side. She smirked and kept her voice low. "I was just going to ring you. Wow, relax will you. Mark rang me last night and wanted to see me, so I got ready and went to meet him. We had a great night together. I spent the night with him." Jane started shouting down the line. Emily held the phone from her ear. "Shut up going on will you. You can come to meet Alex tonight. He's Mark's friend and he let us stay at his house. It was like something from the TV; there was a jacuzzi, a steam room, the man is minted. Honest, it's the nicest place I have ever stayed in my life." Jane seemed to be calming down as Emily continued talking. "Just let me get some sleep and I'll ring you back, but get your best dress on later. Mark said we're going to a posh restaurant tonight. He wants you to come along too. He said he has a friend who wants to meet you." The call ended after a few more minutes and Emily dropped the phone from her hand as her eyes started to close. She was weary, absolutely knackered.

CHAPTER TEN

Jordan sat in his mother's house and he looked bothered today. Something was lying heavily on his mind. He was standing up, sitting back down, itching at his skin, fidgeting, checking the clock every few minutes. Tony dunked his chocolate biscuit into his coffee and nodded over at his son. "What's up kid? You've got a face like a smacked arse. If it's a woman making you feel like this, then bin her off. Nothing but trouble they are. There are just a few chicks out there who are alright but the rest of them are fucked in their head, bleeding psycho's they are, nutters."

Jordan sighed. "Nar dad. I wish it was just woman trouble. I could probably deal with that. It's nothing that I can't handle but yeah, you're right, I'm stressed out. I hardly slept a wink last night, tossing and turning."

Tony sat munching his biscuits and spoke with his mouthful. "Come on then, spit it out. I might be able to help you."

Jordan dropped his head into his hands. He had to get it off his chest, maybe get some advice. "My grafter got lifted last night by the dibble and now it's left to me to clear the debt of ten grand. The firm want their money back and I'm on my arse so I can't pay them. I can't get any more gear to sell either because they won't let me tick any. They want the money up front, so basically I'm fucked."

Tony licked the chocolate from the end of his

fingers. His chest expanded like a pigeon and he sniffed up hard to clear his nasal passage. "Fuck em son, tell them to whistle for their money. They can't have what you don't have can they? Tell them they can kiss your arse."

Jordan blew his breath in frustration. "Dad, you know more than anyone how it all works. They've given me until the end of the week to get the money together otherwise I'll be put in a boot of a car and taken somewhere. You know the score dad. It's Jimmy The Chop and his mob who we are talking about here. He's a fucking lunatic."

Tony bolted up straight and sat cracking his knuckles, nobody threatened his family, not on his watch anyway. "I know Jimmy. I've shit bigger than him, son. I'm mental me when I get going. I'll machete the fucking lot of them, him and his brothers. They call me Tony the fucking tornado," he sniggered.

Jordan squirmed; his dad was so full of shit. He had to calm him down. "Just leave it with me for now. I've got this guy who wants me to do some work for him so I could earn a few quid there. It's easy money really, just driving some brasses to punter's houses and picking them back up when they've finished."

Tony's mouth was wide open. "What, and they pay you for that? Get it done, it's easy money. Plus, you might get a few free sucks."

Jordan's voice changed. "Dad, it's horrible. It's young girls who are off their nappers on drugs. Pretty girls, who've just got messed up along the way. Honest, it's a shame for them. I do have a conscience you know. This would be my last resort if nothing else turns up."

Tony plonked back in his seat. "Yep but ay, if your neck is on the line, then you have to do what you have to do, don't you? Keep me posted on these muppets. If any of them give you any shit, I'll sort it out. I swear on your life, I'll do the cunts in."

Jordan had switched off and his mind was elsewhere. It was his mess and he'd be the one sorting it out, not his father. Elsie came into the room after a short nap. She had bed hair and she made no attempt to straighten it. It looked like she'd been electrocuted. Plonking down on the sofa she nudged Tony in his waist. "Come on then, cough it up, you got paid today, didn't you?"

Tony held a sour expression. "That money is getting put away for our holiday. You can have a tenner out of it, but that's it."

"Tony, I don't have any money. The holiday can go on the back-burner for now. We have to live you know."

"Fuck me woman. I'll never be rich with you, will I? You can have a score and that's it. Twenty quid is enough to get some shopping, isn't it?"

"I suppose it will have to be," she squawked. Tony seemed on edge today. He had a doctor's appointment in a couple of hours, maybe it was that making him nervous. Being without drugs seemed strange to him. He had no reason to get up early anymore. The only reason he was out at the crack of dawn each morning was to feed his habit, but now that was gone, he felt empty. He never saw his friends anymore either. Tony got bored very easily and Elsie knew this was a time when her husband was weak. She could sense it. "Shall we go for a walk in the park with the dog. It's been ages since he's had a good run?"

Tony stretched his arms over his head. "No, I'm going to chill for a bit. I might nip around and see Mickey later too. I've not seen him for moons."

Straight away alarm bells were ringing in Elsie's head, she had to put a stop to this straight away before all his good work was ruined. That was the trouble with Tony, money always burnt a hole in his pocket and he had to spend it. "Don't be going there, love. You've been doing so well, don't spoil it."

"Will you fuck off pecking my head. Listen, I'm having a bad day and I don't need your droning voice down my ear. Fuck off round to Tina's and give me a bit of peace. You're like a fart lingering around me everywhere I fucking go."

Wow, he was in a mood today. He lay down on the sofa and folded the cushion under his head. He flicked the TV on and stared at the screen. Elsie was upset. Half of her wanted to punch his face in for talking to her like that and the other half knew she had to keep her trap shut for now because he was looking for any excuse to go on a mad one.

Jordan left his parent's home and his spirits were low. He'd fucked up for sure. That rat who was dealing for him should have been more careful. He'd told him time and time again about being clever and never dealing where he could be seen. The prick had served a copper up. Yes, a police officer in plain clothes had nicked him there and then. Bang to rights he was, he was going down for this for sure. A few years in the big house for the number of drugs they found on him.

Daft, stupid, prick, there was no other word for him.

CHAPTER ELEVEN

Elsie sat on the wall facing her parent's house. Twenty minutes she'd been sat here twiddling her thumbs, just staring over at the house. Maybe, it was a mistake coming here, she thought. Had too much time passed? Her head was all over the place. The traffic was noisy as it travelled down the road.

Elsie was still perched in the same spot; she hadn't moved a muscle. It was like someone had glued her to the wall. She was motionless. Her neck stretched suddenly, and her eyes opened wide. She pulled her hood over her head and dipped her face down. No, no, she didn't want him to see her. Her heart was beating like a speeding-train and her cheeks suddenly became bright red. Slowly, she peeped out from her fur hood. It was him; he was older than she remembered but she could see it was her dad. Her voice croaked as she tried to speak. It was like someone had a grip on her windpipe, she was suffocating, feeling light headed. She tried again and this time she could get her words out. "Dad," she stuttered from the other side of the road. He'd never hear her like this, she needed to raise her voice. As she stood up her legs buckled, she gripped the red brick wall to the side of her to steady herself. She was desperate now. "Dad," she yelled. The old man across the road shot a look over at her but carried on walking. Did he know it was her, had he just ignored her in the hope that she would leave him alone? Elsie made the decision to chase after him.

It was mid-day and he was probably off to the bookies. He loved a little flutter on the gee-gees and it was part of his daily routine. Her legs were moving faster than they had in a long time. Her breathing was struggled as she got to within a few steps of him. The old man turned his head and snarled at her. His eyes were squeezed tightly together. "What are you gawping at. Don't ask me for any money. I'm sick to death of you bleeding beggars. Every time I go to the shop you're asking me for money. I'm a pensioner. You lot should be looking after me not the other way around. Piss off before you feel my foot up your arse." in

Elsie knew he didn't recognise her. She bit down hard on her bottom lip and searched her heart for the words she needed. "Dad, it's me Elsie." Sydney was frozen to the spot, he stared at her for a few seconds more then carried on walking, Elsie chased after him. He shook his head and sighed. "Dad, can we talk? I've sorted myself out now and I'm not on drugs."

Sydney pulled his grey flat cap from his head and ran his fingers through his fine grey hair. "You shouldn't have come here. I told you last time that my heart couldn't stand any more heartache from you. Just go and do what you're doing and leave me alone."

Elsie was panicking. He was her father. Why was he being so hard hearted? She came close to him and spoke in a soft voice. "I said I'm clean dad. I've not touched drugs for ages. Tony is clean too. We have got our lives back on track now. You were right about me, everything you said was true. I can see that now. Can we just talk for a bit?"

"I've got no money," Sydney sneered. "I tried and tried to help you and you just threw it back in my face. Your mother will have a heart attack if she knows you're back on the scene. She told you last time to never to darken our door again. You broke her heart when you took them kids."

"For fucks sake dad. I've just told you I'm sorry. I know what I did and in time I can start to pay the money back that I took. Tony has got a job now and we will have some extra money coming in. I know I made a mistake by taking Emily and Jordan, just let me talk to you."

Sydney shook his head. "Just let me be Elsie. I don't need this in my life. My ticker has been playing me up and I've had a few near misses. So please, just leave us alone."

Elsie choked up. "Dad, our Emily and Jordan haven't seen you for years. They're your grandchildren. Surely, you can't stop loving them too. They're innocent in all this." Elsie had a point here and Sydney was stuck for words. He loved his grandkids and he'd spent hours with them when they were younger. It would be nice to see them, to hold them, kiss them and make up for all the years that had gone by. But his grandchildren were connected to his daughter, she'd be there with them worming her way back into his life. "What is it you want? Money?" he said angrily. He still wasn't buying that she was clean. He pulled out his old tan wallet from his pocket and dipped his fingers inside. Finding a ten pound note he wafted it in front of her face. In the past this did the trick, she'd have done anything years ago for a tenner.

Elsie closed her eyes and inhaled a deep breath. It was like he'd stuck a big silver carving knife deep in her chest, his words, his voice. "I don't want your money. For the last time I'm telling you I'm clean. I've not touched the gear for a long time. We are even going on holiday with the kids. We've changed Dad, please believe me."

Sydney started to move away. He was agitated. He looked behind him and his voice changed, it was softer now. "Please, leave me alone. Maybe in time we can talk, but all this has knocked me for six. I need to speak to your mother. You hurt a lot of people Elsie, you can't just walk back into our life and expect to start off like nothing has happened." Elsie knew it was going to be hard, but to be neglected by her father was a bitter pill to swallow. What else could she say? Elsie watched as her dad walked along the road. He never looked back.

★

Elsie dropped her head in her hands as Tina banged the kettle on. It was a sad day for her and she was finding it hard to cope. "Tina, he just fucked off and left me as if I was a dollop of shite on his shoe." Why wasn't her life straight forward? Her father should have been overjoyed to see her, praised her for sorting her head out.

"He was probably shocked, Elsie. Fuck me, he's not seen you for how long now?"

"Three years," Elsie whimpered.

"What did you expect, fireworks?"

"I expected a hug at least, a 'well done' or something?"

"Are you from cloud cuckoo land or what? You've told me how bad you were and from what you have told me you really hurt your parents. I mean, your dad saw you on a street corner selling your body. That must have hurt, you never forget something like that."

"Fuck off Tina, you know I hate talking about that. I've not been a brass for ages now. It was just a low time in my life when I hit rock bottom. I was desperate. I only did it a few times."

"The truth hurts sometimes and I'm just saying what I see, that's all." Tina clinked the silver spoon on the side of the cup and placed it on the side. "Just give him time to get his head round it."

Elsie picked up her mug of tea and wrapped her hands around it. "I hope you're right. It's all I've ever wanted. I've missed them you know, my mam, my dad, my sister, I've missed them all. It's the drugs, Tina. It clouds your mind and numbs your emotions. I can see that now, but back then all I cared about was feeding my habit. Look how I nearly lost my kids. Social Services were on my back for years. Two weeks my kids were in care for and it done me in. I cried and cried until they were back home."

Tina opened her packet of Benson and Hedges. She pulled one out and popped it into her mouth. "It's regrets that keep you awake at night love; trust me, I know. Listen Elsie, I've known you a long time. You have been off drugs now for a few months and I'm proud of you. But this is a long road. You can't just expect the world to jump up and do what you want them to do just because you're clean. It's the trust that you broke that will take time to repair. You lied to a lot of people, me included. You're lucky I forgave you and gave you another chance. Fifty quid you nicked from me. I was on my arse too and you never gave a flying fuck."

Wow, Elsie was sorry she spoke. Here she was doing her best to keep her life on track and everybody was just raking up the past. "Leave it out Tina. I know what I've done. You said it was water under the bridge, so stop bringing it up every chance you get. I don't need you going snide on me as well."

Tina sucked hard on her fag. "I bleeding well won't shut up. It is water under the bridge but sometimes you need reminding where you have come from." The two of them sat in silence for a few seconds. "How's Tony doing at work? Is he still working?"

It was a good job Tina spoke first otherwise Elsie was getting ready to go home. "He's enjoying it. A bit too much if you ask me. That Sue's a flirt and I'm sorry I ever mentioned the work to Tony now. It's fucking Sue this, fucking Sue that. I'm sure she's after my man. I'll slice her face up if I hear one whisper that she's coming on to him."

Tina eyes opened wide. "I don't think anyone would be interested in Tony, love. Give your head a shake and have a good look at him. He looks like a ferret," she sniggered.

Elsie's back was up, nobody called her man. "Beauty is in the eye of the beholder. He floats my boat and that's all that matters. Tina, have you got any Space Raiders in? I'm starving. I'm supposed to be on a diet but I can't stop eating."

Tina stood up and dug her hand into the cupboard.

"You better get your head in gear if that Sue is on the prowl. You need to show Tony what you're made of."

Elsie nodded and drew her shoulders back. "Yes, you're right. I'm going to start looking after myself and probably putting a bit of slap on my face too."

"That's the spirit. Show him you can look lovely too."

Tina was taking the piss. Elsie was no oil painting and no amount of make-up would ever sort her spotty complexion out. Elsie sat munching, licking and sucking on her fingers. She froze and looked like she was in deep thought. "I think our Emily is having sex. Don't ask me why I think that. I just do."

Tina chewed on her bottom lip and rolled her eyes. "Bleeding hell, she's nearly seventeen. What do you expect? I was twelve when I started messing about with the boys. The lads on the estate nicknamed me the bowling ball because they'd all had a finger stuck up me!"

Elsie nearly choked laughing. "Eww… That's hanging. I was a late starter. Tony was my first."

"Really? Oh my God. You don't know what you're missing love. I couldn't have had just one man. Variety is the spice of life."

"You're a dirty cow though, you always have been. My body is special and just for my Tony."

Tina burst out laughing and covered her mouth. "You're Tony's probably stuck up that fancy piece Susan as we speak."

This was only meant to be a joke but Elsie spat her dummy out, Tina had hit a nerve. "Tina, you can be a right arse sometimes. I'm already paranoid about him working at her house so don't be making me worse than what I am already."

Tina held her hands up. "Sorry, love. You know me, I can't help having a bit of a joke. Anyway," she changed the subject. "What's made you think Emily is having sex?"

Elsie played with her fingers, twisting them, stroking them. "I don't know, call it a sixth sense or something. She's changed lately and seems distant. She's always at Jane's and she's lost weight. Have you seen her lately? She's like a matchstick."

"The last time I saw your Emily was months ago."

"Well, she has. I might just come straight out with it and ask her."

"You can't just ask her, you need to be subtle, fish about first and see what she says."

"Tina, what will I do if she admits it. Tony will go ballistic."

"So, don't tell him then. This is mother and daughter stuff, so it should be private. You need to make sure she's using protection because the last thing she needs is a nipper. Yes, make sure she's on the pill or get her some condoms. I've got a box full in the bedroom if you need some. Just take some home and leave them in her bedroom."

"We used to be so close, she always told me everything. Do you think that I've been so caught up in my own shit that I've neglected her?"

"No, she's just getting older that's all. My Annie was the same. As soon as she hit fourteen she barely spoke to me. All she used to do was sit in her bedroom all day. I thought there was something wrong with her, but after talking to a few of my friends they told me it was normal. It's their hormones, isn't it?"

"Maybe it is. When I get home, I'll see if I can have a chat with her. I'll tell her about the birds and bees too."

Tina shook her head. "It's a bit late for that don't you think?"

Elsie shrugged her shoulders and reached over and grabbed a cigarette from the packet on the table. "Nicotine, I always need a fag when I'm stressed out."

CHAPTER TWELVE

The wind was howling so Tony was sat in the greenhouse freezing his nuts off, shivering, blowing his warm breath into his hands to try and fight the cold off. Maybe just wearing a t-shirt and his tightest fitting jeans wasn't a good idea after all. Where did he think he was, the bleeding Caribbean? Tony picked up an old newspaper from the side of him. It was quite old and crusty. He'd not read a newspaper for as long as he could remember. He didn't find them interesting, only, when he read his horoscopes. Oh, he loved what the stars had in store for him, especially if he was up in court or someone was looking for him. The stars guided him and helped him sort his life out. He was a Cancer star sign and maybe the traits of this horoscope were bang on with him. Tony was bored so he quickly flicked through the rag, scanning the pages for any nude women. Hold on, he found an interesting story about the notorious Maureen the Mangle. He'd been following the trial of this lady for a while. She was an international diamond smuggler and the word on the street was she was cunning and ruthless. She ran everything from her empire in Spain. Up to now the police had nothing on her until Harry the Cheese turned Queen's evidence and told them everything. Tony carried on reading with interest, nodding his head, biting at his fingernails. What a result, the woman got a not guilty verdict. Tony loved it when one of his fellow grafters got a walk out from court. "Well, done Maureen," he mumbled under his breath.

He froze and sat up straight, he could see someone approaching. He flattened his hair and stood to his feet like a soldier waiting for inspection. Bending down he picked up a plant and started to pull some old leaves from it, brown crispy flakes dropped to the floor. Looking busy was a talent he had and he the art down to a tee. "Hello sweetheart, you must be freezing in here," Sue purred. "Do you want to come in the house until the rain calms down and I'll make you a hot cup of tea to warm you up, you look perished?"

She didn't have to ask him twice, he was already making his way to the door. His tone was confident as he replied. "You're such a lovely lady, Sue. Thanks for looking after me while I'm here. I've never had this much attention in my life. Generally, I have to fend for myself. Her indoors is a lazy cow and doesn't move from the sofa all day. I swear she's glued to it; bone idle she is. Thanks, I'd love to come inside."

Sue giggled and reached over and patted his arm softly. He made her laugh, every time she spoke to him, he had her in fits "That's so nice of you to say that. I don't mind at all. Anyway, I'd only be sat at home all day bored to tears. They say money doesn't buy happiness and they're right, I've never been so alone in my whole life."

Tony had read about this kind of woman in his porn magazine *Big Jugs Monthly*. They were gagging for it, ready for any man that give them the time of the day. He rubbed his hands together as he blew his warm breath onto them. If this woman wanted a quick leg-over then Tony was the man for the job. He'd be in and out of her like a ninja. Like a rat up a drainpipe. "I was freezing my balls off out there. Look at my teeth chattering," he acted out his teeth banging together. "I forgot to bring my warm clothes with me today through rushing about. Not that I have lots of clothes, I've not bought myself anything smart in years. I thought I was joshing it though; I wouldn't need any new clothes if I was dying. I just saved the money for the family instead." Tony was feeling sorry for himself, aware her eyes were on him.

Sue was alert. "You're such a caring soul. Oh, that reminds me. I've got some old clothes of my husbands that I was taking to the charity shop that you can have if you want," she paused. "I hope I've not offended you by saying that? Me and my big stupid mouth again. Sorry."

Tony cut her short and smirked. "Don't be daft. I'll have them for sure if they fit. I've not really got any clothes for work; so I'd be grateful of anything. Made up in fact."

"Alright then, once we have had a drink we can have a look through the clothes and see if anything takes your fancy. My husband has some really nice designer clothing, expensive they were."

Something took his fancy alright and he couldn't hide it, he was drooling as he looked at her. Every wank he'd had for the last few weeks had been over this woman. And, for it to become a reality, wow, it didn't bear thinking about. His mind was filthy and, in his head, he'd had her bent over so many objects having sex, it was untrue. Tony was back in the game alright;

he was the man of the hour. He sat down and rubbed at his goose-pimpled arms and made conversation. "Where does your old fella work, if you don't mind me asking?"

Sue shouted behind her as she stood at the kitchen sink washing out two cups with her candy pink marigolds on. "He works all over the country and, to tell you the truth I'm not sure what he does. I just know he's never home. I bet he's got some dolly-bird on the go. You hear about it don't you, and well, he's never here with me."

Tony was alarmed. "No, he'd never risk losing you Sue. You're a mint bird, he'd need his napper testing if he fucked about on you. You're the dog's bollocks..." Tony rolled his eyes and cringed slightly. He just couldn't help swearing, it just came out.

Sue walked back to him and passed him his hot drink. The steam was flowing from the top of it like a steam engine. Sue's expression changed and she ran a single finger along her long slender leg, tapping it slowly. "Do you think I'm attractive Tony?" Fucking hell, he was going under, he went bright red, he didn't know where to look. He gulped, had the cat got his tongue or what, he was stuttering. He took a deep breath and sucked hard on his lips. "Yes, you're gorgeous. One of the nicest ladies I have met in a long time." Sue smirked and sat down. She was just staring at him now. She was a prick-tease for sure.

After his brew Tony stood in the mirror and twisted his body. "These look mint. I'm probably the same size as your old man. How lucky am I?"

Sue perched on the end of the bed and twiddled

her hair. "You look sexy," she said in her come to bed voice.

Tony looked over himself in the mirror and turned to face her. "Thank you. Nobody has called me sexy in years. Are you taking the piss or what? I think you need to go to Spec-Savers and get your mince-pies checked out."

Sue used a single finger to stroke her cream coloured silk bedding. She held a naughty look in her eyes. "Come and sit here next to me, Tony." Oh my God, this was it, his time had come. Hallelujah.

CHAPTER THIRTEEN

Emily lay on the bed next to Mark. He was holding her in his arms and kissing the top of her head. She was in heaven and nothing else seemed to matter. She never wanted this moment to end. "How are you feeling?" he whispered in a soft husky tone.

"I'm still feeling a bit strange but I'm alright now. I don't know what came over me, I just feel jittery inside and my head is banging." Emily didn't look herself; she was white as if someone had rubbed talc all over her skin. Even the way she was speaking was strange, she was slurring her words.

Mark snuggled in closer. His warm breath tickling her skin. "That's good. I hate it when my baby is not feeling well. I'm here to look after you anyway, you're safe with me." Emily didn't know what was up with her lately, every time she drank alcohol, she started to feel weird. Not a bad weird, just very relaxed and sleepy. Maybe she needed some iron tablets to give her more energy or to sort her diet out and eat healthy food. She was eating fast food all the time now, KFC, Pizza, kebabs, everything that wasn't considered healthy but, why shouldn't she eat this way. It was a treat for her and she wasn't the one paying for it, so it was all gravy in her eyes.

She lifted her head slightly from the pillow and held a concerned look in her eyes. "I hope Jane is alright with Omar, she really hit it off with him, didn't she?"

Mark sniggered and scratched his ball-sack under the duvet. "Omar has his way with the ladies. His smart cars and Rolex watches help I suppose. He's a top-lad, wadded he is and he's not afraid to spend a few quid either. Any girl who gets her claws into him will be made up, he's a generous man. Well, that is until he's had enough of them, then he's a right shady bastard. But," he smirked, "Jane should be alright, if she keeps her trap shut and doesn't start pressurizing him."

Emily cuddled up closer to his warm hairy chest. She played with the sprinkle of dark hair slowly, twiddling it in between her fingers. "Jane will love that, she's not what I would call a gold-digger, but she does like a guy with money. I suppose we all like a guy to treat us to some love gestures if I'm being honest. The emperor penguin finds a lovely colourful rock for his chosen one before they mate, so us ladies are a bit like them I supposed. A token of love is nice." Emily knew this was a fact because she'd watched a documentary about it on the TV with her dad. She loved series like that, and she always found them interesting. The chimpanzees were her favourite. They made her laugh and she was always mesmerised with them.

Mark pulled her head back with a swift movement and looked deep into her eyes. "You don't half come out with some boring shit you do. That's two minutes of my life that I will never get back," he chuckled. His expression changed and he sat thinking for a few seconds. "Emily, I'm not rich. All I can offer you is love, nothing else."

His eyes were sincere and as Emily looked closely at them, they seemed to be filling up. She was alarmed, eyes wide open, frantic. She never meant it to come across like that and she made sure he understood her. "Listen, I don't care about money Mark. You can't miss what you've never had. I love you for who you are. I don't care about material things; love is all I need. Love is worth millions of pounds in my eyes and no amount of cash can buy it."

Her words were from the heart and she was sincere when she delivered them. Mark pulled her nearer and kissed her again. He squeezed her tightly in his firm, toned arms and sighed. "I'm going to look after you babes. You don't need anyone but me. Just us two, that's all that matters. Fuck everyone else."

Emily was melting in his arms, lost in his eyes, so in love. Emily and Mark had both stayed the night at Alex's house again. This gaff was massive, seven bedrooms in total, hot tubs, steam rooms, en-suite, it was top-notch and like nothing she had seen before. Jane had stayed the night too and after meeting Omar a few times now she was already saying she had feelings for him. Emily didn't believe her though. How could she fall in love with this guy when she'd only known him two minutes? Was she just saying it, making it up because she knew Emily was in love and wanted to be the same as her? Both girls had planned to stay here for the full weekend. They'd told their parents they were going to Blackpool with one of their friends who had a relation with a B&B, nobody questioned them.

Mark stretched his arms over his head and checked his silver wristwatch. "I better get up. I've got to nip out, but I'll be back in a few hours. That's alright isn't it?"

Emily nodded, there was no way she was acting like a moaning girlfriend. No, she was going to be perfect. "Yes, I will chill with Jane. We can watch a film on Netflix if Alex doesn't mind?"

Mark started to get out of bed. "Alex will let you do whatever you want, he's sorted. He never stresses, he loves the company." Emily lifted her head from the pillow, it felt like a lump of lead, it was heavy, blurry vision, pounding. Maybe, she was getting a migraine or coming down with the flue. Something wasn't right. She'd suffered with headaches in the past and this felt like the symptoms of migraine. She felt sick in the pit of her stomach, pains, shaking inside, eye sockets aching with pain. She was fine last night though, dancing, singing, full of confidence and then, nothing, she couldn't remember a single thing. It was all a blur to her. "I might just stay in bed for a bit longer. I feel groggy. Honest, I just don't feel myself. If I have a nap, I might be able to shake it off."

Mark looked at her suspiciously. He leaned over and kissed her on her red rosy cheek. "Orr, my poor girl. You just rest and get better," he pulled away from her. "I better get a quick shower before I'm late."

Emily was puzzled. Every day and night he always disappeared for an hour here and there, he was constantly on his phone. She watched him closer and wondered if there was something she was missing. If he was cheating on her it'd break her heart. She couldn't cope with that, no way. Her heart was racing at the thought of ever losing her man. Mark went into the shower. She could hear him switch the water on. He was singing, pelting out a few tunes as he washed his body. Emily peeped to make sure he couldn't see her. Quickly, she picked up her mobile phone and rang Jane who was only a few rooms down the corridor from her. She held the phone close to her ear and whispered. "Jane, can you hear me? Jane," she stressed. There was a voice at the other end of the line, but she couldn't make out if it was Jane's or not. She repeated herself. "Jane, it's Emily. Are you alright?" There were rustling sounds and muffled noises.

"Emily, come to my room, I'm ill." The line went dead, there was no sound whatsoever. Emily sat thinking for a while. Jane was a drama queen and she always over-reacted, she'd probably got period pains or something like that. Yes, she could wait until Mark had left and then she would go and see her. Emily snuggled into Mark's pillow and inhaled his scent; she could smell his aftershave. It smelt so clean and fresh, like nothing she'd ever smelled before. Her dad was still using "Old Spice" or anything he could get his hands on. Cheap shit usually. The bathroom door opened and there he was in his full glory. God, he made her heart skip a beat. Every inch of him was lean and toned, mint he was, sex on legs. His skin was lightly tanned too. Although, he said he hadn't been on holiday, he definitely had a tan. He was a golden colour. Maybe, he used a sunbed. She watched him closely as he dried his body with the white fluffy towel. Emily rolled on her side and rested her chin on her hands. "Why does Alex let everybody stay here? If this was my house, I wouldn't let anybody near it. I'd be scared to death of it getting wrecked."

Mark never made eye contact with her as he replied. "Alex is lonely I suppose. He likes to have people around him. I've been like a son to him. He's a kind-hearted person. He just loves people."

She sat thinking, digesting everything he had said. It was a strange set-up here and she wasn't sure how to put it into words what she wanted to say next, so she just said it anyway. "Why does he have young girls here? I've seen quite a few over the last few months. Are they his daughters or relations?"

Mark started to get flustered and changed the subject very quickly. "Are you staying again tonight? There is no need to go home. I'll take you into town later and buy you a nice dress to wear tonight. Something sexy that shows off your curves. I love you in red, you look amazing in that colour."

Emily's eyes lit up. This was love. Amazing super spectacular love like she'd never ever felt in her life before. This man was treating her like a princess, he'd already bought her so many gifts; perfumes, chocolates, underwear, she was over-whelmed to say the least. "Yes, I'd love to stay over. I thought I was anyway. Nobody misses me at home. I could be dead for all they cared."

Mark walked over to the bed and pecked her on the cheek. He looked deep into her eyes and smiled. "Don't miss me too much, ay?" He walked towards the door and turned and blew her a kiss. She pretended to grab it from the thin air and put it in her pocket. Mark was gone. Emily gripped the pillow and squeezed it with all her might. She was in love, nothing else mattered anymore. She'd found what she was looking for. Her dream man.

★

The room was dark and Emily nearly fell over as she made her way towards the bed. "Jane, it's me Emily. Are you awake?" Emily was stumbling and she nearly tripped over a shoe as she finally made it over to where she was. She quickly found the switch to the light and flicked it on. She was taken back when she clocked Jane for the first time. She was sweating, her eyes were flickering, and she looked like death warmed up. "Oh my God, you look so ill Jane. What's up?"

Jane covered her eyes with her hand. "Please, turn the light off, it's hurting my eyes. Quick, my eyes feel like they are on fire."

Emily looked at her for a few more seconds and turned the light off. There was a ray of light seeping in through the cream coloured window blinds that let in enough so she could see her face. Emily reached over and held her friends' hand. "Do you want some pain-killers? I'm going to get some; I've had a banging headache too. I've just said to Mark about how rough I feel. Do you think we might have eaten something that didn't agree with us?"

Jane murmured as she rolled her head in her pillow. "I can't remember last night at all. What were we drinking? It's all a blur to me." Emily sat thinking; it was weird how she was finding it hard to remember the night before. Maybe they should stop drinking the vodka, they were necking glass after glass of it all night long. Omar and Mark kept going to the bar and their glass was never empty.

"Where's Omar?" Emily asked.

"I don't know. Like I said, I can't remember a thing about last night. I'm not even sure if he stayed in the same bed as me."

Jane lifted the duvet up and looked under the cover, she was shocked and dragged it quickly back over her body. "I'm naked, where the hell have my clothes gone? Oh my God, did I have sex?"

Emily was concerned and positioned herself next to Jane on the bed. "Are you being serious or what?"

Jane sat up and ragged her fingers through her hair. She was getting upset and you could see her racking her brains trying to make some sense of the night before. She was having a panic attack. "I don't remember. It's like my mind is blank. Do you think I've lost my memory or something?"

Emily smirked and shook her head. "Shut up, you daft cow. You know who I am right?"

Jane was stressed. "Of course I do. It's just last night I'm having difficulty remembering."

Emily sighed, "Mark's taking me into town later to buy me a dress. We're going out again tonight, so you'd better get your arse in gear and sort your head out. Are you sure you don't know where Omar is?"

Jane lifted her head up and looked around the bedroom, she looked for any signs of her new man, there was no sign of him whatsoever. "I've not got a clue. When I wake up properly, I will ring him." Jane was in shock and shook her head slowly. "Emily, if he didn't stay here with me, why am I naked? It doesn't make any sense. You know me more than anyone and I never sleep in the nude."

Emily was as confused as her friend. It was so out of character for Jane to be in bed without her pyjamas on. "You were probably that drunk that you took them off. It could have been worse; you could have pissed the bed. So be thankful for that." Jane was in a panic as she rummaged under the bed clothes and patted the bedsheets. No, they were dry. It was all a big mystery.

CHAPTER FOURTEEN

"I'll fucking kill her when I get my hands on her, Tony. Six times I've rang her and she's not answered me."

Tony was lying on the sofa, watching a wild life programme about lions. He never looked at her as he replied. "What love, who are you talking about?"

Elsie launched a pillow over at his head. "Our bleeding daughter, that's who, you dickhead. Something is not right with her Tony. Since when has she stayed out this much?"

"She's only with Jane, where is the harm in that, just relax."

"You won't be saying that when she'd found dead in a gutter somewhere, will you?"

"Fuck me Elsie, why are you saying that?"

"Because I'm worried, that's why."

"So ring Jane then, simple isn't it?"

Elsie scrolled through her phone and found Jane's contacts number. She held the phone to her ear and stared in front of her. "Tony, she's not answering either. This is a joke. What are they playing at? Hold on, I'll ring Jane's mam to see if she's had any contact with her." Elsie sat chewing on her fingernails. Tony continued watching the TV, but he was still listening to his wife. "Hiya, it's Emily's mam. I'm just wondering if you have spoken to Jane. I've tried ringing Emily a few times and she is not answering."

Tony held his stomach and sniggered. He started

mimicking his wife's posh tone of voice. Elsie was smiling and she was trying her best not to burst out laughing. "Right, if Jane rings you will you tell her to tell Emily to phone home?" The phone call ended and Elsie plonked down on the sofa next to her husband. "You should hear her voice, the posh cow, she seems stuck right up her own arse that one. I bet her farts smell of polish, or pine gel."

Tony grabbed her by the arm and pulled her down to where he was lay. "Shut up now and watch this with me. The lions have just fucked up a big buffalo, that's what they're eating now."

"Ewww, Tony, you don't half watch some shit. Why would you want to watch animals being killed like that?"

"It's the circle of life love, that's how it all works. It's a dog-eat-dog world."

Elsie cringed as she watched a bit more, she covered her eyes and screamed out. "Tony, turn it over, I can't watch this, it's rotten. Don't tell me you can't hear that poor animal crying as they sink their teeth into it?" Tony jumped on Elsie and pretended to bite her; she was laughing her head off. "Stop it, you daft bastard, orr, stop it, I'm going to piss myself if you carry on."

Tony roared like a lion and pinned her down, he sank his teeth into the side of her neck. He was acting the goat and loving every minute of it. He yanked his t-shirt off and banged his clenched fist onto his chest. "Me Tarzan, you Jane."

Elsie wasn't laughing anymore, something was wrong. She used all her strength and booted him from her. Her eyes shot to his chest. "What the fuck are them scratches on your back, come here, let me have a closer look at them."

Tony froze as she gripped him from the side. "What are you doing you barmy bastard, get off me."

Elsie pushed him away and stood with her hand on her hips. "So, where have they come from? They weren't there the other day, so where have they come from?" Tony twisted his head to the side and examined his body. He pulled at the skin and raised his voice. "They must have been from the rose bushes. I was cutting them down yesterday and I fell into them. I'm lucky they didn't have my eyes out."

Elsie sucked hard on her gums. "Do you think I came over on the banana boat?"

Tony reached over and gripped his t-shirt and quickly put it back on. "You always have to go and spoil it, don't you? There we were having a bit of a laugh and you go and get all paranoid."

"If I had scratches all over my body, you would have something to say, wouldn't you?"

"Sort your head out woman. Fuck this, I'm going out."

"Go on then, off you trot, don't let me stop you." Tony was in a huff and marched over to the set of drawers in the front room. He dug his hand deep into the drawer and picked something up, quickly he shoved it into his pocket. "Don't expect me back anytime soon you stress-head."

Elsie sat down and rammed her middle finger in the air to him. "Sit on that, you prick." Tony was gone. The moment he'd disappeared, Elsie grabbed her coat from the back of the chair and headed towards the front door. Wherever she was going she was in rush to get there.

Tony marched down the road like a man on a mission. He rammed his hands deep into his pockets as the wind picked up. His hair was blowing up in the air and his nose was starting to dribble slightly with warm clear liquid. Tony seemed to know everyone in the area. As his feet pounded the pavement every person he passed nodded at him. It was "hiya love, hiya mate," non-stop all the way down the road. He was well known for sure, maybe for the wrong reasons but still they all knew him. Tony reached the shopping fort and smiled. This was going to be his first instalment on the family holiday he'd promised his daughter. It was the first task he'd ever completed without messing up. He could never be trusted with money in the old days and here he was with two hundred quid in his pocket doing something sensible for a change.

Suddenly he heard a voice shouting from behind him, loud echoing tone. "Yo, Tony, wait up."

Tony squeezed his eyes together and tried to make out who it was running towards him. He dug his hand in his side pocket and gripped a small blade. If this was someone wanting some beef, then they were getting stabbed up for sure. The man had his hood pulled up covering his identity and so he still couldn't recognise him. "Where you off to pal?" Tony looked closer and smiled. It was his old mate Toddy.

"Fuck me mate, when did you get out of the big house?"

Toddy chuckled and reached out his hand to Tony. "Two weeks ago. I'll tell you what Toe, this sentence broke my fucking back. It was hard, gruesome. It's not like the old days when you can walk about on the landing, it's pure bang-up. Nightmare."

"Well, I've only been in for bed and breakfast so to speak and that was enough. I was rattling my balls off too. No medication, no fuck all. The screws just leave you to do your roast. Twats they are." Tony was pleased to see Toddy and gave him another hug. "Great to see you. You look good too. You've banged some timber on though, you fat fucker."

Toddy slapped his hand against his podgy stomach. "You can say that again. Two stone I've put on. So jail might have done me good after all. Where you off too anyway?"

"I'm just going to pay the deposit for a holiday for our lot. I'm off the gear now and sorting my head out. I've even got a job."

Toddy burst out laughing. "Are you having a laugh or what? Since when have you been on the straight and narrow?"

"A few months now. I feel miles better for it too. Got myself a little gardening job on the side, money in my hand, so it's all good."

Toddy was shocked to say the least. "I'm going for a few beers with the old gang if you fancy it. Just that pub over the road."

Toddy pointed at a boozer not far from where he stood. "Come on lad, you can pay your deposit later. Come and see the firm, we'll have a laugh." Tony squeezed the money in his pocket and stood thinking for a few seconds. It was a few pints they were talking about, nothing more. What's the worst that could happen?

★

Elsie was slumped on the kitchen table. Tina banged the kettle on and stood at the side of her friend. She held a curious look. "So, tell me again what's happened."

Elsie's mood was low. "He's got scratches on his back, Tina. Don't try and defend him, I seen them with my own two eyes. No wonder he's not been bothered with me for sex when he's sticking it up somebody else. I'm a fool, why didn't I see it?"

Tina patted the top of her shoulder and tried to calm her down. "You don't know that for sure. Have you asked him where they're from?"

"Fucking dead right I did. The lying bastard said he fell into a rose bush when he was at work. I'm not bleeding green Tina. He's been at it."

"You're going a bit over the top if you ask me. Let's look at the evidence. Tony is an ugly cunt to start with, so don't have him down as a man that women are throwing themselves at, because he's hanging. He has nothing to offer a woman. Plus, he only goes to work, and the rest of the time he's sprawled on your sofa. I think you are barking up the wrong tree there love. Tony is a lot of things, but he's never a love-cheat, he's bloody rotten to the core." Tina raised her eyes. So what, it was the truth in her eyes.

Elsie squirmed and steam was coming out of her ears. Her man was sexy and he would always be. "Oh, fuck off Tina. I come here for some support, not so you can slag my husband off. He's got scratches on his back and I'll get to the bottom of them if it kills me."

"Like I said, he doesn't move from your sight. He goes to work then he's back home again. So, unless he's sneaking somebody in your gaff when you're asleep at night it doesn't make sense."

Elsie shook her head and yanked her coat off. "Give me a cig Tina. For fuck's sake I don't need the extra stress of this as well as worrying about the kids."

Tina passed her friend a cigarette. "Here, let's hope this calms you down." Elsie lit up and sucked in a large mouthful of smoke, she must have been gasping. "What's up with the kids? You've never mentioned that you were worried about them before."

"I did, I told you last week. I'm out of my mind with worry about Emily. She's staying at Jane's all the time and switching her phone off."

Tina sighed, "And, you've never been young, have you? Come on Elsie, you're not thick. She's got some male attention so just leave her to it. You've told her about the birds and bees, haven't you? She's not daft."

"Tina, I've got a gut feeling something is not right. You know when you just know?"

"Oh, fuck off Mystic Meg. What are you, a psychic now or something?"

"I'm telling you, mark my words, something is fishy."

There was a pause as Tina puffed on her cig. "Ay, I've met a man. Well, he's alright and I think he's got potential. He's a bit of a fat fucker but he seems really nice. I met him in a pub when I was out with a few of the girls from the darts team on Saturday. I swear, he was treating me like a queen, he bought my drinks all night and then asked me to go back to his place.

He said he had a big house with hot-tubs in and all that. I just gave him my phone number. I'm not into all that one-night stand stuff. I want something nice for a change. And, the good thing about him is that he knows nothing about my past. He's not from the area."

Elsie smiled and sat back in her chair. "You deserve it, chick. I mean, the shit you've had in your life, you should have been dead by now."

Tina nodded, "Tell me about it. I just hope this one is different. My knight in shining armour."

"Is he good looking?"

"Erm, he's alright. He's no Brad Pitt, but beauty is in the eye of the beholder or so they say."

"I hope it all works out for you. Just remember me if he whisks you off to his big house." The two of them giggled.

Elsie swigged her drink and sat deep in thought for a few seconds. "Do you think he's banging the woman he works for - Sue?"

Tina spat out her mouthful of coffee and nearly choked. "Is he bleeding hell you daft get. Sue is a classy woman. Do you think for one moment she'd have a hobo in her bed, stinking the place out?"

Elsie sucked hard on her bottom lip. "He's not a hobo. And, you hear about stories like this all the time, she might fancy a bit of rough. She could be lonely, after all, her husband is always away working. I might just pop around there one day, just to see how the land lies."

"You're talking out of your arse. If it makes you feel any better, then go around to see her. At least then your mind will be at rest." Elsie never replied, she just sat looking into thin air.

CHAPTER FIFTEEN

What an absolute disaster. How had he let himself get like this? Tony was on the floor in the boozer and he was steaming drunk. Toddy was a party animal and he made sure everyone in his company was necking as much beer as possible. He was a free man now and he wanted to celebrate his freedom with everyone there. Tony only meant to have a few drinks with the gang, but he just got caught up in the moment. There he was pulling money out of his pocket like it was nobody's business. He'd spent the deposit money hours ago. Oh yes, he was buying everyone drinks, even people he didn't know. He was everyone's friend. The landlord tapped him on his shoulder as closing time came. "Come on mate. It's time to go home. Go and get your head down pal, you're wasted."

Toddy was well gone; he was wrecked and didn't even know what day it was. Tony's eyes opened slowly as he took a few seconds to focus. He lifted his head slightly and you could see he was in pain. His hand touched the front of his head and his body wobbled as he tried to sit up straight. "Just give me a minute boss. Fuck me, how long have I been asleep?"

The landlord chuckled. "I'm not sure. One minute you were up dancing and the next you just collapsed." Tony tried to smile, but reality was hitting home. He dug his hand deep into his pocket and you could see the pain in his eyes as he rummaged about in it. The landlord was eager to get him out, he shot a look down at his watch. "Come on lad. I want to get to bed, it's been a long day."

Tony staggered to the exit. "Cheers pal," he shouted, as the door bolted behind him. Tony scanned the area. It was pitch black and there was hardly any traffic on the road. It had just started to rain and small water bombs from the sky started to hit his body. He'd fucked up and he knew it, he'd dropped a right bollock this time. Reaching inside his coat he pulled out his mobile phone, a cheap basher phone and nothing to write home about. Elsie had got it him so she could keep in touch with him. "Jordan, it's me son. I don't suppose you can pick me up. I've got myself in a bit of a state and I'm stuck in Cheetham Hill." There was shouting down the phone. "No son, I've just had a few beers with the lads. On my life I've not touched any drugs." Tony had a lifeline; Jordan was on his way to pick him up. He made his way to a nearby bus-shelter and sat on the plastic bench inside it. His head rocked against the plastic glass and he sighed. "Fuck me, why, why, why? He muttered under his breath.

Within minutes Jordan arrived and honked his horn as he spotted his old man quivering at the bus stop. Tony stood up wobbling from side to side. What a state he was in! The silver BMW came to a halt not far from where Tony was stood. As soon as he saw his son he staggered towards the car and fell into the passenger side. "Fuck me it's cold out there," he slurred. He blew warm breath on to his hands and rubbed them together as he flicked the rain from his matted hair. "I was freezing my balls off. Thanks for the lift, you're a saviour. Your mam is going to go sick. It's nearly one in the morning. She'll be sat at the front door like a fucking Rottweiler waiting for me to come home. You know what she's like."

Jordan raised an eyebrow. "It's your own fault, you never learn, do you?"

Tony could hear a noise behind him, he quickly twisted his head and spotted a young girl sat on the back seat. Her perfume was strong, and he got a whiff of red roses, a sweet fragrance. "Are you alright love? I didn't see you there. Sorry for swearing. I'm pissed, just ignore me."

The girl just carried on looking out of the window, she never replied. Ignorant cow. "She's a bit-tired dad. She's been working all night," Jordan said as he burned his eyes into her through the rear-view mirror.

Tony turned back around in his seat and nodded his head. "Where does she work, behind the bar somewhere?"

Jordan's rolled his eyes, "Yeah, somewhere like that."

Tony knew this wasn't true, but he didn't want to delve any deeper. It was Jordan's business and if he didn't want to tell him, then that was fair enough, no harm done. Tony was agitated. "Orr son, you need to come home with me and tell your mam that you picked me up. She's been acting a bit crazy lately and I'm scared of what she'll do next."

Jordon chuckled. "No way pops. You're a grown man, go and face her yourself."

Tony was worried, he knew he was up shit street.

He'd blown the money for the deposit and he was back to square one. Up the swanny without a paddle. "Where are you going anyway?"

Jordan was a bit sheepish and didn't answer straight away. "I've just got some running about to do, you know how it is."

Tony nodded and cracked his knuckles. "Yes lad, I do. Anyway, how have you gone on with Jimmy The Chop. I hope he's backed off. It's been playing on my mind."

Jordan gulped and his grip tightened on the steering wheel. "Yeah, yeah. It's all water under the bridge now. Everything is fine. It's sorted."

Tony smiled. "That's my boy. You're a chip off the old block you are. Nothing keeps you down for long."

Jordan looked into his mirror and met the eyes of the young girl. She shook her head and snarled at him. What the hell was up with her?

★

Tony slid his key into the lock and took a deep breath. He slowly opened the door and his eyes were all over the place. With caution he went inside and closed the front door with a gentle push behind. Where was she? Was she hiding? He wasn't sure. With the slightest movements he tip-toed into the hallway. He could see Frank now wagging his tail and getting ready to bark. He rushed towards him and cupped his hand firmly around his mouth, squeezing it shut. "Ssshh, you barmy get. Do you want to wake her up and have me hung drawn and quartered?" The dog was excited and started pissing as it jumped about. Enough was enough and Tony booted Frank right in his hind legs. "Fuck me, you dirty bastard. How many times have I told you about doing that? For fucks sake, look at the state of me now."

The air changed and a chill ran down the back of his spine, hair standing on end slightly. He turned slowly and there she was, waiting for him with a face of thunder. "The dog has just pissed all over my foot, look at my trainers now."

Elsie went nose to nose with him and her eyes met his. "So, let's hear what excuse you come out with this time."

"I've nothing to say. I've been for a few scoops with the lads and got a bit carried away that's all. There's no crime in that is there?"

"You just don't get it do you?"

"Get what?"

"You can't just go and get wrecked when you feel like it. I've been worried sick about you."

Tony could see she'd let her guard down slightly and took control. "I hate it when we argue. It blows my mind up and I just need to get away from you. I've not touched drugs, I've had beer. So, stop stressing. Maybe a few spliffs with Toddy, but no hard stuff."

"Did you pay the deposit?"

His eyes were wide open and he rubbed the end of his nose as if ten ants were running across it. "Yep, first instalment done and dusted."

Elsie smiled. "I'm sorry for kicking off before. It was just the scratches on your back got my mind doing somersaults."

Tony kicked his wet shoes off and plodded into the

bedroom. "You're mental woman. As if I would risk losing a beauty like you." He winked at her and started to get undressed. Elsie was still suspicious and from the corner of her eye she watched his every move.

CHAPTER SIXTEEN

Jordan sat outside a house and tapped his fingers on the dashboard repeatedly. Where the hell was she? She was supposed to be finished fifteen minutes ago. This job was doing his head in already. Jimmy The Chop had called his role 'security' and had given him no option but to work off his debts. These girls were never on time. His neck stretched as he peered out of the car window. A large house looked back at him and he could see a few lights were on inside. He stared at the dwelling and looked for any sign of movement. Nothing. What should he do next? Should he just sit here until she came out? A light switched on in the hallway, he sighed and turned the engine over. At last. The young girl wobbled towards the car and he could see she was in a bit of a panic. He reached over and opened the car door. "Where the fuck have you been? You should have been here fifteen minutes ago. I don't have all day, you know; time is money."

The girl sat in the passenger seat and clicked her seat belt across her body. She was a lovely looking girl, long red hair, green eyes and a perfect smile. She never replied to him and carried on looking out of the window. Jordan snarled at her. Where were her manners, an apology would have been nice? "Oi, are you fucking deaf or what? I've just asked you a question" he snapped. She twisted her head slowly and looked directly into his eyes. There was so much sadness there. What was up with her?

"He kept me longer than he should have. I told him his time was up, but he stood in front of the door until he'd finished off. What could I do?"

Jordan wasn't sure what she meant. "Finished what off?"

She opened her eyes wide and stressed her words. "He couldn't come, he was trying all the time, but something was wrong with him. It was probably the drugs he's had. He's a dirty old bastard, he knocks me sick. I've told Alex before that I don't want to come here but he just doesn't listen. They treat us like pieces of meat, it's horrible."

Jordan felt a wave of emotion run through his veins. The poor thing, she must have only been nineteen. She should have been at home tucked in her bed, not roaming the streets. "What's your name then. You can tell me that, can't you?"

"Lizzy," she answered in a soft voice.

"How long have you been doing this? I'm not being funny but you're stunning and wasted here. I'm sure you can get money some other way."

Jordan was concerned and he had every right to be. Lizzy shook her head slowly. She looked straight ahead and licked her lips. "You don't know my story, so don't judge me. I do what I do to survive, not because I like it."

"Feisty one, aren't you?" he chuckled.

"I'm just telling the truth; everyone is quick to judge when they know shit about my life."

Jordan was warming to her, there was something about her that he found attractive. "What's your story then, go on, we've got at least twenty minutes before we get you home. I'm all ears." Jordan made sure the radio was turned down and he was eager to hear how this young girl had lost her way.

"Nosey, aren't you? Why do you care about my life? I'm just a brass. That's all you need to know."

"Wow, fuck me. Calm down will you. I was only asking."

Lizzy sparked a cig up and opened the window slightly to blow the smoke out. She looked over at the driver and examined him in more detail. She'd always sat in the back of the car before and she never took much interest in her driver. "I met a guy when I was sixteen. He told me he loved me, and I believed him." Jordan didn't know what to say so he remained silent as she continued. "He never loved me. It was just part of his plan to get me mixed up in this sick twisted world we live in. He groomed me, he got me ready for all them dirty bastards."

Jordan was gobsmacked and felt a chill run down the back of his neck. "I don't know what to say Lizzy," he said.

"You don't have to say anything; it was my own fault for being so thick. He used to take me out, buy me clothes, everything a girl my age was looking for. I thought he was the real deal."

"So, what changed?"

"Every time we went out for a drink, he was always making sure I had a skin-full, drink after drink he brought over to me. I was only used to the odd glass of wine back then."

"Lightweight, aren't you," he smirked.

Lizzy was starting to relax and she seemed to be warming to Jordan. "Each morning I woke up in bed and I couldn't remember a thing about the night before. My boyfriend said it was because I'd drank too much but I knew then something wasn't right. So, the next time we went out I pretended that I was drinking my drinks as normal and acted like I was pissed out of my head."

Jordan was involved now and he was hanging on her every word, eager for her to continue. Her eyes closed as she told him the rest of her story. Her emotions were running high as he could see a teardrop rolling down the side of her cheek. "He thought I was drunk. He took me in the car to a house full of Asian men. Once I was inside, he just flung me on the bed and each of them had sex with me. I tried screaming, but nobody could hear me, or nobody cared. He came back for me a few hours later and took me back to his flat and put me in bed. He never said a word."

"Fucking hell, what an arse-hole he is. The dirty bastard."

"Tell me about it. I'd run away from home to be with him and he'd promised me the world. I can never go back home now, not now, not ever. I've caused my family so much pain."

"So, you're still with the guy?" She dropped her head low and her lips quivered.

"No, he's moved onto the next girl. I have to work to live in the house. That's what he's told me. I have nowhere else to go, so I've got to carry on doing what I'm doing."

Jordan was annoyed. "You can come and get your

head down at my gaff if you want. Nobody should have to go through that just because they have nowhere to live."

Lizzy reached over and stroked his arm. "That's nice of you, but I'm stuck where I am for now. I have been stashing a bit of money each week and when I have enough, I'll just get my belongings and leave. There are other girls there too, about three more. He's done the same to all of them. He drugs them and takes them to punters, the prick."

Jordan blew a laboured breath. This was some sick twisted shit. The guy should have had his bollocks cut off for what he was doing to these young girls. "The offer is still there if you change your mind, just bear it in mind for the future. I'm here if you ever need me. I'll give you my number before you leave."

Lizzy looked at him and just stared for a few seconds. "You're nice. Nobody has ever given me the time of day, never mind tried to help me. It means a lot to me, more than you know." Jordan's good deed was done for the day and he felt better about himself. "So how long have you worked for Jimmy then?" Lizzy asked.

"I don't work for that nob. I work for myself. I owe him some money, and this is how I have to pay it back. All because I got done over and lost a lot of money."

"They all piss in the same pot, they have no values. I found that out a long time ago"

"You're right there. Once I've paid what I owe, he won't see me for dust. I'll set up on my own and fuck him right off."

"Good luck with that. I've heard he's a head the

ball, a lunatic."

"Yes, he is. Why do you think I'm driving you girls about? He said he was coming through my mam's front door if I didn't sort out the dough that I owed him. I can't have that can I? I had no other option."

"No, your family are precious. I realise that now." Lizzy pulled a small jacket over her body. Her eyes were closing, she was completely knackered. She drifted off to sleep.

Jordan had reached his destination. He pulled up outside the house and turned the engine off. It was time to wake Lizzy up. But, how could he send her back into the house knowing what lay behind those walls. He sat thinking for a few seconds and sighed shaking his head. This wasn't his problem, he had enough of his own. It was just a crying shame that Lizzy had nobody in her life to help her get away from the world she was involved in. He reached over and gently patted her shoulder. "Lizzy, we're here. Come on, wake up."

The young girl began to stir, her eyes opening slowly. She looked bewildered as she fully opened her eyes and took a few seconds before finding her bearings. She looked out of the window into the darkness and swallowed hard. "Thank you, not just for driving me home but for listening to me. I don't talk to anyone about what I do and it was nice to have a friendly face, who sort of understands me."

Jordan was involved again. She was pulling at his heart strings. How could he let her go back in the house now that he knew what was happening to her? She was selling her body, and those dirty bastards were touching her in places she didn't want to be touched.

He swallowed a large mouthful of air and sucked on his bottom lip. "Come home with me. I'll tell them that you weren't at the house when I came to pick you up. I care about you and I don't want you putting yourself in danger. I don't want anything in return, no money, no sex, fuck all, just to know you are safe."

Lizzy gasped, she was having a panic attack. Her eyes flicked one way then another, she squeezed her fingers into tight balls and bit down on one. "No, I have to go back. They'll hunt high and low for me. They've told me that before, when I was late home one night. One of the girls who went missing never returned and the story is that they found her and did her in. I don't want to die."

Jordan banged his palm on the steering wheel and his voice got louder. "Nobody will find you. I can hide you away until you're ready to leave. You don't need anything. Just come with me and sort your head out for a bit. After a few days you'll feel better and everything will look different."

Lizzy was shaking from head to toe and she wasn't making sense anymore. She gripped the car door and fumbled to open it. "I'm not ready yet. This is the only home I've known. I can't go back to my family. How could I when I've been selling my body? My parents would never forgive me. I'm broken now, lost."

Jordan reached over and grabbed the back of her skimpy dress. "You can do what you want. Just get back in the car and let me take you to safety."

Lizzy wriggled free; she was frantic to get away. "Stop being so nice to me! Just go home. I'll be fine. Thank you for caring, it means a lot to me. But just leave me be." Lizzy disappeared and he could hear her heels clip up the long path towards the house. She turned back to look at him one last time. He punched his fist into the dashboard and dropped his head. At least he'd tried, what else could he have done?

CHAPTER SEVENTEEN

Tony was working today but he was distracted, always looking over his shoulder. His head looked one way, then the other. What was he searching for? The weather was fine so there was no reason for him to be sat in the small wooden shed at the bottom of the garden skiving. Peeping out from the small window his eyes squeezed together. He nodded his head and rubbed his hands as he spotted Sue pulling up in her car. The corners of his mouth started to rise and he stood up to straighten his clothes. He quickly rubbed some soil on his cheeks and smeared some of the dark brown grit across his forehead. He grabbed a metal spade in his hands and stepped outside and started digging a patch of turf. Here he was getting paid to sit on his arse all day doing nothing. What a piss-taker.

Sue twisted her head and spotted him from the corner of her eye. "Shall I make us a nice cuppa Tony?" she shouted across the garden. She didn't need to ask him twice. He downed tools and he was already on his way over to her. "What a lovely day it is, spring is surely on the way. We'll start planting some flowers soon, in time for the summer. I've already started to plan the colours. I can have red and pink carnations over there, and maybe some yellow and cream ones on the higher ground. What do you think?"

Tony was caught off guard and stuttered. "Yes, but

let the weather settle first. I've been weeding today. I've yanked loads of them up from the back of the fence. And, yes, we can start planting some flowers in the next few weeks. Just let's do the groundwork first."

They headed towards the front door and Tony was holding her shopping bags for her. What a gentleman he was. She must have been on a spending spree, there were lots of clothes and shoes. He would never have done a tap for Elsie, he'd just lie on the sofa and watch her heave all the shopping in on her own, he always turned a blind eye. There was more go in a sick-note. "Can I just nip to the loo?" Tony asked as he held his crotch with desperation in his expression.

"Yes, of course. Just put my bags down here and I'll sort them out later." Tony left the hallway and rushed upstairs. The toilet door was facing him, but he detoured passed it. He was as quiet as a mouse as he entered the bedroom. Tony knew exactly what he was doing and headed straight for the silver jewellery box on the high gloss, white dressing table. Lifting the lid up slowly with the slightest of movements, his hand hovered for a few seconds. Quickly, he clutched a diamond ring and studied it for a few seconds. This was what he was looking for, something that was worth a few quid. He rammed it down the front of his boxers and made sure it was lodged under his ball sack. There was no waiting about, he slammed the lid back down and made sure everything was as he found it. Twisting on his feet he was out of the room as quick as a flash. Tony was sweating, hands clammy, small beads of sweat rolling down his forehead. Tony closed the toilet door behind him and sat down on the toilet. His heart was racing and he had to calm down. It was time to examine his stolen goods. His eyes were wide open. This was a beauty and worth a few grand for sure. He turned the ring one way then another. All his worries would be over now, he could pay for the holiday and even have some spending money. This was the life-line he needed, a second chance. He stashed the ring away, inside his sock this time and flushed the toilet behind him. His cheeks were beetroot when he made his way back down the stairs and he looked shifty.

Sue was sat at the kitchen table and she was waiting for him. "I've put you some cake out. Lemon drizzle, it's one of my favourites. I hope you like it. I've put you a large slice out, I know you like anything sweet." Sue was flirting and he could tell by the way she licked the white fluffy cream from her finger. She slid it in her mouth and sucked it out slowly, making sure he could see her. Tony had no appetite whatsoever and he was nervous in case she'd sussed him. He sat down and reached over for his drink. He swallowed hard. "I'm going to get off early today Sue. The wife is at the doctors and I said I would go with her."

Sue rolled her eyes. "Oh, right. I thought we could have spent some time together today. But, not to worry, we'll catch up another day." She licked the edge of her rosy red lips and flicked her hair over her shoulders. Tony was agitated as she stood up and ran her fingers through his hair. He could smell her perfume, her sweet floral aroma that drove him mad for her body. "It's a shame you have to leave, I thought we could have had some time together. You know, special time," she purred in her sexy voice. Her hand slid down the front of his t-shirt and she bent her head slowly and kissed his neck. He couldn't turn her down, he was like butter in her hands. The way she smelt, the way her body curved, her long blonde hair, no, he had to have her. He wasn't thinking straight anymore. The two of them kissed passionately and Tony was lost in the moment. She was dragging his clothes off in a wild frenzy. He only had his boxer shorts on now and his white tennis socks. With a flat palm she pushed him onto the table and lifted his leg up. With her teeth she gripped his foot firmly. Sue was kinky for sure and sucking his toes was a guilty pleasure. Her face changed, as her hand dragged off the sock. Tony flapped about, remembering what was in there, but it was too late. Sue held the diamond ring in her hand and studied it. The shit was going to hit the fan for sure. She lifted her head up and looked at Tony then looked back at the ring. The penny dropped and she moved away from him as if he was diseased.

"That's my ring isn't it?"

Tony was stuck for words, he had to think quick. "Yes, it is. I was going to buy you a ring to thank you for all you've done for me and I needed your ring size. I was going to bring it back to you, honest, I was."

I suppose it was a good effort from Tony but she was onto him. Her voice was louder. "No, I don't believe you. How could you steal from me when I have done so much for you? Move away from me you deceitful bastard."

Tony held his hands up and started to get his clothes back on in a panic. "Sue, on my life, that's the truth. Why would I ruin what we have here? I'm not that kind of guy. Come on, how many times have I been in here and never touched a thing. And, I could have, couldn't I?"

She walked up to him and drew her hand back and swung it forward with speed. The slap landed right across his cheek and made a loud noise. "Get your belongings and get your stinking rotten, thieving hands out of my property before I ring the police on you. I trusted you. I, I…" she stuttered.

Just the mention of the old bill sent him into a panic. He went white. "Sue, love, come on. I would never steal anything from you. I love it here, and us," he was frantic.

"What about us?" She growled at him and moved away from him. He'd not seen the side of her before, she was no pushover. She was the one calling the shots. "Just go and never come back here. You were a mistake, a daft mistake that I'm already regretting. You're nothing more than a street rat, a dirty thief, with no respect for nobody."

Tony hovered, he dropped his head and his voice was soft. She was right, and he knew it. "Sorry, there are no other words for it. If you think I'm a thief, then there is nothing more to say. I'll go." Sue's eyes burned into him. The sooner he was out of here the better. His feet trudged towards the front door. He was hoping she might have had a change of heart, but she never did. He'd fucked up big time. Tony booted the front gate as he left the property. He could have been the Lord of the Manor here, made for life. But now he was back to square one. What a plonker.

★

Tony sat in Mickey's and he was on a complete downer. He'd just confided in his pal all about his antics with Sue. Yes, he told him about the sex too. Mickey rubbed his hands together. He was amazed and still not sure if Tony was filling his head with shit. But, either way, he loved the story. "Fucking hell, so you were bollocks deep in her? Standard that mate. Ay, I wonder if I knock on and ask if she needs a gardener she'll take me on? I could do with a good shag. I've not emptied my bollocks for years."

Tony booted at his leg. "Are you having a laugh or what. I was special. Do you think she'd have your sweaty todger stuck up her when she's had mine first?"

Mickey burst out laughing and fell back onto the sofa. "It's a shame about that ring though mate, I bet it was a right few quid. Trust you to get caught."

"Tell me about it. I take two steps forward and three steps back. What am I going to do now? I can't tell Elsie what happened, she'll go ballistic. I'll have to say Sue's going on holiday for a few weeks, that should get her off my back for a bit."

Mickey chewed on his lips. "You'll have to get your arse back out grafting then won't you, because Elsie will be wanting some cash."

Tony was alarmed. No, he was past grafting for drug money, he was off drugs, he was clean. Plus, he didn't have the nerve for it anymore. What else could he do though? Mickey was right, his missus would be wanting some cash from his work soon. Maybe he could set a job up? One last hit, a big one, a game changer. But he was no big-time gangster, he was just a poxy shoplifter, a house burglar, nothing more. Tony sat thinking and tickled the end of his chin. A plan was hatching in his mind, his eyes opened wide. "I'll get that ring Mickey; I'll screw the house over. I know where the alarms are and all the CCTV. Plus, she has other rings, I'll take the fucking lot. It would serve her right for cheating on her old man." Tony rubbed his hands together and nodded his head. He was back in the game.

Mickey was itching at his skin, sweating and he held a cunning look in his eye. It was that time again. He never said a word he just reached over and started to get the stuff ready to smoke the heroin, silver foil and lighter. Tony was struggling and you could see his fingers roll into tight balls at the side of his legs. Don't be an arse Tony, walk away, you've been doing so well, he told himself. But there was another voice in his head that was getting louder and louder, gripping his thoughts. Music played softly in the background as Mickey melted into the chair, his eyes glossed over and every now and then they opened, nothing he was saying was making any sense. Why was Tony still sat here? He should have left and gone home to his family. He bit down hard on his fingernails and chewed at the small piece of skin hanging there. His body rocked and he was moving to the edge of his seat. His hands were shaking as it moved towards the drugs. He stopped and froze. What the hell was he doing?

CHAPTER EIGHTEEN

Emily lay in her bedroom just staring at the ceiling. She'd only been home a few hours and already she was pining for Mark. She lived and breathed him, he was constantly on her mind, he was well and truly under her skin. Elsie opened the bedroom door and popped her head inside. "Bleeding hell, are you home? I thought you'd moved out."

Emily rolled on her side and she was happy to see her mother. She stretched her arms over her head as she replied. "Mam, I'm just living my life. You are always telling me to get out more and now that I am, you're stressing out. I can't win."

Elsie waddled over to the bed. "I'm not stressing out; I just miss our chats. Move over, I'll chill with you for a bit." Emily was in no mood for talking but she shuffled her body over the bed and let Elsie take a place next to her. "So, tell me his name then. Don't even try to lie because I know you have a boyfriend. I can see the changes in you. You do your hair, even put make-up on. Since when did you ever bother with any slap?"

Emily giggled and covered her mouth with her hand. She was excited to open-up and tell someone about the new man in her life. "I have met somebody. He's so cute. Mam, he treats me like a princess and I'm totally in love with him."

Elsie squirmed. How could her daughter be in love

when she'd only been seeing this guy for a short time? She brushed the comment off and spoke in a sarcastic voice. "It's puppy love, it's not real love. That will come when you're older."

Emily growled and her voice changed. Nobody was putting a dampener on her new relationship. "No, it's real love. I know what I feel in my heart and this is the man I will marry one day. We have just connected; he knows me inside out."

Elsie looked at her daughter and sniggered. "Bleeding hell, keep your knickers on. I was only making a comment. If you say you love him then who am I to question you? When are we going to meet him, because if it is true love, we need to give him the seal of approval? Your dad will want to vet him; you know what he's like."

Emily was in a panic. "No way, mam. Do you think I'm bringing him here for you lot to embarrass me? Dad would sit there farting and you would be laughing your head off. It's not what I want him to see."

"We're your family though. We are who we are, you can pick your friends, but you can't pick your family, remember that."

Emily brushed off the comment and changed the subject. "Where is my dad? Is he still working?"

Elsie looked her daughter proudly in the eye as she reached over and twiddled with her hair. "Yes, he's still grafting. He's doing so well too. He's not touched drugs and all he keeps talking about is taking us all on holiday. I'll tell you what, he must have really taken on board what you said to him."

"So, we're still going on holiday then?"

"Yeah, that's what you wanted, so that's what you're getting."

Emily wriggled about in the bed. She was uncomfortable. "I'm not sure I want to go anymore. I didn't have a boyfriend when I said that to him. Things have changed now and well…" she paused. "I don't want to leave him."

Elsie sighed, "Fuck me, don't make it too easy for this guy. You sound a bit desperate if you ask me. You need to play it cool and be a bit of a player. Men just walk all over you when you wear your heart on your sleeve. Don't reply to his texts too quickly, tell him you're washing your hair some nights and let him miss you."

Emily saw her arse. "No way, I'm spending all my free time with him. We get on so well and he feels the same way about me as I do for him. He said he loves me."

Elsie sat up on the bed. This was news to her. "How old is this lad?"

Emily's cheeks were beetroot and she looked away as she answered her. "He's the same age as me. But age is just a number."

This was all too concerning for Elsie and maybe she'd let things slip. She should have been keeping a closer eye on her child. "Are you having sex with him?"

Emily was distraught and covered her eyes with both of her hands. "Mam," she shrieked. "You can't say things like that to me."

Elsie looked bewildered, "Why not? You're my daughter and if you're having sex then I should know about it. I mean, you could get pregnant, you could contract a sexual disease. You don't want a scabby fanny, do you?"

This was getting worse by the minute; Elsie didn't have a clue how to word this conversation. She should have got some leaflets from the family planning clinic, gathered some information from the professionals before she tackled this issue. "Mam, just leave me alone now, you are sending me under. If I need any advice, you would be the last person I would come to."

Elsie's face dropped. She wanted the bond that was between mother and daughter, the closeness. She wanted to be the person Emily could talk to whenever she needed help. Her daughter's words had cut her up and inside she was wounded. Elsie didn't move straight away, she sat on the edge of the bed and looked at her daughter and smiled. "Listen, you know I'm crap with words, but you know what I mean don't you? I will never judge you or make any demands. I just want you to be safe. There are a lot of men out there who will take advantage of you, given half the chance. I just want you to be safe. You can't blame me for that can you?"

Emily had overacted and she knew it. She tried to make amends. "Jane has a boyfriend too, so we are both safe, we have each other's back. I'm not daft, am I? God, with you and my dad, I'm probably the most streetwise kid round here. Remember when you sent me to the front door to the loan man and told me to tell him you were in prison?"

Elsie giggled. "Oh yes, ay, you were a mint actress. You even threw in some tears too. I thought the loan man was going to give you some money at the end of your performance."

The air was cleared and they both sat laughing together. No more words were spoken about having sex, it was brushed under the carpet and forgotten about. "Tina should be here soon. She's calling around for a cuppa. She's only gone and bagged herself a man. I told her that she should cling onto him with both hands because he sounds a decent guy. We both know what kind of men she mixes with and apparently this one is different to the rest."

Emily always had a lot of time for her mother's friend and she'd helped Emily a lot when her mother was off her head on drugs. Tina always made sure she had food, gas and electric in the house. She was a kind and caring soul. "It's about time she found a nice man. She's getting on a bit now, she'll end up on the shelf if she doesn't act soon. I hope it works out for her mam because, let's face it, she's never had any luck with men. What was he called? The man who blacked her eyes?"

Elsie thought for a moment before she shouted out. "Len, bloody hell, I remember him. He nearly left her for dead. He battered her black and blue."

Emily shook her head and sighed. "But, what does she expect when she does the job she's doing? How on earth can you meet a decent man when they're going to a brothel where you work."

Elsie's jaw dropped. How on earth did she know that Tina was a brass? She'd thought she'd always kept it under wraps. She looked at her hands as the memory of her own torment came flooding back into her mind. It was a bad time in her life, a time when she would have done anything to fill her veins with drugs. Did Emily know her mother's story too? "Tina did whatever she had to do to keep her head above water. Sometimes when people are that low, they make choices they have no control over. She's got a big heart and whatever she does for a living will never make me treat her differently. So, I hope you don't judge her either?"

Emily played with her fingers and she was thinking about what she was going to say next. "Mam, I know how hard it is when you have no money or when your addiction takes control of you. I've lived through addiction with you both and I know how it changes a person. I'm just glad that all that is behind us now. Look at you and my dad now, you've both turned a corner. I'm proud of you both."

Elsie choked up and realised how grown up her daughter really was. She wasn't brain-dead, she was wise and knew a lot about life and what went on in it. Elsie choked up and her eyes flooded with tears. She knew she'd been a crap mother in the past and every day she was trying to make things better. "I went to see your grandad you know. I've been waiting to tell you, but you've always been in and out of the house so fast that I've never had a minute with you."

This was great news and Emily rubbed her hands together with excitement. "That's brilliant. Did he ask to see us? Jordan will be over the moon, he misses grandad. It was the only the other week that he was talking about him. Orr, they were close, weren't they?"

Elsie had to stop her, put her in the picture before this got any bigger. "Emily, he didn't want anything to do with me. He told me to leave him alone. I told him I'd changed but he wanted fuck all to do with me."

Emily froze, she had to digest what was being said.

"What, he told his own flesh and blood to leave him alone?"

"I know, but you have to remember what I did to my family. I let them down, time after time. They were good to me. You and Jordan basically lived there when I was bad on the drugs. I have to thank them for that. If they hadn't looked after you two, then social services would have been involved and you both would have ended up in care."

Emily snapped and banged her hand on the bed. "But, he's our grandad. Why has he cut us out of his life? I thought he loved us?"

Elsie put her arms around her and kissed the top of her head. "Ay, don't ever think that he doesn't love you. That man would have climbed mountains for you both. He loved you both to bits. To him and my mam, you were the apple of their eye. Don't you remember all the pretty dresses she bought you? She knitted you so many cardigans too. You were like her daughter, not mine."

Emily was angry, rage was climbing up her throat and smashing its way through her teeth. "Bullshit mam, if somebody loves you, they just don't close the door in your face. If they loved and cared for us, how could they let you take us from their house?"

This was a story on its own, a secret Elsie had never told her children. Her shoulders sank and the shame she'd carried for all these years seemed to be weighing her body down. It took a few seconds but Elsie knew it was time to come clean. Her voice was low as she revealed the truth. "That was my fault. I never told you the real story. I was off my head on the shit and went banging on the front door looking for money. I was off my napper and desperate." Emily pulled the blanket tightly over her shoulders and sat with her back against the wall. She was always like this when she was feeling uneasy, the blanket was never far from her side. "I was screaming and shouting outside the front door, making a show of myself. I barged passed my mam and dragged you both out of bed. I told them that if they didn't give me any money then I was taking you both home with me. They called my bluff and let me take you. There was nothing else they could do; I was a nightmare. Usually, they would just give me some money and send me packing, but not this time. Your dad tried to take you both back a few hours later but he ended up kicking off with my dad and the rest is history."

This was all news to Emily, no wonder she'd been shunned by her family. She looked at her mother and shook her head. "I don't know what to say. I suppose they did what they thought was right. It was you who was the nightmare. What else could they have done?"

"I know that now but you know what I was like when I was twisted."

Emily could never understand the need to take drugs and even after several counselling sessions in school, she still couldn't get her head around it. "I think you should go and see him again. It must have been a shock to him, seeing you after all this time. Let it sink in and go back. I'll come with you if you want. I'd love to see my nana and grandad again."

Elsie was nibbling at her fingernails. "I don't know about that; I don't think my heart could stand the rejection. I was just going to take it on the chin and leave them alone."

"Stop being silly. I'll come with you. Just let me know when you're planning on going."

There was knocking on the front door and a voice shouting. Elsie jumped up from the bed and chuckled. "That will be Tina. Get out of bed and come and see her, she's not seen you for ages. You can both talk about the new men in your life." Emily smiled; she could talk about Mark all day long given the chance. She picked her grey fluffy blanket up and followed her mother out of the bedroom.

Tina was white as a ghost and struggling for breath as she entered the flat. Elsie raised her eyes and helped her sit down. "That bleeding lift is broken again. I've had to trudge up them bastard stairs. You should report it to the council, nobody should have to climb them stairs every day. Bang the kettle on Elsie, I need something to wet my whistle."

Elsie walked into the kitchen and left her daughter to entertain her friend. When Tina finally caught her breath, she smiled over at Emily and looked surprised. "Oh, you look lovely, have you changed your hair or something?"

Emily blushed, she hated compliments. She never knew how to handle them. "Erm, I've got a bit of make-up on, that's all. My hair is more or less the same as I always wear it."

Tina scanned the young girl again. "You've lost weight, that's what it is. Your face is a lot thinner." Emily had lost some blubber and her puppy fat had disappeared.

"Thanks Tina," she replied.

"My mam tells me you have a new man in your life. Fill me in then."

Tina didn't need asking twice. "He's lovely. I can't believe my luck really. He's not from around here so that's good because he knows nothing about me. I've been up to his house and it's a million miles away from the life I live here. His house is massive, lots of bedrooms, more than I've ever seen in any house. He treats me nice and he's always on the blower asking me to meet up."

Emily loved a love story and snuggled into her blanket on the sofa. "So, do you think he's the one, the man you're going to spend the rest of your life with?"

Tina burst out laughing. "I wouldn't go that far. It's only early doors yet but he's got good potential let's say."

Emily was itching to tell her story too, here it was, it just rolled from her tongue. "I've met a guy too. I've just told my mam and she tried telling me about the birds and the bees in her own way."

They burst out laughing and Tina could only imagine what had been said. "That's nice Emily and that explains why you look different. You looked like you're wrapped up in love. Every inch of you is glowing."

Elsie wobbled back into the room with two mugs hooked around her fingers. "Grab one then, instead of looking at me. For fucks sake, the handle is burning my finger."

Emily moved quickly and took the piping hot mug from her mother. Elsie sucked her finger and tried to cool it down. "Ay, I've just seen your Tony on the estate with that Mickey. He didn't see me, but I seen him."

Elsie was on the edge of her seat and sat thinking for a few seconds. "No, it wouldn't have been Tony, he's at work today. He won't be home for another couple of hours yet."

Tina was alert, she knew what she'd seen. "No, honest, it was Tony. I know what he looks like."

Elsie was still in denial and she was having none of it. "It must be your eyes. I've told you to go and get them checked out. Tony is at work."

Tina was questioning herself now, was it Tony or someone who looked like him? "Well, he must have a double because I could have sworn it was him."

"No, my boy is grafting his balls off. If he'd finished work early, he would have come straight home here, oh hold on," she paused. "He does have an appointment at the doctors today but I'm sure he said that was at half four. I'm not sure now."

Emily interrupted them both. "He'll be home when he's finished doing what he's doing, stop worrying about him, he's a grown man."

"It's your dad we are talking about here" Elsie butted in, "he's been a bit edgy lately and I'm sure he's been struggling with coming off the drugs. In fact, that's what he's going to the doctors for, to up his dosage."

Tina rolled her eyes but kept her thoughts to herself, she had no time for Tony and didn't trust him as far as she could throw him. He's was lower than a snake's belly in her eyes, no one would ever make her see any different. "I was just saying to Emily how much she's changed; she looks great doesn't she?"

Elsie shot a look over at her daughter and sat tall.

She was proud of her. "Yes, it must be this new man in her life. What's his name again? I'm not sure if you told me."

Emily was a bit cagey; did she really want anyone to know his identity? He'd already told her that he didn't like people knowing his business. But this was just his name, nothing more. "He's called Mark and that's all you two need to know. I'm not saying anymore because my mam will start stalking him on Facebook. You know what she's like Tina."

"Don't I just Emily. You keep his surname to yourself love. The last thing you need is her messaging him when she can't find you."

"I'm not that bad, Tina" Elsie sounded offended, "I just want to make sure he's from a good family and that."

"You just keep clear of him, mam. When it's time I will introduce him to you but for now back off and let us get on with it."

Tina pulled her mobile phone out and started to log into Facebook. "I'll show you my new man. I've had a look at his Facebook profile and checked him out."

Emily and Elsie sat closer together so they could see the photograph. Emily seemed concerned when she saw the picture for the first time, it was a blurred image and she couldn't make out the face properly. "I think I've seen him somewhere before. Where did you say he lived?"

Tina shook her head. "No, you won't have seen him before he doesn't live around here, he's from Bolton."

Emily got a text alert and was paying no attention to what they were saying now. She grabbed her mobile and clicked on the messages. It was from her true love, her heart desire. Elsie had a swan neck and tried taking a butchers at her daughters phone but she got caught in the act. "Oi, stop trying to look at my messages! See what I mean about her Tina? She's a nosey cow!"

Tina nudged Elsie in the waist and made sure she couldn't read anymore. "Leave the girl alone for crying out loud. No wonder she doesn't tell you anything."

Elsie chuckled and sat down with her arms folded tightly in front of her. "I'll find out who he is. You know me when I have a bee in my bonnet. I'll just get our Jordan to put the word out and then I'll know everything."

Emily knew she was winding her up. "Whatever mother, good luck with that. Anyway, some of us have got a life. I need to get ready. I'm off out again."

Tina smiled. "Good on you girl, it's about time you had some fun instead of being sat in here every day looking after these two."

"Correct Tina. They can look after themselves from now on because I'll be moving out soon."

This was news to Elsie, her eyes opened wide and she spoke in a stern tone. "Over my dead body are you moving out! You're still a kid. So, get that thought right out of your mind. Your dad will go sick if he hears you saying stuff like that, so get it in your head now, you're here until you are eighteen."

Emily rolled her eyes. She wasn't going to get lippy; she knew better. "Oh, mother. What is up with you lately? Where has your sense of humour gone? I'm joking!"

Emily left with a smirk spread across her face. Tina winked at her before she left. Elsie was on one, she just sat there staring into space. Tina clicked her fingers in front of her eyes. "Hello, is anyone in? Elsie, it's me Tina."

Elsie give her head a quick shake and she was back in the moment. "Did you hear what she said Tina? She's a baby still. How can she even think about leaving home?"

"She's grown up now. You can't start putting rules there after she's had none for years. You're lucky she has turned out the way she has. It could have been a lot worse."

"Still, I'm not happy with it all. I'll word Jordan up and get him to find out who this geezer is. He seems to have a strong hold on her, she's not thinking straight."

Tina slurped her cup of tea as she watched her friend from the corner of her eye. Elsie was still in deep thought.

CHAPTER NINETEEN

Emily sat with Mark in the corner of the pub with Jane and Omar facing her. They were out on the piss again. Emily, being honest with herself, was sick to death of drinking all the time. Before this she had only had the odd bottle of Wicked sat on the park with Jane but Vodka was a whole new level to her. Omar didn't let any of their glasses get empty either and as soon as they finished one drink, he had another lined up for them. The boozer was packed. Lots of people were in tonight dancing and singing on the karaoke. Emily loved singing but she didn't have the guts to get up tonight. She had a lovely tone to her voice, and some people had commented that she could have do something more than just be a bathroom singer. Mark was anxiously checking his wristwatch every few minutes as his eyes darted at Omar. They both held the look for a few seconds as if they were intimating something to each other. Mark reached over and grabbed his jacket. "Emily, I've just got to nip out. I won't be long." Her face dropped and she had a sinking feeling deep in the pit of her stomach. But, what could she say? She had to keep her mouth shut. Mark bent down slightly and kissed her on the cheek. He could sense something was wrong by the look on her face. "Are you okay, doll?"

She couldn't look at him; it was written all over her face. "Yes, I'm fine. Just a bit tired."

Mark patted the top of her shoulder. "I'll be back before you know it and we'll have a great night. Get a few more drinks down you and you'll feel fine."

She found it hard to raise a smile, her heart was heavy and something was on her mind. When Omar went to the bar, Emily moved over to Jane and folded her arms tightly in front of her. "See what I mean, he's always going on the missing list. I wonder what he's up to. Do you think he's got another girl on the go?"

Jane shot a look over to Omar who was stood at the bar. "I think they're both shady, something doesn't sit right with them. At first, I thought Omar was an alright guy, but there are a few things with him that bother me."

Emily's eyes were wide open now, she moved in closer making sure nobody was listening. "Like what," she whispered.

"I'm not sure, but every time I go to bed with him, he's nowhere to be seen in the morning. I found Alex in the bedroom the other morning when I woke up. I shit myself and screamed."

"What was Alex doing in your room?"

"I've not got the foggiest idea; I just know he looked shifty."

Emily's heart and mind were racing. "It's funny you should say that because I've woken up with him in my room too."

The girls both shot a look at each other and froze. Jane was panicking. "Emily, something is wrong. I drink with these guys and know nothing about the night before when I wake up, it's like I blank it out. I can't remember a bleeding thing."

"Me too."

There was a silence between them. Jane dropped her head low and reached over and touched Emily's hand. "Do you think they are drugging us or something?"

Emily was alarmed. "Fuck off. Mark loves me. Why would he do something like that?"

Jane squeezed at Emily's fingers until they turned white and growled at her. "You know something isn't right. We're not daft. I tell you what, let's watch our drinks tonight and don't touch them. We can pretend to be pissed and see what happens."

"No way, why would we do that? Like I said, Mark is all over me, he'd never do something like that."

Jane held a sour expression as she watched Omar on his way back over to the table. "Well, I'm not drinking anymore. You can if you want but count me out." Omar was back and handed them both a drink. You could cut the atmosphere with a knife. Emily reached over and grabbed hers. She made a point of drinking it so Jane could see her.

Omar placed his arm around Jane and snuggled up to her. "What's up with your mush?"

Jane could never hide her feelings and she squirmed over at him as she pushed him away. "I don't feel too good. I want to go home. Can you drop me off?"

"You've not been here for long. I'm not driving to Manchester when I'm already half cut."

"Fine, I'll get a taxi," she snarled. Jane was adamant that she was going. She was scared and feared what would happen next.

Omar took a few deep breaths and pulled her closer, he whispered in her ear. Emily was trying to listen in, but she couldn't hear a thing. Jane started to shout out in a loud voice, everyone was starting to look at her. She bolted up from her seat and made sure everyone could hear what she had to say. "I said, I'm going home. How dare you tell me what I can and can't do. You don't own me."

Emily tried to keep her calm, but Jane was in the zone and nobody was stopping her now. She barged past Emily and headed for the doors. Omar was frantic and followed. Emily was about to follow, but Omar pushed her back to her seat. "You just stay here. I'll sort her out."

Emily was in two minds what to do. Would she like someone interfering in her relationship? The answer was no. She sat back down and kept her eyes on the door. Jane was big enough and daft enough to look after herself. After a few minutes later Omar arrived back in the pub. He was stressed out and pumping with rage. He stormed over to the table with his hands ragging through his hair. "You better sort that slag out. I've invested time and money into her, and she thinks she can treat me like a dickhead. Go outside and see her before I run back and punch her fucking face in."

Emily was gobsmacked. What the hell was going on? Omar was usually laid-back and happy. Suddenly, he was a different person and Emily was frightened of him. She edged passed him. "I'll be back soon."

"Just sort her out," he growled.

Jane was stood near a wall and she was upset. Emily ran to her side and hugged her. "Bleeding hell, what's going on. What did he say to you?"

Jane was blubbering, her words stuck in her mouth.

"He's a prick, he's not dictating to me what I can and can't do. He doesn't own me, the dick. He said he would shave my hair off if I didn't do what he told me to."

Emily calmed down and they both sat on a nearby wall. Emily looked over at her best friend. "So, are you going home?"

"Dead right I am. I'm going to get a taxi. My mam will pay for it at the other end. There is no way I'm staying here, it's not safe. These are bad men, honest, I want out of this as soon as possible."

"Wow, what am I going to do then? My mam thinks I'm with you. You were my alibi."

Jane pulled a sour face. How selfish was her best friend, she was just thinking about herself? "And, you think I'm arsed about you and Mark. That man in there has just ragged me about and threatened to do me in. I can't stand him. I knew there was something wrong with him, he's shady. He's a control freak. He bought me gifts and showed me a good time yes, but I'm not into him anymore. I suggest you cart Mark as well while you can. Let's go home."

Emily gritted her teeth together and she was ready to whack Jane. She took a deep breath and spoke in a clear voice. Her cage had been rattled. "Stop being a drama queen. You just can't stand to see me happy, can you? Go on, admit it, you're jealous of me."

Jane let out a sarcastic laugh. "Are you crazy? Why would I be jealous of you? You've got nothing I want."

Emily was fighting her corner. "I have Mark, I've seen the way you flirt with him. You only went out with Omar so you could be near my man. I can see right through you. You're a dirty slag."

This was fighting talk. Jane went nose to nose with her best friend and her hot breath sprayed over her face as she spoke. "Oh, have you heard yourself, give your head a shake. He's the first man that has ever given you the time of the day and you're all over him. It's sickening to watch. You can't see the woods for the trees, but you just watch. He'll show his true colours soon and, you'll see who is right. I'm getting a taxi; you can sort your own story out for your mam."

Jane walked off. Emily was fuming. She wanted to run over to Jane and kick ten shades of shit out of her. Taking a few seconds to calm down, she started to make her way back inside the pub. Hold on, she froze and quickly moved out of sight. Her neck stretched as she peered over to the car park. Mark was sat in the car with a girl. She could see him laughing, his arms around her shoulder. Her stomach churned and vomit was bubbling up from her stomach. What should she do? She couldn't just stand there and do nothing. Tears flooded her eyes as she motored over to the car park. Emily's clenched fist pounded on the passenger side window. "Open the door you slag. Who do you think you are, sitting with my boyfriend?"

She banged on the window several times. Mark got out of the driver's side and rushed to where she was. "Fucking calm down will you. If that window goes in, then you'll be paying for it."

Emily slammed her palm onto his chest. "So, how long has it been going on. I trusted you, how could you do something like this to me."

Mark let out a laboured breath and shook his head.

"What the hell are you going on about? It's my cousin, Lizzy. I pick her up for work sometimes and drop her off."

The girl sat in the car had no emotion on her face, she just looked straight through Emily like she wasn't even there. "Fuck off Mark. I'm not daft. Don't take me for a fool."

"On my life. I swear down to you, she's my cousin." Mark twisted his head slightly and shouted Lizzy to open the car door, "Lizzy, tell this nutter you're my cousin and I've just picked you up from work."

Lizzy was in no rush to get this guy off the hook. The corners of her mouth started to rise, and she spoke with a cocky tone. "Yep, he's my cousin."

Emily's eyes flicked one way then another, she didn't know what to believe. "So, every time you go missing, you're picking her up?"

"Yes, I've just told you."

Emily's face was beetroot. What a plonker she felt. She'd made a show of herself. How was he ever going to forgive her for this? It took a few minutes for Emily to digest what had gone on. Her head dipped low and she was on the verge of crying her eyes out. Her voice was low, and she cringed as she spoke. "I'm sorry. I just seen you together and flipped out. Lizzy," she said as she looked at her directly, "I'm sorry, I just seen red and rushed over without thinking."

Lizzy scowled and didn't even reply. Mark stood there right in front of her and his chest expanded. "I'm not having all this you know. Trust is a big thing to me and if you're one of them paranoid birds then we can say goodbye now. I'll drop you off and that will be the end of us."

Emily choked, her jaw was wobbling and her heart beat double. "Mark, I've said I'm sorry. I just didn't know what to think. I've overreacted, I can't say anymore."

"Go and wait back in the pub. I'll speak to you when I've finished here." Emily was like a scolded child. Her feet moved slowly as she obeyed his orders.

Jane had been watching the disturbance from afar. She had seen everything. She watched Mark get back into the car. Her eyes were all over him making sure she didn't miss a single thing. Suddenly, Jane covered her mouth with her hand. She stood on her tiptoes and held her phone up in the air directed at the car taking a photograph. As soon as she had the image, she examined it on her phone. A cunning smirk filled her face. "I knew I was right," she whispered under her breath.

★

Emily sat in the corner of the pub with her arms folded tightly in front of her. Omar was eager to see what had happened. "Well, is she coming back in here or is she going home?"

She was on the spot, nervous to tell him the truth. Her voice croaked. "Jane's gone home. She's rang a taxi. I tried to reason with her, but she was adamant that she was done with you."

"Are you having a laugh or what? Has she really gone? Fucking hell, she's messed things up now."

"What has she messed up?" asked Emily.

He was anxious and sat cracking his knuckles. "I

just need to make a phone call. I'll be back in a minute."

Mark was back and she found it hard to maintain eye contact. Lizzy was with him. "Get me a brandy," she said to Mark.

"Do you want a drink Emily? Maybe a double to help you calm down and sort your napper out."

He was a sarcastic bastard and all of a sudden, this loving boyfriend had turned into a heartless monster. He should have just laughed it off and told her how foolish she had been. Mark trudged over to the bar; he was playing the victim for sure. Lizzy plonked down on the chair and eyeballed Emily. "So, are you his new girl?" New girl, what did she mean by that? Yes, she was his new girlfriend but to refer to her as a 'new girl' was a bit odd.

Emily sat up straight, she didn't like this girl's attitude. "Yes, we've been going out now for a few months. We're in love."

Lizzy burst out laughing and rolled her eyes. "Oh, right, so you're his girlfriend. Where are you from?"

This bitch was doing her head in and if she carried on with this attitude, she was going to get a piece of her mind, cousin or not. "I live in Manchester, why where are you from?"

Lizzy was cagey. The less people knew about her the better. "I'm from all over me, love. I like to think I'm a bit of a gypsy. How old are you?"

Emily was aware that her age was still a secret and there was no way she was confiding in this witch. "Eighteen, nearly nineteen."

Lizzy frowned and the side of her cheeks creased. "Really, you don't look that old, you still look like a kid to me."

Emily pushed her breasts out as far as she could and replied to her. "I've got a baby face, soft and smooth skin. That's what makes me look young."

Lizzy bent slightly to the left and saw Mark still at the bar. Once she was aware of where he was, she placed her feet on the chair opposite her and chewed rapidly on her chewing gum. "So, you really like Mark then?"

Was this a test or what, why she so interested in her love life. "Yes, he loves me, and I love him. We're going to get a place together soon."

Lizzy was amused and she couldn't hide it, she smirked and rolled her eyes. "Mark tells me that you have a friend too?"

"Yes, but she's just gone home she had an argument with her boyfriend Omar."

"So, let me get this right, she was seeing Omar?"

This was like a cross-examination, Lizzy was delving deep and wanted to know the ins and outs of a cat's arse. "Yes, I thought they were really getting on, but Jane just switched. She's like that sometimes. She'll probably phone me later telling me to tell him how sorry she is."

Mark was back, he placed the drinks on the table and sat down next to Lizzy. It seemed like Emily was getting the cold shoulder. She had to make this right, get back in his good books. "Jane's gone home. She had a massive argument with Omar and stormed out."

Mark sighed and she could see his temper was rising. "Where's Omar? Did he just let her go?"

"No, he went outside after her and Jane said he

man-handled her. She was upset, crying she was."

"I'd have chinned the daft cow. Omar has looked after her and spent a right few quid on her."

Emily didn't want to get into it any deeper. She remained silent. Tonight had been a total nightmare. It was just one thing after another. All she wanted to do was make things right between them both, but how could she do that when Lizzy was sat there like a spare part?

Suddenly, Emily went white in the face, colour being sucked out of her complexion. She looked like she seen a ghost. Oh My God, what was Tina doing in here with Alex? If she spotted Emily, she would be straight over and then her secret would be out. Elsie was laid back, but when it came to Emily lying to her, she would go ape. She would have done her in. Head dipped low, she scurried into the toilets, her heart pounding inside her chest. Think girl think. She locked the toilet door behind her and sent Mark a text. "I will meet you outside, I feel sick and need some fresh air." She pressed the send button and stood behind the door having what looked like a panic attack.

CHAPTER TWENTY

It was after midnight and it was pitch black. Tony had been planning this graft for over a week now. Mickey had chickened out and wanted no part of it. He'd turned snide lately, always fobbing Tony off, not wanting to spend any time with him. Word on the street was that he had a job, but he'd never told Tony. Maybe he had a new pal, someone else he was grafting with. Tony was dressed in dark clothing and all you could see were the whites of his eyes. He was making small steps forward, ducking and diving. With the slightest of movements, he creaked the side gate open. The night was eerily silent and every time Tony heard a noise his heart skipped a beat. His heart pumping, his feet unsteady, he scrambled towards the back window. Digging deep into his coat pocket he pulled out a large screw driver and lunged it deep into the window frame to prise it open. That was a bit loud, he thought to himself, he had to quieten down before he woke somebody up. The window pinged open after what seemed like forever. Taking deep breaths Tony used the small black drain pipe at the side of him to help him gain entry to the house. He didn't have long once he was inside, he had to be quick before the alarm went off. His face betrayed his panic, his were eyes looking one way then the other. He gripped the small cupboard open and his fingers were all over it as he tried to press the red light that was flashing. "Quick,

quick," he whispered under his breath. That was close, very close indeed. Another few seconds and the alarm would have been blaring. Tony tiptoed into the hallway. His nose twitched at the smell from the vanilla plug-in freshener. For crying out loud, his nose was sensitive, and he was doing his best not to sneeze. His eyes closed tightly, and he pressed his two hands firmly over his mouth as a blast of air surged through his nostrils. He froze, heart racing, small beads of sweat dribbling down the side of his forehead. Why was he just stood there? After all, he'd never been what you'd call a sneak thief, his crimes were usually petty; shoplifting and car crimes. Tony was unnerved, something didn't feel right. His feet seemed to be glued to the floor.

Taking one or two deep breaths he continued. He was here now and he needed that ring to pay for the holiday he'd promised his family. He had to see it through. Elsie wasn't daft and every day for the last week she kept asking him why he wasn't in work. Of course, he'd lied and made up more excuses. He'd told her Sue was unwell and she didn't want anybody around at the house. What a load of codswallop. It was wonder she hadn't uncovered the truth. Perhaps she was too worried about Emily to be bothered tracking her husband. The first stair creaked as his hand gripped the bannister. For crying out loud, he had to be more careful. With the smallest of steps, he slowly made his way up the stairs. He could smell Sue's perfume, her aroma, her lovely sweet fragrance. Perhaps, he should just own up and beg her forgiveness, she might have some sympathy for him then. Tony dipped his head behind the door, his eyes trying to focus. Nobody was in bed. He entered the bedroom and scanned around, nothing, he was safe. This was going to be his best job ever. Easy peasy, like taking candy from a baby. He walked straight over to the jewellery box and opened it. His hands moved frantically, where the hell was it?

"Is this what you're looking for? I've been expecting you." A voice echoed from behind him. Sue switched the light on in the bedroom and there Tony stood in his full glory, caught red-handed. "You dirty, no good bastard. How dare you ever come back here! I should have your fingers cut off and rammed up your arse."

Sue was no longer the sweet innocent woman. She was alert and ready to strike him if he made a move. Tony started to run towards her, he was getting off. She was a woman, what chance did she have against him? "Move out of my way you slapper, before I snap your jaw" he snarled as he ran at her but just before he reached her, a man jumped out from the darkness and whacked him over the head with a plank of wood. Tony didn't know what day it was as he fell to the ground like a lead weight. A small dribble of red claret seeped down the side of his head. The man booted Tony in his stomach several times as Sue just stood there and smirked. Tony was lifeless on the floor.

"Mickey, thank you for warning me about him. Imagine what he would have done if I'd have been here on my own." She rubbed at her arms as the goose-pimples started to appear on her skin.

"He's a wanker anyway. I owed him that for the way he's treated me over the years. I just couldn't sit back and watch an innocent, beautiful woman like yourself be robbed like that."

Mickey was the hero of the hour. What a Judas he was!

"Get him out of here. I can't stand the sight of him. And, Mickey, when he's gone come back and I will reward you for your help. Two-hundred pounds we said, didn't we?"

Mickey was already dragging Tony along the floor; he was pumping with sweat as he replied. "We sure did, my lady. Give me five minutes to launch this scruff onto the streets and I'll come back for it."

Tony moved about in the bushes. It was dark and only the street lamp enabled him to see. What the fuck had happened? He wasn't sure. His body crumbled as he tried to sit up. He looked like he needed medical help, the gash at the side of his head was still pouring blood. There were moans and groans as he rolled onto his side and scrambled over the hedge. He'd had worse beatings before and he was used to this feeling. Tony sat up straight and drew his legs up to his chest, his eyes wide open. He was remembering what had happened.

"Mickey!" he growled as spit hung from his mouth. "Fucking Mickey, you double-crossing twat. Just you watch now. I'll have you for this, mark my words you'll pay."

★

Elsie was watching the clock on the wall. The noise was doing her bleeding head in. In her hand she held a letter, a scruffy piece of paper. Every now and then she re-read whatever was on the letter. Her eyes clouded over every time she read it. Jordan had just come in and by the looks of him he wasn't having a good day either. "Fuck me, could this day get any worse? I'll be glad when it is over."

Elsie lifted her head up and held a puzzled look. "What are you going on about? What's up?"

"Nothing mam, just forget I said anything. Where's my dad?"

Elsie gritted her teeth together. "Fuck knows. He's up to something. All day he's been sat here on edge. He forgets that I know him inside out."

Jordan plonked down on the sofa. "Is Emily in bed?"

"No, she's at Jane's again. I hardly see her anymore."

Jordan squirmed; this wasn't right. He'd seen Jane earlier and she was on her own. There was no sign of his sister. "I don't think she's with Jane. I saw her on the estate before and she was on her jacks."

Elsie was concerned. "Do me a favour, I know it's late but just bell Jane phone and ask to speak to Emily."

Jordan held the phone to his ear and waited for the call to be answered. "Yo Jane, I know it's late, but can you put Emily on, I need to speak to her?" Jordan's face changed as she replied, his grip on the phone tightening. He walked out of the room and spoke. "How long has it been going on? Where does he live?" He was gathering all the information he needed to get his sister back home where she belonged. The call ended and he stood on the spot for a few minutes. Elsie was on the hunt for him now and when she found him in the hallway, she knew by his face that something was wrong.

"So, what's going on? Don't lie to me either because I heard the conversation."

He walked back into the front room and walked over to the window. Slowly he pulled back the curtains. "She's not there, she's with some guy called Mark."

Elsie was right behind him. "Well, I knew she had a boyfriend so she's probably just spending a bit more time with him. You know what it's like, son."

"Mam, Jane said she's not been staying there for a few weeks. This guy lives in Bolton. Do you know she met him on the internet?"

This was a whole new ballgame and the colour drained from Elsie's face. She cracked her knuckles. "Oh my God, I bet he's a kiddy fiddler. How stupid is she? I thought she knew better. I've warned her about stuff like this."

Jordan paced about the front room. Where was Tony when they needed him? It was the same every time there was a crisis, he was nowhere to be seen. What a waste of space. The rage pumped through Elsie's veins, Emily had changed, she was never a liar. Elsie was breaking down, in a desperate state. "Where the fuck is she then? We need to find out where this peado lives. I'll cut his balls off and make a necklace out of them if he has so much as laid a single finger on her."

Jordan was distressed. "Wind your neck in, will you? If you would have kept a closer eye on her none of this would have happened."

Elsie let out a laboured breath. "Oh, how did I know I would get the blame for this? She's never had a boyfriend before so how am I supposed to know what she was going to do, the silly cow. Ring Jane back and get an address of where this Mark lives. I don't care what time it is; I want Emily back home here, where

I know she is safe." Elsie ragged her fat chunky fingers through her tatty hair and plonked back down on the sofa. "I'll ground her for this, on my life, how dare she lie to me. I've always given her my full trust, but she's fucked it now, she'll be staying in, grounded."

Jordan was back on the blower to Jane. This was serious now and he wanted to know everything. How long it had been going on, how she met him and where he lived. Yes, he needed to know everything.

CHAPTER TWENTY-ONE

Emily sat in the corner of the room with her knees held up to her chest. Her body was shaking from head to toe and she'd been crying for hours. The room was in darkness and even though she'd stayed at Alex's house lots of times before, she'd never been in this room. It was a place under the house, a cellar transformed into bedrooms but they were more like luxury prison cells. Keys jangled outside the door and her eyes filled with fear. She cowered into the corner and closed her eyes. "Please, not again, please, please," she sobbed. The door opened and the light from corridor outside crippled her eyes. A large shadow appeared. As she lifted her head up, she could see large feet stood near the doorway. A man walked into the room and flicked the main light on. He was foreign and he was talking to someone behind him in his own language. Emily didn't have a clue what he was saying, it was all gibberish to her. Large hands clawed at her body, fingers like bunches of bananas. The man gripped her cheeks and squeezed at them with force. "Tonight, you work. Get cleaned up." Emily raised her arms to try and break free and several deep purple bruises were visible on her skin. In fact, she was covered in them; on her legs, arms, stomach, she was in a right state. The man still had a firm hold of her, his eyes drilling into hers. With a swift movement he flung her back against the wall and let out a menacing laugh.

"Lizzy," he shouted behind him. "Get in here and sort this one out. Make sure she's scrubbed up and ready for tonight. She has three to sort out. And get her smelling nice, she smells like donkey shit."

Lizzy strolled into the room and shot a look over at Emily. She knew how to handle this guy, she smiled at him and walked to his side. The prick was a control freak and she knew if everything didn't go his way, they both would get a good beating. "She'll be ready, don't worry. Just give me a few hours with her and she'll look like a new woman." The man held his head high and nodded. He loved using force to get what he wanted. He turned and left the room. Lizzy held her ear to the door and rushed back to Emily. She pulled the wet strands of hair that were stuck to her cheek and shook her head. "You have to do what they say otherwise they'll beat you. What's your name?"

Emily's shoulders were shaking, she was in floods of tears. "I want to go home, please help me to go home."

Lizzy remembered how she'd felt when she first come here and sadness filled her eyes. She sat down and placed her thin hand on the top of Emily's knee. "It's hard, I've been here for months, maybe years now. I've lost count. Who got you involved Omar? Mark?"

Emily choked, her breathing struggled. "I've been seeing Mark for a few months, he was perfect and then he just," she burst out crying, hysterical as she tried to speak. "He turned on me and started hitting me if I wouldn't do as he asked. He told me he was in trouble and he owed money. The only way he would be off the hook was if I slept with a guy to clear the debt for him.

I loved him that much, so I agreed."

Lizzy chewed hard on her bottom lip. She knew the rest of the story without Emily having to tell her. She stopped her dead in her tracks. "And, you slept with a man, and Mark told you he loved you more than anything in the whole wide world."

Emily snivelled and nodded her head. "Yes, how did you know?"

"Because Mark was my boyfriend too, he promised me the world, told me he loved me, treated me like a princess and did exactly the same thing to me. Mark, Omar and the others are always on the lookout for young girls. They groom them and make them think they're safe."The word 'groom' smashed against Emily's brain. She always thought of herself as on the ball with stuff like this. Why on earth had she not seen this coming? Lizzy checked no one was listening and sat back with her thin frame against the wall. "He drugged me at first and I never knew what was happening. When I did find out, it was too late, there was nothing I could do about it. Mark told me how much he loved me and made up a cock and bull story to keep me doing it. He told me we would get a home together, marriage, yep, the prick had me right over." Emily was having a full-blown panic attack; it was all making sense now. She gripped her knees as tightly as she could and squeezed at the pale white flesh. Lizzy could see she was distressed but it didn't stop her talking. "I get shipped out all over the show now. They take me to houses where the dirty bastards are waiting for me. Dirty old men mostly who want kinky shit like smacking their arses. I don't mind that kind though, it's the ones who want to do the sick stuff to you that I hate."

Emily had a look of terror in her eyes. What the hell had she got herself into? With a frantic move she clasped hold of Lizzy's hand, she dug her fingers deep into her flesh. "You need to get me out of here. I'll do whatever you want, just help me."

Lizzy sucked hard on her lip. If she had a pound for every new girl who'd asked her the same question, she would have been a rich woman. She couldn't make promises she couldn't keep. "Where does your family think you are?"

"My friend's house. My best friend was seeing Omar but she finished with him, otherwise she would have ended up here as well. She told me something wasn't right, but I was so wrapped up with Mark I couldn't see anything other than my love for him. I was such a silly bitch."

Lizzy stood. "We need to get you ready for tonight."

Emily was distraught. "There is no way I'm doing it again. They can't make me. Please tell them I'm not well, say anything but please don't let them dirty horrible men touch me anymore."

Lizzy turned on the spot, she wished she could help this young girl but her hands were tied. She never replied, she just walked away.

Emily had been sat in her 'cell' more or less all day. Every now and then someone would pop their head inside and just look at her. She was offered food and something to drink but she refused anything they brought. She wasn't daft, she knew there would be drugs in her food, something to help her relax. The door opened and Mark stood with his hand resting on the doorframe. "You look lovely," he said.

Emily snarled at him. "Fuck off will you. People will be looking for me soon and guess what, when they find you, you'll be sorry. I trusted you and you lied to me."

Mark walked further into the room; he held no remorse for his actions. "I'm doing a job that's all. Plus, we had a good time too."

"You told me you loved me, what happened to that? Was that all lies?"

Mark sat down on the side of the bed. He didn't speak straight away. "Emily, I did love you and most of what I told you was true at the time. I'm in too deep now and there is no way out for me either. You see I had a gambling habit. A big, big, habit and I owed Alex a lot of money. When I couldn't pay what I owed, he left me for dead. I didn't have a choice then, I had to do what he wanted."

Emily was frantic. "Help me, we can run off together and I'll never tell anyone what's happened here. You can have a fresh start, no more looking over your shoulder."

"No, no. These guys don't mess about. They know where my family live, they wouldn't be safe."

"Stop being an idiot. All this here," she held her hands out and pointed them around the room. "It will stop soon and you'll end up in prison for a long time. I'm willing to forgive you, to put it behind us and start again. When are you ever going to get this kind of chance again? Get out now before it's too late."

Mark dropped his head low and slowly ragged his fingers through his hair. "Come on, you need to go in the other room with the girls. Alex has some guests coming over tonight and he wants you to entertain them."

She snapped at him and pushed her flat palm deep into his chest. "So, that's a no then?" He never replied, he stood up and walked towards the door. "Well, you're nothing but a coward. You'll see when all this comes out. I'll tell them everything I know. Every little detail about you. Go on, fuck off you rat."

Mark slammed the door behind him nearly taking it from its hinges. She was alone now, left in tears, with nowhere to run.

CHAPTER TWENTY-TWO

Jordan hammered on Jane's front door in a panic. He stood back and looked up at the bedroom window. Jane's mother opened the door and held a look of disgust on her face when she saw him. "Hi, can I speak with Jane. I'm Emily's brother."

Jane's mam stepped back from the door and closed it slightly as she spoke. For all she knew this man could have been a thug, a thief, he could have run into her home and nicked all her belongings. "What do you want with my daughter. Is she in trouble?"

Jordan shook his head. "No, nothing to worry about. I just need a few words with her."

The woman didn't move straight away, she was thinking. "I'll close the front door then I'll go and get her." The front door slammed shut on him. What a cheeky cow this woman was, who the hell did she think she was. Jordan could hear every word from inside the house. "Get him away from the front door. What will the neighbours think?" Jordan was ready for snapping. He had a good mind to run into the house and kick fuck out of this toffee-nosed bitch. She was no better than him, she was up her own arse.

The front door swung open and Jane stood there looking flustered. With one hand on her hip she snarled at Jordan. "What do you want?"

He stepped forward and held a firm look. "Oi, cocky bitch, lose the attitude before you get a slap."

Jane swallowed hard and realised now that this guy would put her in her place if she carried on. She backed down. Her voice was low. "My mam is going sick. You know what she's like. Just keep your voice down before she hears you."

"You better come with me; I need to find Emily." Jane sighed and all the colour drained from her face.

"Ssshhh, I said. My mam doesn't know anything about it." She was testing his patience.

"So get your coat and come with me before I go right in there and tell her all about what you have been up to. And I will, you know, I'll tell her everything."

Jane growled at him and turned on the spot. "Go and wait in the car, I'll be there in a minute." She slammed the door behind her.

Jordan sat in the car tapping his fingers on the dashboard. He kept looking at Jane's house and sighing. She'd been ages. He honked the horn several times and he was getting ready to go back to the house to drag her out. Jane finally emerged from the house but there was no urgency in her walk. The car door opened and she plonked herself on the passenger seat. Jane pulled down the mirror and doubled checked her make-up. "I look hanging, look at the state of me."

Jordan flicked the engine over and spoke. "Like I'm arsed what you look like. We're going to sit down in a minute and I want you to tell me everything about this cunt who my sister has been seeing."

She gulped. "I don't know much. She'd been talking to him for ages before she told me. I went on a few dates with them and I was seeing Omar, his mate."

"Omar, is he a Paki?"

Jane was beetroot. "Well sort of. He didn't act like one though, he was like us."

This was getting worse by the minute. "Is he a Paki or not, which?"

Jane looked out of the window and replied. "Yes, he is. But don't be saying anything to anyone. My dad will go ape, he's already warned me about seeing foreigners. He said I would go in care if I ever brought one home."

"So, go on, tell me more."

Jane fiddled with her hair and sat back in her seat. The more she thought about this, the more she realised how wrong it had all been. She started to confess. "This is between us. I'll tell you as long as you don't tell my parents, I want my name keeping out of it, otherwise I'll deny it. Honest, I'll say you're making it up."

Jordan agreed, he just needed her to spill the beans. Jane licked her dry cracked lips and played with her fingers. "I knew something wasn't right. I think they were drugging us."

Jordan slammed the brakes on the car and gripped her by the arm. "What do you mean drugged?" His temper was boiling and his ears were pinned back.

Jane hung her head and her voice was low. "They used to take us out each night and buy our drinks, not just one, nine or ten Vodkas each night. I don't even remember going to bed some nights. I knew something was wrong and I mentioned it to Emily, but she wouldn't listen." Her eyes filled up and her bottom lip trembled. "I think they brought men in to have sex with us. They took us to this big house, that had lots of bedrooms and they said it belonged to this guy who loved having people staying with him."

Jordan was boiling over inside but tried to keep a lid on his emotions. He took a breath. "Where does this guy live do you remember?"

"I think so but I'm not sure." Jane carried on speaking. "I started to have flashbacks; I knew then that something wasn't right. I kept having a vision of men on top of me, touching me, feeling me, doing stuff." Jane broke down and cried. "It wasn't my fault, I never said they could do that."

Jordan held his stomach. He felt sick. This was on a whole new level. He thought he would just have to give this Mark a back hander or a kick up the arse - how wrong could he have been! Taking a few deep breaths, he urged Jane to continue as he cringed. "Omar was never there in the morning when I woke up. I thought that was strange to start with, and it was the way I felt. I had this sick, weird feeling inside. I never thought anything about it until I got away from them that night in the pub. He tried making me stay but I told him straight I was going home. I think if we hadn't been in a public place, he would have locked me up and kept me there. I pleaded with Emily to come with me. Look, I even took a photo of Mark kissing another girl in the car park. I never sent her it because I was pissed off with her and I thought if she wanted to stick up for him then I'd leave her to it. I'm sorry now, because if she's not answering her phone and she's not come home, where the hell is she?"

Jordan took the phone from her hand and zoomed in on the snap. He could see the name of the pub on the car-park wall. This was a lead, somewhere to start.

He passed her phone back and googled the boozer. Bingo it was in Bolton. He studied the map and held a puzzled look on his face. This was the area he picked the brasses up from. Lizzy had been picked up from here before. Jane was a mess, shaking, hands trembling. "Will she be alright? I'm sorry I didn't tell anyone what was happening, but I thought it was just a bit of fun. They were treating us nice at first, buying us gifts, perfumes, bags."

It was all too much for Jordan to take. Was this girl thick or what? "Are you on this planet? The pair of you have been groomed, why the fuck do you think they took you out of the area? And, presents? What the fuck were they buying you stuff for? Think about it you clown!"

Jane was hysterical, tears streaming down the side of her face. "I was raped, I know I was. Oh My God, my mam will go mad. I've tried to block it out but I can't get it out of my mind."

Jordan dropped his head onto the steering wheel. He was heartbroken. Sucking in some air he had to get his head back in the game, time wasn't on his side. "Right, I'm going to go up there and have a scout around, if I can't see her then the police will have to be involved. I'll drop you off and I'll go and get my dad to come with me. He's going to go sick. God help these men when he gets his hands on them."

Jane banged her head gently against the window. "Please, don't tell my mam. I'll do anything, just don't tell her." Jordan never replied, he couldn't promise her anything anymore, this was serious.

CHAPTER TWENTY-THREE

Elsie was staring at her husband while Tony was staring into space. "So, go on, you tell me your version of events and then I'll tell you what I know. Don't fucking lie to me you wanker because I'll know and God help you if you're lying."

Tony was in a bad way. His eyes were swollen and dried blood was stuck to the side of his head. "Elsie, do I look like I need you stressing me out now? I've been jumped. Four of them held me down and kicked fuck out of me for fuck all. They were saying I'd robbed them but on my life, I know fuck all about what they're going on about."

Elsie had to put him in the picture, give him a clue of what she knew. "So, are you still working for Sue?"

Tony gulped, his mouth went dry. "Nar, she was ill and when I went back to start work, she said her husband was back and she no longer needed my services."

Elsie snarled at him. What a dirty no good lying bastard he was! "Oh, and you never thought to tell me. So if you've not been working where have you been going through the day?"

"I've been chilling with a few of the lads. In fact, I was trying to get some money together for this fucking holiday. Honest to God, you're doing my head in. Fuck off out of my face and leave me alone. I'm suffering here, look at the state of me."

His wife walked slowly towards the door, she watched him with eager eyes. Her hand stretched across to the small wooden table and she gripped an old wine bottle by the neck. With a swift movement she turned on the spot. "So, this letter I've got saying you've had your cock shoved up Sue is a load of shit then?" The bottle skimmed past his head, shattering to tiny pieces around the room. He covered his head and tried to protect himself as she started to look for other missiles to launch at him. "That explains it all; the new boxers, the washing all the time, the new clothes. You're a cheeky twat and I want you out of here you fucking scumbag. Our Emily is missing and you've got your scabby cock shoved up some fancy piece."

Tony ran at his wife. "Calm the fuck down will you. I've never touched Sue. Fucking hell, do you think she would look at someone like me?"

She slapped him across the face with force. "So, you're saying if she did look at you, you would have slung one up her?"

"No, you daft cow. I'm saying I never touched her. What does the letter say, go on, fill me in because it's a load of shit! It's someone trying to cause trouble between us. You're my woman, always have been. I've got eyes for no one else. So, turn it in."

Elsie broke down and collapsed on the floor. It was all too much. The thought of her man with another woman made her skin crawl. Tony stood back and held his hands up in the air. There was no way he was admitting anything, so he changed the subject. "What the fuck is this about Emily being missing? Since when and why have I just found out now?"

"Since last night. She's with her boyfriend or so I believe."

"So, why are you saying she's missing then?"

Elsie scrambled to her feet and plonked down on the sofa. She sighed and ragged her fingers through her hair. "Jordan has gone to find out what's going on. She's lied to us and said she's been staying at Jane's and she's been found out because we rang Jane and she's not there."

Tony paced the front room. "So, if she's not staying at Jane's where has she been staying? I want her home now! Where is she?"

Elsie had to take her time to speak, she was sobbing. "Jordan has gone to look for her, apparently she's been staying with this Mark guy."

Tony cracked his knuckles and a spray of spit left his mouth as he spoke. "Get Jordan on the blower. I'll go with him to get her and I'll make sure this Mark gets a good slap. Fuck me, why didn't you tell me what was going on. How many times have I told you to keep an eye on her?"

"And I have. She's never done anything like this before. You know she's a good kid."

The front door slammed shut and in walked Jordan with Jane behind him. Tony wasn't waiting for any meet and greet; he went straight for Jane. "Where the fuck is Emily? Don't be chatting a bag of shit to me because I'll drag you around to your parents and tell them what's been going on."

Jane was in pieces and sat down as Jordan started to fill the family in on where Emily was and what had been happening. Elsie went white and Tony ran into the kitchen and came back with the biggest knife he could find. Then he rummaged behind the sofa and pulled out a machete. "Take me there now. If a single one of them has laid a single finger on my girl I will deal with them. She's a fucking baby, my baby."

Jordan turned to Jane, "You need to come with us. We might need you to get to Emily if they are hiding her."

Jane fell to her hands and knees. "I don't want to go back there. Please, I'll come with you but I'm going nowhere near the house. These are bad men, very dangerous people."

Tony lost his rag and grabbed her by the throat. "And, I'm fucking dangerous too. If my girl is there then I will take the lot of them out, now move your arse before I drag you by every hair on your bastard head."

Elsie was putting her coat on too and she was ready for war. Jordan shot a look over at her and spoke. "You're staying here in case she comes back. This is a man's business. You wait here."

"Over my dead body. If my girl is in danger, then I'm coming too. I can handle myself; don't you worry about me."

Tony agreed with his son. "Stop being stupid. I don't want to be worrying about you too. Stay put here. I'll ring you as soon as there is any news."

Elsie was still playing up but she knew she was going nowhere. She marched over to the window and pulled back the net curtain looking at the area below her. "Just bring her back safe. Please, just bring her back home."

Tony paused; his bottom lip quivered. "I'm bringing her home; don't you worry about that."

The three of them were gone leaving Elsie in silence.

CHAPTER TWENTY-FOUR

Tina was with Alex in the pub and it was fair to say she was enjoying the night. She had her glad rags on; a black fitted dress, red shoes and a handbag to match. Her hair was on point too, it looked bouncy and shiny. She'd really made an effort tonight, you could tell. Alex reached over and held her hand and smiled. He looked directly into her smoky blue eyes. Was he going to propose? He just stared at her for what seemed like forever but didn't say anything. Finally, he cleared his throat and spoke. "You make me smile Tina and I feel like I can trust you with anything. You make me so happy and although I've known plenty of women, there is something special about you. You just get me. We've connected."

Tina was taken back, lost for words for the first time in her life. Things had been going great with this new guy and he'd told her some of his deepest secrets. He ran a brothel but so what? It didn't bother her, he was just making a living and she didn't judge. It was the same kind of job she'd been in for years, so she kept quiet. He never knew that about her though, there was no way was she telling him she'd sold her body for money. She'd stretched the truth of course and told him she'd worked on the reception at an escort agency. She lied and told him she just took bookings and nothing more. "Tina, I want to put a business deal to you. I want it to bring us closer together. As you know

I have girls working for me but to tell you the truth, it's driving me mad. I want you to run the agency. You have worked with these kinds of girls before and I know you could keep them in line. I'll pay you well, I just need you to be discreet and well," he paused as he touched her cherry lips with his warm wet lips. "I want us to be a team."

Tina didn't flinch, she had to hold it together and play it cool. She could do this job with her eyes closed. She knew this kind of world inside out. God knows she'd had the experience. She twiddled a strand of hair around her finger and looked as if she was thinking. She didn't answer him straight away and kept him hanging. She lifted her glass up and took a small zip of her wine. Her voice was low and she checked nobody could hear her. "You said a team, how is that going to work because in the past it has meant someone taking all the money and me doing all the work. I'm not doing anyone's donkey work."

Alex snuggled in closer. He could smell her sweet perfume, the fragrance he'd bought her. "I'm not like that, I'll make sure you earn when I do. I know you know everything about me and up to now you've never judged me. Most women run a mile when I tell them what I do, but you never flinched. You're one in a million and I want you to be part of my life as well as my business."

Bleeding hell someone pass me the tissues, this guy was pulling the big guns out tonight. The bullshit was rolling from his tongue at speed and by the looks of Tina she was falling for it. What was wrong with her, usually she was on the ball and could smell a rat a mile away. He'd pulled the wool over her eyes for sure, she was smitten, lost in his eyes, believing every word he was telling her. "So, would that mean me moving up here to Bolton?"

Alex sucked hard on his lips and he was making a rod for his own back but he needed her on board. "If that's what you want. As you know I have a big home with plenty of space for the both of us. Some of the working girls stay there too but I'm sure that wouldn't bother you."

Tina had been back to his house on a few occasions and always felt at home there. Yes, there were girls there too but there always seemed to be a party going on or some kind of celebration. It all made sense now, these were the working girls, the entertainers. Tina had a real chance to change her life and maybe she'd never get that chance again. As she'd told the world and his wife before, she'd never had any luck with men. Alex was a Godsend after all the heartache she'd endured. It was a no brainer; she liked this man and he treated her like no other man had ever treated her before. He was a gentleman, opened doors for her and pulled chairs out for her before she sat down. What more could a woman ask for? Usually, with the men she met, she'd be lucky to get a chip butty off them on the way home from the pub. A quick leg over and they'd be snoring next to her in bed. That had been her life for so long now and she knew she deserved more. Yes, she could manage some girls, it wasn't rocket silence.

"If this is what you really want then I'll take your offer and move my stuff in over the weekend. I have a few loose ends to tie up in Manchester first, then I'm all yours."

Alex rubbed his hands together. "I'm glad you have agreed to work with me. Not only will I have a lovely sexy woman on my arm. I will have a business partner who will make my life a lot easier."

This was all happening too fast. Tina seemed to be sucked in by him and couldn't see the wood for the trees. If this had been one of her friends, she would have been telling them that there was something not quite right going on here. It just goes to show you that love can certainly blind you. Mark came over to the table and plonked down next to Alex. He patted Mark on his arm. "Here he is, my wing-man. Tina meet Mark, he works with me. He's been a diamond this man has and he's kept things ticking over for me. Mark, Tina has agreed to come onboard and she'll be the one managing the girls from now on, so you can relax for a bit."

Mark weighed Tina up. He wasn't as trusting as Alex; he was paranoid and wanted to know the ins and outs of a cat's arse hole. He wanted to keep the circle as small as possible and the less people who knew about his job, the better. Of course, Alex hadn't told Tina about where they got their girls from, no, the snidey fucker never breathed a word. He kept his cards close to his chest and made out he was whiter than white. Mark was edgy and hated meeting new people, she could be dibble for all he knew. "So, how did you two meet?"

Tina was flattered that he was interested in her love life. It wasn't much of a love story, but it was the most important thing in her life at the moment and nothing else seemed to matter. She never really saw her friends much anymore and the afternoon chats she'd had with Elsie had gone out of the window. "We met on a night out. We just clicked from the moment we got talking. I never believed in love at first sight until now," said Tina.

Mark raised an eyebrow; he had an eye for a classy lady and Tina was far from one. She was mutton dressed as lamb; a desperate woman looking for a husband to spend her twilight years with. He could tell by the way that she spoke that she was common. You can't polish a turd. He wanted to know more about her and threw some more questions over at her. "So, which area are you from?"

"Manchester, I lived there all my life. I always planned to move away but I kind of got stuck in a rut and never did. I love my home and where I live and moving up here to Bolton will probably give me a big culture shock, but I'm sure I will cope."

Mark was full of questions, but Alex cut him short, "Stop worrying, it's all in order."

Tina smirked and snuggled closer to her man. "He won't be worrying anymore. Especially now that I'm here to ease his burden."

Mark brushed her comment off and spoke directly to Alex. Who did this daft bint think she was talking to? She wasn't his boss. She was just some washed up slapper Alex was boning for the time being. Alex never kept a woman for long. He was always in bed with one of the working girls given the chance. Why would he close the door to these sexy young girls with firm toned bodies in exchange for this wrinkled old bitch with saggy tits. It was just a matter of time before she got carted and Mark would be there to give her the marching orders when it did. He didn't like Tina, he had a gut feeling about her, a feeling that she wasn't the person she was making out to be.

Outside, Jordan and Tony had finally located the pub and were plotted up in the pub car park. Jordan patted his leg and nodded slightly at his father. He was tooled up, ready for action. Jane was sat in the back of the car whimpering. She just wanted this to end and all the way on the drive up here she had been pleading with them to take her back home. Everything was hitting home now, the extent of what had happened. She'd been groomed and didn't have a clue about it. Jane was more concerned about her parents finding out. It was inevitable though, of course they would be informed when all of this came out.

Tony was a live-wire. He reached over and patted the top of Frank's head who was sat in the back of the car. This animal would rip them apart once he'd given him the right command. He'd tear them to shreds. Frank often accompanied Tony when shit was going down. The dog had his owner's back and he was dangerous when he needed to be. Tony gripped the dog's face and looked deep into his chestnut brown eyes. "Don't you let me down Frank. I want you to tear the cunts apart. Every single one of them."

Jane's sobbing was getting louder. This was no place for her, she should have been at home, protected from what lay ahead. Frank was restless and trampled all over her legs, she pushed the dog away with force and snapped. "Can you move this flea-bitten mutt from me please? Look, he's slavering all over me."

Tony twisted his head over his shoulder and gritted his teeth together tightly. "This flea-bitten mutt will help get my daughter back, so shut the fuck up and pipe down before he turns on you."

Jane squeezed herself into the corner of the car and tried to ignore the dog. He seemed to know there was a job to be done and he was raring to go. Jordan nodded his head slowly. "Jane, this is the boozer right?"

"Yes, now can I go home? You don't need me anymore," she said timidly.

They never answered her. Tony was out of the car in a flash. If his daughter was in this pub, then she was coming home with him no matter what and God help any man that stood in his way. Jordan was the leader here today and he was the one calling the shots. "Dad, you wait here while I have a quick scout around. If I spot her, I'll be straight back."

Tony was bouncing about on the spot. "Nar lad, I'll come in with you and we can rush the bastards."

"Just wait here with Frank. If you come marching in here with the dog, you will just bring it on top. I'll be as quick as I can." Frank cocked his leg up and pissed up the brick wall, the animal must have been nervous too. Jordan took his time looking around, he was checking every nook and cranny. There was no sign of his sister. He went to the bar and got the attention of the barmaid. "Hiya love, has Mark or Omar been in tonight?"

The busty barmaid came to where he was stood and leaned over the bar slightly. "Yes, but you've missed them. They were in earlier."

Jordan was in a panic, what now, where did he

go from here? "Oh no. I should have met them both about some business. I don't suppose you know where they live, or have their contact number do you?"

The woman shrugged her shoulders and huffed. "Sorry love. I don't."

Jordan backed off. His spirits were low. What was his next move? Maybe Jane could help him find the house. He stormed out of the pub and met his father. "They've been and gone, fuck knows where. We need to try and get Jane to remember where the house is. Come on, get back in the car."

They both motored over to the parked car. Jane was sat biting her fingernails, eager to hear what had gone on. "Was she in there? Is she okay, did you see Mark or Omar?"

Jordan was fuelled with adrenalin now. He looked straight behind him and spoke to her. "We've missed them. We need you to try and remember where the house was where they took you."

Jane was gobsmacked, the pressure was back on her now. "I'm not sure, I can't even think straight. How do you expect me to remember, I'm not even from around here?"

Tony punched his clenched fist into the side of the chair. Frank cowered and lay down shaking. He could sense his owner wasn't happy and when this happened, he always gave him a wide berth. Jane held her head with both her shaking hands. "I don't know, all I remember was that there was a street near it called Marry Street. I remembered it because I said to Emily that is was a sign that she was going to get married."

Tony flipped out. "My daughter won't be getting

married to no fucking peado. When I've finished with him, I'll cut his dick off and ram it up his shitter."

Jordan was all over it, he had his google map opened and he was zooming in on the street. "It says here fifteen minutes away. Jane sit up and start taking things in. It might jog your memory when we get closer, you might recognise the house."

The engine roared and Jordan wheel spun the motor out of the car-park. He was wasting no time and put his foot down. He was swerving in and out of the traffic while Tony was quiet. His eyes never left the road. He popped a fag into the corner of his mouth and opened the window a tiny bit for the smoke to escape. Jane had her face glued to the window when they reached Marry Street, surely, she could remember where the house was from here? They were both hanging on her every word. "Do you know anywhere? Is it familiar to you?" Tony ranted.

"No, I mean, it might be, I just don't know." Jordan crawled down the streets nearby, looking at every house, imagining his sister was somewhere inside one of them. Elsie might have been right, perhaps this was too big for them to deal with, it might have been better to get the police involved and then at least these bastards would have had the book thrown at them.

Suddenly, Jane sat forward in her seat, lips moving but no words coming out, she gripped the top of Tony's seat. "I think it's just down this street, it's a massive house with iron gates, I'm sure the gates are electronic." Jordan was eager to get to the end of the road. His eyes scanned every nook and cranny. Just as the car came to the end of the street Jane screamed at the top of her voice. "There it is, that's the house." The brakes slammed on and they all jerked forward.

Frank was near enough on Tony's knee. Jordan turned the engine off and looked in the rear-view mirror. "Are you sure, it's that one there?"

"Yes, yes, look at the gates. I remember them now."

So here they were, no plan, no team behind them, what on earth did they think they were going to do? If they were team-handed in there, it could be a massacre. Jordan's head was in turmoil. This was the same house where he'd dropped Lizzy off. This could only mean one thing, Jimmy The Chop was involved and if that was true, they were in a whole new ball game. This would be a blood bath. Jimmy was ruthless, a lunatic, a gun merchant. Jordan sat frozen, he had to fill his dad in on the whole story because they were on dangerous ground. Tony was fuelled with anger. "I don't give a fuck who's behind them doors. My daughter is in there and I'll do whatever I have to do get her back. These cunts don't know who they're messing with."

Jordan tried to calm his old man down. "Right, right, just be quiet while I think."

Jane dipped low on the back seat, she was shaking like a leaf, upset and scared of what lay ahead. "There is a cellar under the house, look at the small light shining through the window," Jordan stated. Tony considered himself a sneak thief and this was right up his street. But he'd never had a job this big before, it would be tricky and dangerous, but he was willing to give it a try. Jordan was thinking aloud.

"I know Lizzy who lives here, if only I could get hold of her then maybe I could get into the house.

She'll know where they are keeping her. Am I thick or what, why didn't I put two and two together and suss this lot out?"

Jordan spoke about his work now for Jimmy The Chop and everything he knew about the crew. They needed to calm down and come up with a plan otherwise they would all be in body-bags before the night was over.

CHAPTER TWENTY-FIVE

Emily sat in her cell and prayed they would just leave her alone. She could hear voices outside and her heart raced knowing they would take her soon. She made a quick sign of the cross and pressed her two flat palms together, she was praying. Thick black mascara ran down from her eyes and onto her cheekbones as she pleaded, "Lord, if you help me now and take me home, I'll be a better person, I'll never lie, or pinch stuff again. I need your help; I need this to stop. Please listen to me, help me please." These were desperate words, she had no one else to turn to.

Keys jangled outside the door; the time had come. A large Polish man was in the doorway. He was massive with big banana like fingers and bulging biceps. He spoke behind him in a foreign accent before he came into the room. Emily scrambled onto the bed and drew her legs up to her chest, trembling. "Please, just go away and leave me alone. I swear, if you bring another man near me, I will kick him right in the bollocks You can do what you want to me but I won't do this anymore. Go on, beat me but you won't change my mind. My mind is made up and I would rather be dead than sleep with another man. You lot will rot in jail for this, you're sick in the head. I'll tell everyone about what has happened here, mark my words."

She was rambling, anything to keep them away from her. Was this girl crazy? She was dicing with death. The man stood tall and his nostrils flared. He walked over to the bed and just stared at her for a few seconds before his shovel like hands reached over and gripped her hair. "Any trouble and I will shut you up once and for all," he hissed. Emily didn't stand a chance. What was the point in fighting back? She was wriggling about, scuffling with her attacker. The man pulled a tablet out of his pocket and rammed it down her throat. He sealed her mouth with his hand and dragged her head back. "Swallow it bitch," he growled. The tablet went as he dragged her to another room. The door was slammed shut behind her and she was alone again. It didn't take long for the tablet to kick in, she had blurred vision and her eyes closed slowly. Her body was folding in two and she was barely able to stand. As she looked behind her, she could see the bed, the place where her body was used for these sick men to do what they wanted to her. Her breathing was shallow and she seemed to melt into the bed. She was trying to talk but her words were prisoners in her mouth. Her hands gripped the side of the bed as she fell back onto it, her eyes staring at the ceiling, like she was in some kind of trance. She could see a shadow approaching her, she heard a man's voice in the distance. Her mind was asleep now and all that was left was an empty shell. Emily could feel his cold hands on her flesh. She tried to move but she no longer had any control. She could feel his warm stale breath, his stubble digging into her breasts, his hands touching her in places she didn't want to be touched.

"No, please no!" she tried to cry but nothing would come out.

★

Jordan sprinted back to the car. He was gagging for breath and distressed. He opened the car door and plonked back into the driver's seat. "I've had a good look around the area and I can't see a way in. The gaff has got CCTV all over the place. As soon as we get inside, they'll be on to us."

Tony's ears pinned back. He could have done with a spliff to calm down, his heart was racing and he was having a full blown panic attack. "There must be a way in. Fuck me, have you ever been on a big job? I knew I should have gone myself."

"I've looked and unless you want them onto us straight away, there is no way in," Jordan snapped.

Tony shuffled about in his seat. "Fuck it, let me out of this car, I'm going myself. Fucking hell, sending a boy to do a man's job. I should have known better."

Jordan watched as his dad left the car. "Wait up, don't go fucking this up. Think about it first before you get us all done in."

Tony had already started to walk away. He twisted his head back over his shoulder and spat a big ball of phlegm behind him. Frank was going ballistic in the back of the car and running from one side of the backseat to the next. "Shut that fucking mutt up will you while I think," Jordan screamed.

Jane panicked; she'd never been as scared in her life. She was wide eyed and looked like she was going to pass out. With shaking hands, she touched the top of Frank's head and spoke to him in a low voice. "Come here lad, lie down, come on." Frank wasn't listening and he continued jumping about. Jordan opened the car door and paused for a split second before he left. "I can't let that daft cunt go in there on his own. He's a live-wire. I'll have to go with him." Jane licked her dry cracked lips and turned her head away. The sooner this was over the better.

Tony crept about the garden using low, slight movements. He could see the house from where he was. He stretched his neck and could see lights on inside the gaff. "Calm the fuck down Tony," he whispered to himself. "Come on lad, get your shit together." The branches crunched underneath his body as he moved forward. The ground was hard and smelled of shit. He'd scurried towards a small window that was low to the ground. This could only lead to the cellar. Rummaging deep into his jacket he pulled out his old faithful screw driver and gripped it tightly. Looking one way then another he rammed it into the side of the window and prised it open. Splinters of wood fired out at him like bullets from the barrel of a gun, but bit by bit the window started to open. Once he completed the job, he pushed the window open firmly. This was going to be a tight squeeze, very tight indeed. Tony shoved his head inside first; it was pitch black and he couldn't see a thing. His breathing was rapid and he was struggling to hoist his body all the way through the window. Moaning, huffing and puffing he was nearly inside. Tony was as quiet as a mouse now and his sneak thief days were all coming back to him.

Once he got in, he made small steps as his fingers fumbled along the wall. Surely there was a light switch somewhere, something to help him see? After double checking he was alone, he found the switch and flicked it on. His head spun around and gave him a second to gather his thoughts. There were empty boxes and bottles of wine piled high but there was nothing here of value. Tony held his ear to the door and listened carefully. There wasn't a sound. His hand gently gripped the round brass door handle and turned it slowly. It was do or die time; he needed his daughter back. Tony patted his pocket. His blade was stashed there and ready for use. If they wanted a beef, then he'd give it to them. Taking deep breaths, he opened the door. A small ray of yellow light sprayed from the room at the end of the corridor and there were muffled noises. Tony stuck close to the corridor wall and slowly made his way towards it. He tried each door he passed but they were all locked. The noise was getting louder and he could now make out a man's voice. He weaved in and out of the doorways. He'd not lost his touch; he was as light as a feather. He looked confused, where next, what was his next move? Should he stay put or just run into the room and one-bomb them all?

Suddenly there was a noise behind him, he had to get out of sight. His quickly hid in a doorway, his heart was beating like a speeding train. A large Asian man wobbled out of the room and he was angry. Another man appeared from a room in front of him as Tony listened in. "I'm not paying for that one. She's barely awake. I pay for a good time, not that. I want another girl, one who is more entertaining."

The Polish man shook the man's hand. "I'm sorry Amid, I will get Lizzy for you. You like her, don't you?"

The man was still grumbling as he waddled down

the hallway. Tony looked behind him and he could see a small light flickering from where the man had just emerged. He waited until the coast was clear and rushed back. The door was a jar slightly and with the smallest of pushes he rushed inside. A body lay on the bed, candles were lit round the room, the vanilla fragrance dancing in the air. Tony stood with his back against the wall, examining every part of the room. Slowly, he approached the bed, his eyes opened wide and his breath stuck in his windpipe. There she was, his little girl, his daughter. Tears, fountains of big fat salty tears burst from his eyeballs, like jets of water. He sat down on the bed and touched the side of her cheek with his fingers. "Princess, it's your dad. I'm here with you." Emily was in a world of her own. Her eyes flickered but she never moved. Tony inhaled a large mouthful of air and cringed as he spotted the bruises on her body. Enough was enough, he didn't care what happened anymore, his daughter had been wronged and he was ready for anyone who stood in his way. Tony held a menacing look in his eye and gripped the sharp knife he had stashed in his pocket. His voice was low as his head bent slightly to his daughter's ears. "Princess, I'll be back soon. Everything is going to be alright, honest; everything is going to be fine." He bolted from the side of the bed and stormed out from the room with the blade in his hand. There was no more ducking and diving, he was on the rampage, ready for any cunt that stood in his way.

Tony headed to the door he'd seen the men disappear into and growled at the men stood there chatting. His eyeballs wear bursting out of their sockets.

The knife cut through the air as he waved it one way and then the other. He didn't need to explain why he was here, there was no time for that. Tony sprinted at them and jumped in the air with the blade held in both his hands. As he landed, he plunged it deep into one man's shoulder. "You dirty bastards, I'll fucking do you both in for what you have done to my daughter," he screamed. He was like a mad man as blood sprayed around the room. Tony was dancing about with the blade held tightly in his hands and before long he'd damaged both men. He stood over them and he was getting ready to make the final blow, to end them both when suddenly, without warning, his body went crashing to the ground.

Mark stood over Tony and booted him a few times. He screamed over at the injured men. "Who the fuck is this joker, how did he get in here and what the fuck have you two been doing if someone can just walk in here?" There was no reply from his workers. They were badly injured and the biggest man was blowing bubbles of blood from his mouth. They both needed urgent medical help. Tony was lifeless, out for the count. Mark gripped his legs and dragged him through the room. Once he was on the corridor, he found an empty room and flung him in there. He'd deal with him later. He needed more men to check the grounds. They needed to make sure this clown was alone.

Ten minutes later Tony stirred on the bedroom floor. He wasn't sure what had happened as he lay motionless. He groaned with the pain pounding in his skull. His vision wasn't good and everything was blurred.

Where was his baby? How could he save her now?

CHAPTER TWENTY-SIX

Elsie was a bag of nerves. She'd not moved from the window for over an hour. Where was Tina when she needed her most? She'd not seen sight or sound of her for weeks. Elsie was chewing at her fingernails and had gnawed them down to the bone. The skin was red and starting to bleed. Every two minutes she was checking her phone but there was nothing, no missed calls or messages. Jordan and Tony's phones were just ringing out. Maybe she should just ring the police. This was serious and her daughter's attackers needed dealing with good and proper, but her man and her son were involved now and she didn't want them getting arrested too. Her head was all over the place. She popped another cigarette into the corner of her mouth and flicked the lighter underneath it. Her cheeks sank in and it seemed like forever before she blew the thick grey cloud of smoke from her mouth. Elsie looked out of the window again. Everything seemed so quiet, even the traffic on the road below was quiet. She turned her head and looked at the clock on the wall. It was ten-thirty, her boys had been gone for hours now. Surely they had found her by now? But, if they had, why hadn't they rung her? That was the first thing they would have done, let her know her daughter was safe. There was a knock at the door. She froze and held her palm over her chest. It was the police; she was sure of it. They'd come with the news to tell her Jordan and Tony had been arrested and Emily still hadn't been found. Her feet seemed stuck to the ground. The knocking continued and she finally plucked up the courage to answer the door. Her eyes filled up with tears and she was shaking as she twisted the lock on the front door. Elsie stared at the person there, a hand grabbing the door frame to steady her feet. Her mouth was dry and she was constantly licking her lips.

"Dad," she croaked. After staring at him for a minute she invited him in but neither of them could say anything. When he sat down, she examined him closely. He looked older than she remembered and he still held sadness in his eyes, a shiny glaze that could have developed into a tear at any second. Elsie was nervous and was twiddling her fingers. What should she say at a time like this? Talk about the weather, the price of bread, she wasn't sure?

"Do you want a drink, dad?" He shook his head. He'd been here for over five minutes now and not said a word. Why was he here? "Dad, you have to speak you know, don't leave me hanging here, what's wrong?"

He sucked hard on his bottom lip and a dribble of clear liquid dropped from his nose. Reaching into his pocket he pulled out a white cotton handkerchief and dabbed it softly clearing it away. "I don't know why I'm here to tell you the truth. When I saw you the other day, I was adamant that I was not going to let you back in our lives and cause us anymore heartache, because that's what you did you know. You hurt every single person who loved you. I lay awake with your mother every night wondering if this would be the night when we got the knock at the front door telling us you were dead. Do you know how that feels? Waiting, scared to death that we were going to have to bury you."

Elsie looked at the floor, the shame and regret for the choices she'd made in life came flooding back. "Dad, I was in a bad place back then. I know I hurt the people who cared about me most, but I was an addict, someone who I am not proud of being."

Her father cringed and you could see the pain in his expression as he took himself back to the time when his daughter was a junkie. "You got lost and there was nothing any of us could do to bring you back. It was like I was shouting you and you never heard us. Oh, I've done some serious soul searching, as has your mother. We blamed ourselves. We thought it was us who'd let you down, but as time went on Elsie, we could see we weren't the ones who let you down, you were the one in control of your own decisions. Nobody but you. You had a happy home life; a loving caring family and we gave you everything you wanted. Granted, money was short sometimes, but there was always food on the table and you had clean clothes on your back. It was a lot more than some families had. I tried my best."

What could she say to this? Was it true? Was she going admit she was the one at fault? After a few minutes she sucked hard on her bottom lip. "You're right dad, you were a great father and both of you worked hard to give us the life we had. I was young and foolish but all that's changed. I've not had drugs for ages and I'm not that person anymore. Tony has kicked it in to touch too."

Just the mention of Tony's name made her father

squirm in his seat. "I've come to see it for my own two eyes. Your mother is sceptical, but I wanted to come and see you and give you another chance."

Elsie burst out crying and ran to her father's side. She was heartbroken. "Dad, I'll never let you down again. On my life, you will see how much I've changed and you'll be proud of me. Thank you so much for giving me a chance."

She wasn't out of the woods yet, he still had his barrier up, he just patted the top of her shoulder. "Where are the kids? I've missed them so much. When you took them both a part of me died. I was lost without them; you'll never know how much heartache not seeing my grandchildren caused me. They're adults now and I've missed so much of their lives thanks to you."

Elsie panicked, bloody hell, if she told him the truth about what was happening, he would never believe that she'd changed. Emily was in danger and he'd judge her as a mother and find a reason why it was her fault. Maybe, Emily would be okay and this ordeal would be over soon. But what if Tony got arrested for battering Emily's man? What if Jordan was locked up too? Her head was in bits. Should she tell him the truth or cover it up? Elsie lied; she was taking no chances. "Emily is at her friends and Jordan is out with the lads. I will tell them you've been and they will be over the moon, they still talk about you and my mam and they're always singing your praises regarding the way they were brought up by you."

Her father smiled, a warm red glow filling his cheeks. "They were good kids, no trouble whatsoever.

We were as proud as punch when we used to take them out. As good as gold they were."

Elsie was agitated, Emily was still lying heavily on her mind. There was no way she could sit here for hours with her old man pretending nothing was wrong. "Dad, I have to pop out, but what if I call around to see you both tomorrow with the kids?"

He stood up and knew he'd outstayed his welcome. He stared at his girl and the corners of his mouth started to rise. "Our family will be complete again. Happiness, that's all I want before I go to my grave - happiness."

Elsie was on the verge of crying again. His words went straight to her heart and meant the world to her. She'd dreamed of this day, wished for it for years and now it was here. Her happy ending, her family back in her life again. Elsie watched him leave and pecked him on his cheek. "Thanks, dad," she whispered after him. It looked like Elsie was in shock when she came back into the room. Her steps were slow and she looked a bit unsteady on her feet. Her cheeks were bright red like she was having some kind of hot flush. She plonked down on the sofa and wafted a piece of paper in front of her face. The gentle breeze from the open window cooled her down. Elsie looked at the clock again and sighed. "Fuck this, I can't sit here any longer," she mumbled to herself. She grabbed her coat from the back of her chair and stormed out.

CHAPTER TWENTY-SEVEN

Tina walked along the hallway in her new home. She'd landed on her feet alright. She'd never seen anything like this house in her life. She smiled as she slowly walked along, smelling the fragrance of furniture polish and floral scents - this was nothing like her own gaff which always smelt of damp and stale cigs. There were two double doors in front of her, she'd never been in this part of the house before. She twisted the brass knob on the door and dipped her head inside. It was dimly lit and there was an eerie silence. Her high heels clipped along the marble floor. She was the lady of the manor now and held her head high. She felt like royalty, a woman of substance. Tina stopped; she could hear whimpering. She tried opening the door where the noise was coming from but it was locked. Tina tapped on the door with the end of her knuckles. "Hello," she whispered. She held her ear to the door but there was no reply. She was puzzled. She carried on walking and noticed that another four doors were locked shut too. There was something fishy going on here. Why was someone crying behind the door? She turned on the spot and went back through the double doors.

Spotting Lizzy she asked her, "Hiya love I've met you briefly before. I'm Tina and I'll be running things in here from now on. I'm trying to get in the room through the double doors do you have a key?"

Lizzy was spaced out, she'd been working all night. "I think one of the lads has them. Mark usually takes care of things down there. I don't go down there unless someone's with me."

"So what's behind the doors. I heard someone crying."

Lizzy was in no mood to socialize, she started to walk away. "Like I said, speak with Mark. He'll answer any questions you have."

Tina could have punched this cocky bitch right in the mouth, she had attitude, and lots of it. Maybe she should put her in her place now and show her who was boss. She shouted her back and stood with her hands firmly placed on her hips. "Oi, cocky face. I only asked you a question, so lose the attitude."

Lizzy had no respect for no anyone anymore and this woman could take a running jump if she thought she was jumping through hoops for her. She rolled her eyes and grinned. "I don't have an attitude, I just told you to go and see Mark."

Oh, she was pushing her buttons now, Tina had steam coming out of her ears. "It's the way you said it darling, may I suggest you talk to me in the correct manner." Tina was speaking like a school teacher, posh and sounding all her words properly. Lizzy huffed and wiggled off without a care in the world. It was way past her bedtime and she was dead on her feet. Tina stood debating whether or not to run after her but how would that look on her first night? No, she stayed calm and went to look for someone who could answer her question.

★

Jordan tried to trace his father's footsteps. He could see where he had entered the house but there was someone there now and they were boarding up the window.

"Fuck, fuck, fuck," he whispered under his breath. Tony must have been sussed. Otherwise, where was he? He had to think on his feet, time wasn't on his side. Jordan made his way to the gate and pressed the intercom. He could hear a foreign voice cackling on the line. "It's Jordan, I've come to see Lizzy." He cringed waiting for a reply. After a few seconds he was buzzed in. His heart was in his mouth, his palms were clammy and small beads of sweat were starting to form on his forehead. When he reached the front door, a large man was waiting for him. "Alright pal, I work for Jimmy and drive the girls about. Can I speak with Lizzy, there's been a problem at one of the client's houses and I need to make sure she's alright?"

The man shouted another man and now the two of them were stood blocking the front door weighing him up. He repeated himself and this time he made sure he was going inside. "I fancy an hour with Lizzy too, she's a filthy cow and it's just what I need after the day I've had."

With that he was in, his plan had worked. Jordan's eyes were all over the place. He made small talk with the men and he was led to a room not far from where he was stood. "I'll go and get her, she's a feisty one - are you sure you don't want one of the other girls?"

"I like my women rough and ready and she ticks

all the boxes," Jordan sniggered "she'll do." They were gone and Jordan sighed with relief. This could all go pear-shaped at any moment and he wasn't sure what his next move would be. He paced the floor, looking one way then the other. It seemed like forever before Lizzy came to the room. She pulled a sour face as soon as she saw him. "What the fuck are you doing here, I was in bed?"

Jordan made sure the door was shut and kept his voice low. "I need your help Lizzy, shit's happened and they've got my sister Emily here."

Rubbing her eyes it took a while for the penny to drop. She went white and started ragging her fingers through her hair. "I've seen her; I've been with her. How can she be your sister? It's Mark who brought her here."

"Can you take me to her? My dad is in here somewhere too."

Lizzy froze, she had to think about this. She was putting herself in great danger. She changed her mind. "I don't want any part of this. Do you know what will happen to me if they know I'm helping you?"

"What? Are you going to let my sister go through what you've been through? Come on Lizzy, have a fucking heart, she's still a kid."

Lizzy was in a panic and wanted no part of it, she began to edge towards the door. "I'm going, check the door at the end of the corridor but keep my name out of this. I value my life. I'm sorry, but just leave me out of this."

Lizzy disappeared and Jordan was in two minds to run after her and give her a good slap. How selfish was she? And, here he was thinking of helping her. She could get to fuck now; she could sort her own shit out. Jordan stood behind the door; he could hear a woman's voice nearby. He poked his head from the doorway and squeezed his eyes together to try and see properly. He spotted Tina. Fuck me what was going on here? This was some fucked up shit. His head went into overtime; his mind was racing. Was it her who'd got his sister involved in this shit? Why was she here? He waited until she passed the doorway. He had one thing on his mind now and that was to find his father and his sister.

★

Emily struggled to stand up from the bed. Her head was spinning and she started to be sick. This girl had cried so many tears over the last few days and all she wanted was her parents, her family, somebody to stop this nightmare. The door creaked open and she wasn't sure if she was imagining things. Jordan ran over to her and cradled her in his arms. "I'm here, sshh, I'm here now. I'm taking you home." Emily was still drugged up and nothing seemed to be registering. Jordan saw the bruises on her body and squirmed. This was bad, very bad indeed. This was a police matter and he wanted to make sure these sick twisted bastards paid for everything they'd done to his sister. He helped her to walk but all that was on his mind was to get her out of this place without her being hurt any more than she was already. The front door wasn't far from where he was and his only hope was to walk out with his sister and pretend it was Lizzy. He grabbed a coat from the edge of the bed and placed it over Emily, pulling the hood up so no one could see her. He had to keep his cool, never flinch and act normal. He could hear music, laughing and shouting from another room. Using all his strength he yanked his sister up at the side of him and tumbled down the corridor. Nobody was about, he was home and dry. "Oi, where are you going?" a deep voice shouted behind him. His arse fell out and his bottom jaw started shaking. He was so close to freedom he could smell it.

"I'm just taking Lizzy on a job pal, she's pissed up but a bit of fresh air will sort her out. It's a regular client so she'll be fine." Jordan waited and made no eye contact.

The man started to snigger and buzzed the door open. This was working, his plan was actually working. He just needed to get out of the gate and he was home free. The walk down the garden path seemed like it would never end. Just as he got to the gates the door started to open. His eyes welled up and he squeezed Emily's hand in his. "You're safe, Emily, it's over." Jordan couldn't breathe when he got to the car. He ragged the door open with shaking hands and dipped his head inside. Where was Jane and the dog? Where the fuck was the dog? This was getting worse by the minute. He had to keep his sister safe and go back for his father, he couldn't leave him there, he needed to find him. Emily was still out of it. He laid her down on the back seat and covered her body with a coat. Jordan ran back to the driver's side and started the engine. He needed to park up somewhere safe, a place nobody would find them. The engine roared as he sped off. There was no time to waste.

After he'd parked the car he ran back to the house. He was huffing and puffing as his feet pounded the pavement. Jordan knew this time that he would have to do things differently. He needed to find a way back inside the house, his dad was still in there. His feet crunched over the branches and the trees were hanging low blocking his vision. The silver moon was bright and gave off just enough light so he could see. It was only now that he could feel the fear pumping inside his veins. The vein at the side of his neck seemed like it had a heartbeat, his adrenalin overflowing. He sprinted to the side of the house. A window was open nearby and a light was on inside the room. This was his only way in. He gripped the window as he hoisted himself inside. This was not looking good, a woman's voice started to scream and she ran at him with what looked like a candlestick in her hands. "You thieving fucker," she yelled. Jordan was wrestling with her, throwing her one way then the other. He would never beat a woman, but this bitch was like a bloke. Her grip was strong and she was holding her own. He gripped her face and he could see her now for the first time.

"Tina," he yelled, "It's me Jordan, you fucking idiot, get off me."

Tina broke free and ran to switch the light on. Her jaw dropped. "What are you doing here?"

He moved about just in case she launched something at him. "Our Emily has been here, they kidnapped her and made her do stuff. Jane was with her too, but she got away. These pricks are groomers. They take young girls from the street and drug them so men can have sex with them."

He tried to tell her as much as he could in the time he had. Tina staggered and looked like she was going to pass out. She pointed at the key in the door as she tried to get her words out. "Lock it, close the door." Tina collapsed onto the small chair near the side of the door, she looked bewildered.

Jordan stood behind the door and spoke in a low voice. "These cunts have ruined our Emily; how will she ever get over this? My dad is in here somewhere too. He came in first to try and find her, but fuck knows what's happened to him. I need to find him because he must be in here somewhere."

Tina was flabbergasted, how could this be? Alex was a gentleman, a kind caring guy. She needed to hear it again to make sure she wasn't hearing things. "Are you sure? Alex said he has a few girls working here for him and he wanted me to run them, he never mentioned anything about girls from the street."

Jordan pumped with rage. "As far as I know, Emily met a guy called Mark on Facebook, she got chatting to him and ended up meeting him. Jane went with her too and met a guy called Omar. Jane told me she was drugged too and once they were out of it these dirty twats brought men in to have sex with them." For fuck's sake how many times did he have to tell her what was happening. He didn't have the time for this.

Tina was gagging into her hands, her cheeks were bright red. She looked directly into his eyes and pleaded with him. "I knew nothing about this. I swear on my son's life. I met Alex on a night out and I've been dating him for weeks. He's not into grooming and having sex with young girls."

"He's in with Jimmy The Chop, Tina. I've been driving these girls about and dropping them at punter's houses. I owed a bit of money and to cut a long story short I had to work it off."

Tina bolted up from her seat. "Where is Emily now? Don't tell me she's still here?"

Jordan had to quieten her down, she was loud and somebody could have heard her. "I've just blagged it in here and got Emily out, but my dad is in here. I need to find him and once I've got him, I'm going to phone the police on these sick twisted bastards. There is no way they are getting away with this."

Tina was already getting her clothes on. She knew in her heart the story was true and she wanted out of here. The sooner the better. "I'm coming with you. I want no part of this. I thought it was too good to be true. I should have gone with my gut feeling. It's never let me down before. How could I have been fooled like that?" In a flash Tina was ready. "You stay here and I'll have a wander around and see what I can see. There is no point in you coming out yet until I know where your dad is. I'll be straight back."

Tina was gone and he was alone. His heart was racing and he couldn't keep still. He listened carefully and he was sure he could hear a dog barking. Shouting, screaming, a dog barking again. "No, sack this," he mumbled under his breath. He needed to find his dad. He couldn't sit here any longer biting his fingernails. Jordan swung the door open nearly taking it from its hinges. He ran towards the disturbance. His body froze, his dad was there with Jane and Frank was stood in front of them ready to attack.

"Come on you dirty cunts," Tony screamed, as he swung a machete about in the air. "I'm not going nowhere until everyone of you is on your arses."

Jane was stood with her back against the wall and she'd finally found her voice. "All of you will rot in jail. We were innocent girls, untouched and you've ruined that. Scum bags you are. Tony, waste them, make them suffer."

The odds were against them and Jordan stormed towards his dad and stood by his side. He yanked a silver pistol from his pocket and pointed it at Alex and his boys. Shit had just got real. "Come on then, let's have it," Jordan ranted. Alex stood tall and Mark came to his side. None of them showed any fear, they stood tall and looked at their opponents nodding their heads. Tony had never been one for thinking about things first. He was ready for war. Mark was eyeballing Jordan and any second now something was going to happen. Alex sneered over at Tony. "And, do you think you are going to walk out of here alive?"

Tony was bouncing about on the spot. His cage had been well and truly rattled. He'd had enough of this bullshit and he wanted revenge for his daughter, his girl. Without thinking he raised the silver blade over his head and stormed into the men. "Come on you fuckers," he screamed at the top of his voice. This was a blood bath already and Jordan made a beeline straight for Mark while Jane stood holding Frank by his collar. He was barking and jumping about as Tony screeched over at her. "Let him go." The red nosed pit bull jumped into the air. He was a foot soldier now. He knew this was war and he savaged a man's arm who was trying to grip him. Tony was struggling and Alex seemed to be getting the better of him as Frank lunged and bit into his leg. Blood splurged from Alex's leg and he was howling in pain. Tony saw his chance and took him down, booting him and punching him until he curled up in a small ball on the floor. Jordan was going blow for blow with Mark, but it was time to end it, time for the gun to come into play. His hand squeezed the trigger as Mark tried to grab the pistol from his hand. It was pointing one way then another; a loud bang, smoke and a body folded in two came smashing to the ground.

Tina ran into the room now and yelled at the top of her voice. "Stop it, for crying out loud, stop it." She was hysterical and ran to cover Jane as the men scuffled. Frank howled and fell to the floor; he was bleeding from a large gash in the side of his stomach and blood was pumping from it. The poor mutt limped to the corner of the room and fell to the floor, his tongue flopped to the side of his mouth and his breathing was shallow. Upstairs, the front door burst open and police rushed the place. It all happened so fast, handcuffs were put on everybody and bodies were dragged about.

Jane collapsed to the floor. She was shaking from head to toe. "It's them, arrest them," she howled. Tony was on his knees covered in claret. Jordan stood tall and his nostrils flared as he watched Alex's men being dragged out one by one.

Tina spoke to the female officer in a desperate voice. "I made the call, go down the corridor, that's where the girls are. I will give a full statement. These people here are innocent and had no part of the gang."

They uncuffed Tony and Jordan but told them to stay put. Tony asked if he could go into the next room and get his coat as he was starting to shiver and the officer let him.

Now the WPC was on her radio asking for more assistance. The nightmare was finally over. When he came back Tony paused, his heart was in his mouth and from the corner of his eye he could see Frank. He let out a scream from the pit of his stomach and raced to his four-legged friend. "Frank, come on mate, don't you be dying now, come on mate." This was such an endearing moment and it seemed like everyone in the room stopped and watched this scene. "Somebody help him, get somebody quick. He needs help, help him please." A police officer came to assist and radioed for a vet, but it didn't look good. The dog was struggling for breath and his eyes were closing. Maybe it was time for Tony to say goodbye, to tell the animal how much he loved him. It looked like Frank was taking his final breath.

CHAPTER TWENTY-EIGHT

Emily lay in her bed. The duvet was tucked tightly under her chin and she was staring into space. She didn't look good, there were dark circles under her eyes. Her body was thin and scrawny. A tear rolled down her cheek landing on her top lip. The sun was trying to burst into her bedroom, but it was blocked out by the dark brown curtains and only a small yellow ray of sunshine seeped into the room. The door opened with a slight squeak and Elsie stood hovering at the doorway. Ever since her daughter had been brought home safely, she was heartbroken and unable to talk about the ordeal. She blamed herself, hated that she'd let it happen. If she would have been more on the ball and put her own shit on the back-burner this would have never happened.

The aftermath had been horrific. Mark had was recovering from gunshot wounds and Alex from several stabs wounds, but they were now due to face trial. Tony and Jordan had been questioned by the police and after an investigation they were released with no further action. The pair of them were still recovering from very bad injuries and the doctors had told Tony that, in time, he may need an operation to fix his leg but he was now on a higher payment from the Benefit Agency, so every cloud had a silver lining...

Elsie's voice was low; you could barely hear her. "Are you awake love?"

Emily raised her head slightly from the pillow and

made eye contact with her mother. Elsie edged into the room and sat on the side of the bed. There was a silence while Elsie was thinking about what she would say. How could she even put this into words, she didn't have a clue. Should she just hug her, cradle her in her arms and tell her everything would be alright? But, that would have been a lie. You didn't need to be a rocket scientist here to know nothing would ever be the same again in this young girl's life. Elsie touched the top of Emily's shoulder softly. "How are you feeling? Do you fancy a piece of toast? You've not eaten anything for days."

Emily rolled on her side and faced the wall. "No thanks, I'm not hungry."

"You have to eat something love; you'll make yourself ill if you don't eat."

"If I'm not hungry then you can't force me to eat. Just leave me alone."

Elsie choked, her emotions were bubbling in her throat. Should she just walk away and leave her for a bit? She may have needed some time to get her head around things. She raised her voice. "No love, I won't leave you alone. This is why all this has happened, because I left you alone. I'll never forgive myself for this. Go on, say it, you blame me. I deserve it, punch me, whack me, just don't push me away."

Emily twisted her body so she could see her mother. "It's my own fault mum, not yours. I just got caught up with Mark and thought that he loved me. He's not the man I thought he was, how could he let them do that that to me? He said I was special, his princess."

Elsie was in tears again. "He's a bastard love, a dirty no good bastard who will go to jail for his crime. The lot of them will. When those men stand in the dock, I will make sure everyone there knows what evil sick cunts they are."

Emily squeezed her mother's hand. "I'm scared mam. Everyone will know what's happened to me. I feel dirty inside. Will that feeling ever go away?"

"Of course it will love, we are going to get you all the help and support you need. You and Jane are going to be fine. It's not your fault. You're young and your only crime was trusting somebody you thought was genuine."

"I loved Mark, and part of me still does. Is it wrong to feel like that? Am I ill? Messed up in the head? He let me get hurt but he said he cared about me. If he cared about me how could he let those men do what they did to me? You don't treat someone you love like that, do you?"

Elsie was snapping, temper boiling up high in her throat. "That's what these kinds of people do, love. It's all part of the plan to get girls to trust them. You weren't to know. It's a dangerous world out there and I should have prepared you for it. Maybe, I should have had more talks about what was on the news because there are always stories about young girls being groomed on the internet. I should have made you aware of it."

Emily was sobbing, the hurt was deep in her heart and there was anger too, rage burning inside her for being such a fool. "I want to see Mark mam. I want to look him in the eye and ask him why? I want to ask did he really love me or was it all just part of a game?"

The poor girl, she was so mixed up and her head was all over the place. In her own mind she thought this man would have been her husband in time. He'd got inside her head so much that and had let her down like she'd never been let down before. She would struggle to find love again, the wall around her heart was growing bigger by the day. She would make sure no man would ever fool her again - love was nothing but a distant memory now. She would never trust another man for as long as she lived.

Tony was lying on the sofa talking to Jordan. "This court case can't come quick enough for me, son. I won't rest until them twats are behind bars. I feel sick to the pit of my stomach every time I think about it."

"It's some fucked up shit, dad. I just hope Emily can cope with all the trauma when she has to give evidence. Jane's head is in bits too. Her mam has had her at the doctors and she's on tablets to help her sleep. Fucking hell, she's only a kid, she shouldn't be going through stuff like this, none of them should."

"Well, our Emily is not going down that road, pill popping is not going to solve anything. That's how I started out because when my old man was kicking fuck out of me, I needed something to help calm me down. The doctor wasn't arsed about how long I was on them either. My mam just handed them out like fucking Smarties, anything to keep me quiet." Tony hated talking about his childhood but every now and then he poured his heart out and told his family a little bit more about his early years. "I was hooked on sleepers by the time I was seventeen. Bad that. Isn't it? The doctor stopped giving them to me, so I started to search for other stuff to sort my head out. It's a vicious circle you know, and one thing leads to another. Anything to just feel calm."

Jordan cracked his knuckles. "Did you ever have it out with your dad when you got older because if you were bullying me, as soon as I was big enough, I'd have put you on your arse." Jordan watched his father while Tony was fidgeting about. You could tell he wasn't happy talking about his past.

"Just let's say he got what was coming to him. I fucked him off out of my life a long time ago and to tell you the truth I've never thought about the old cunt or even missed him. He was no dad, no role model, so why did I need him in my life? Change the subject now son, it's making my blood boil!" Jordan wisely kept quiet.

Elsie come back into the room and she was white. "Tony, I'm worried about her, she can't just lie in bed every day. We need some help for her, counselling, therapy, something."

Tony was hurt deep in his heart and it was visible all over his face. He'd felt pain before but nothing as gruelling as this. He had no control over this, his baby was hurting and there was nothing he could do to take the pain away. "I thought Jane was coming over. Maybe, when they sit down and talk things through things will be a bit better."

"Emily wants fuck all to do with Jane she said. At the end of the day she left her up there with them guys, didn't she? What kind of mate sells her best friend out when something like that was going on? To tell you the truth I can't even look at her without wanting to punch her lights out. I mean, why didn't she let us know what was going on? Is she a fucking retard or something?"

Tony nodded, he had to agree. "Just let's play it by ear for now. She will calm down and see sense when they start talking. Anyway, once this court case is over I've got something up my sleeve that will cheer her up. I made her a promise and I'm sticking to it."

Jordan huffed and shook his head. "Dad, stop chatting shit, don't promise things you can't deliver. She's had enough let downs without you adding to them. For once in your life just tell the fucking truth. I'm sick of hearing your lies if I'm being honest."

Tony was up in arms now, why did nobody ever believe a word he said. "Watch this space my laddo. That's all I'm saying. You'll eat your words when I show you." Tony was still bruised and his eyes were a purple and yellow rainbow of colour. He was lucky to be still breathing. He'd been to hospital and walked away with ten stitches in the side of his head and lots of aches and pains. His worst injury was in his leg. A large gash was still visible where a blade had dug deep into the muscle. Jordan was lucky too, he only had minor injuries, a few cuts and bruises but there was someone who was still injured that everyone in the household was giving extra love and affection to. Frank was a warrior for sure and after a visit to the vets he was set for a remarkable recovery.

"Frank, come on son, come over here and get on the sofa." This was a privilege for the animal and usually he only got a prime seat in the house if nobody was about. Frank limped towards his owner like a soldier returning from war, his eyes were blood-shot and you could see his back legs were still in pain. Fortunately, the gash on his tummy had missed his vital organs but he'd had to have twenty stitches and was wearing one of those lampshades round his neck to stop him from picking at the wound.

Tony patted the space next to him and urged Frank to jump up. The poor animal was struggling, he didn't have much energy and he was in too much pain to make it. Tony reached down and scooped him in his arms. Once he was next to him, Tony spoke into Frank's ear. "You done good lad. You protected us and probably saved us from a good arse-kicking. From now on I'll take you out more and every time I get my jobseekers allowance you can get a nice bit of steak for your tea. You'd like that wouldn't you?"

Frank looked at Tony and probably thought the same as the rest of his family when he was promising stuff. If the dog could have talked, he would have told him to stop chatting shit. Frank knew more than anyone that the promise of steak was just another of Tony's lies.

★

Jane popped round later that week. She went straight to Emily's bedroom but paused as she was about to go in. She was frozen staring at the wooden door. Finally, with the palm of her hand she pushed the door open. Emily was awake and spotted her straight away. "What do you want? I suppose you're here to tell me that you were right? Well, save your breath because I already know, so there."

Jane was in no mood for drama, she wanted a friendly ear, someone to talk to. Her spirits were low and this usually confident girl was in bits. "Emily, I've not come here to argue. We have both been through some horrendous shit and I need you by my side so we can both get through this together."

Emily sat up in bed and growled at Jane. "You left me. If you knew what was happening, why didn't you come back for me. I would never have left you knowing what was going on. You're just a selfish cow, like you've always been."

Jane moved across the bedroom towards Emily. "It wasn't like that. I would never have left you if I'd have known what was really happening. Those men drugged us, had sex with us. Not just you, me too. So you're not the only one who's going through shit here, it's me too."

Emily was rattled and anger filled her veins, rage pumping through her blood. "Oh, how did I know it would be about you. I loved Mark, I mean really, really, loved him with every bone in my body. You were just after a free ride with Omar, you weren't in love like I was."

Jane wasn't standing for this, she needed to fight her corner. "Mark was coming onto me too. I never told you because I knew how much it would hurt you, but yes, he wanted to meet me when I was away from you."

Emily ran at Jane and plunged her nails deep into her eyes. "You're lying, you evil bitch, why would you say something like that?"

Jane was holding her own and she was getting the

better of Emily who was still weak, "because, it's true, you daft cow. You thought he loved you when he didn't give a shit about you. I took photos of him kissing another woman in the car-park when you were in the pub, but I never sent them you because you would have dismissed it anyway. He's fucking brainwashed you. He never loved you."

Elsie and Tony came flying into the bedroom and pulled the girls apart. "Whoa, turn it in, you mental cases. You two are supposed to be friends. What are you fighting for?" Tony shouted.

Emily was gagging for breath and collapsed onto the floor as Jane straightened her hair. "I've told her the truth Tony; she can't handle it."

Emily was trembling from head to toe. And there it was, the truth had hit her in the face and knocked her for six. She lifted her eyes and they welled up with floods of tears. Emily broke down crying. "I know; don't you think I know he never loved me."

Jane wriggled free and went to her friend's side and hugged her. "Don't cry, I'm sorry, I'm sorry for leaving you. I was scared, shitting myself in fact. But I come back for you. Ask your dad, I was terrified but still came and showed them where the house was."

Tony nodded, "She did love, she was petrified and she still came with us. That's a true friend, that is."

Elsie shot a look at Jane. She wasn't letting her off so lightly and still held a grudge, you could see it in her eyes. Emily let out a scream from the pit of her stomach like a wounded animal. There was so much pain leaving her body. Elsie ran to her side and pushed Jane out of the way, she put her arms around her daughter and rocked her gently. "You get it all out, go on girl, let it go and cry."

This was all too much for Tony. How could he stand there and watch his own baby suffer like this? He needed to get out of here before he lost the plot. He booted the door open and smashed his clenched fist into the wall. "God help me; I'll rip their fucking heads off when I get my hands on them." Tony ran out of the house before he hyperventilated. He was in no mood for anybody today and God help anyone who crossed him. He was on the war path and somebody was getting hurt today without a shadow of doubt.

Tony scurried through the estate. He didn't seem to know where he was going, he walked one way, then another. Finding a brick wall, he plonked down on it and cried his eyes out. The heavens opened as he lifted his head towards the sky. "Please, take this pain away. God, if you let her be alright, I'll never do wrong again. Do what you want to me, but please help my girl. She's innocent and doesn't deserve this." Tony's heart was breaking. This was a father's worst nightmare.

Tony had been sat on the brick wall for over half an hour. He was soaking wet and shivering. Looking around the estate he seemed to be going back over his life and the choices that he'd made. From the corner of his eye he spotted someone, and he gritted his teeth tightly together. Without a second thought Tony sprinted towards Mickey and ragged him all over the show. "You fucking Judas, you set me up, you double crossing twat." In seconds Mickey was on the floor curled up in a tiny ball. Tony was dealing with this traitor alright, he was kicking and punching him like there was no tomorrow. If a passer-by hadn't stopped him, he would have finished him off. Mickey was on the floor and barely moving. As Tony stood back, he screamed at his mate. "I thought you had my back, you scumbag. Don't you ever darken my door again. Every time I see you, you should expect a good hiding. You may as well move from around here because I'll let everyone know what you did. You're a snitch, a rat, a grass, a fucking German." This was bad news for Mickey, a few of the younger kids from the estate had heard what he'd just said and they were eyeballing the grass now. Tony started to walk away. His job was done here. He knew now that the word was out and Mickey wouldn't last long on the estate, he was a marked man.

A grass.

CHAPTER TWENTY-NINE

Tina stood in the kitchen and gawped out of the window as the kettle boiled on the kitchen side. The steam was rising from the spout but she just twisted her head and looked at it. Elsie looked over at her and brought her back to planet earth. "Make a brew then instead of just watching the kettle boil." Tina was still dressed in her pyjamas. There were dark circles under her eyes and she looked like she'd not slept properly. Tina grabbed two cups from the side and placed a spoonful of coffee in each of them. "Tina, I have two sugars, bleeding hell, get with it will you."

Tina tried to snap out of. "I can't think straight anymore. I'm on some tablets from the doctors and they just freak me out. It's like I'm here but I'm not, if you know what I mean?"

Elsie went over to finish off making the cuppa. "Go on, sit down over there. I'll make us the coffee. I'll wait all bleeding day if I wait for you."

Tina stumbled to the kitchen table and sat down. Her fingers ragged through her hair and you could see she was struggling today with her emotions. "I still can't believe it. He seemed such a nice man. I thought he was genuine. Everything about him was everything I was looking for. Why didn't I see it? I'm not usually daft and I can normally smell a rat a mile away. God knows I work in a brass house I know this kind of men inside out."

"They're tricky fuckers Tina. They get you where they want you then pull you in. They're professionals. The police said there were ten other girls there who they had working for them. Mark had pretended to love them but he just used every single one of them. I mean, how will they ever get over what he's done to them? Our Emily is trying her best to cope, but I can see it in her eyes that she will never get over what them cunts did to her. The police said one of the girls called Lizzy has given evidence against Mark that will put him behind bars for a very long time. Personally, I would hang the lot of them. Prison is too good for them, they should string them up, every single one of them."

"The police have had me down the station too. They wanted me to go over every detail. Do you know Alex is married and his wife lives in Cheshire? He'd set this up years ago with Jimmy The Chop and every time he was away from home his wife thought he was away on business. What a lying bastard. I feel for his wife. Imagine finding out that your husband is part of the sex trade, picking up young girls and drugging them so they will have sex with men. I feel sick inside every time I think about it."

Elsie slid a hot drink over to her and sat down. "I'm dreading the trial. They've asked for Emily to give evidence by video link, but she said she wants to be there in the courtroom to say what she has to say to Mark. She wants to see him get sent down."

Tina was alarmed. "Do you think that's a good idea? She's still only a baby. If you can keep her out of that courtroom, then I think that would be for the best.

You don't want her seeing him again, do you? It will just upset her even more."

"Jane and Emily are adamant that they want to give their evidence in the dock, so I just have to go along with it."

Tina placed her hands around the hot mug. "I'll be taking the stand. I have no doubts about that. What they did was wrong and I want to make sure the lot of them rot in jail for it. The sooner it's over the better for me. I can't wait to put it all behind me and move on. I could have been homeless; I was giving everything up for Alex. I was leaving my home, this area, the lot."

"Lucky escape if you ask me," said Elsie. "I have to tell my dad what's happened. I told you he came to see me, but I never mentioned anything about what had gone on. He wants me to bring the kids around to see him, but I've just been putting it off. I'll have a word with Emily when I get home later. She'll be happy that he's been asking about her. She's missed my parents. Every night for months she cried her eyes out when she left there. It was a big void in her life. I feel so guilty about it all. I didn't see back then how much my kids would be affected by it all."

Tina nodded and took a small sip from her mug. "We all fuck up in life, love. The thing is, you must put it behind you and learn by it. Life is one big lesson and we are all learning each and every day."

Elsie shot a look over at her friend, this was one of the most sensible things she'd ever said to her since she'd known her. "I'm dreading seeing my mam. I can't see her being as forgiving as my dad. He said she's looking forward to seeing me but somehow, I don't believe him. I'll just have to front it and see how she is when we go there. We have years to make up for. I just hope she's not living in the past and wants a relationship with me."

Tina tapped her fingers on the table. "Of course she will. For fucks sake you're her daughter. Surely she's missed you. She wouldn't be human if she's not."

"I hope your right. Do you think I should take her some flowers and chocolates, a piece offering?"

"That would be nice. It would break the ice and show her you have changed."

★

Jordan sat with Lizzy in a local café. She'd been in touch with him and wanted to meet him. Jordan was facing her and waited for her to speak. After a few deep breaths she started. "I've told the police everything. I'm sorry I never helped your sister when I was there, but you must understand how terrified I was. I've been in this world for so long I feared ever leaving it."

He reached over and stroked her hand. "I understand. You did the right thing in the end and that's all that counts. Have you been back home to see your parents?"

She choked back the tears. "I've been in touch but I'm not ready to face them. It's been a long time and I just need space to sort myself out. I'm lost at the moment. I've been through a lot and it will take time for me to start get to grips with it. Your sister will be the same. You just need to be there for her, listen and support her." These were wise words from the heart. Lizzy ate some chips slowly, eating them one by one.

"Jordan," she said in a soft voice. "You tried to help me when I was at the house and I'll never forget that. You knew what I was doing and still you never judged me and wanted to help me. I'll never forget that for as long as I live. I ran it over my mind every day after you said it. Your words kept me going, helping me face another day."

"I cared about you Lizzy. You're beautiful and I just didn't want to watch you falling apart. You can still make something of yourself and put this behind you. I would like to see you again if you want?" Jordan was smitten with this girl. It was obvious by the way he looked at her.

"You can have any girl you want. Why do you want some mixed-up girl who has been through hell and back? I'm damaged goods."

He smiled and edged closer to her. "You're right, I can have any girl I want but I don't want anyone else. I think you'd be worth it in the end. Your past means nothing to me. I've made mistakes too, Jimmy The Chop is in jail now but I'm sure he won't forget the money I owe him. He'll have his boys booming my door in sooner or later. I'll build my empire back up now and when they do come calling, I'll be ready for them. I can earn good money doing what I know best. Drug dealing is not the best career, but it's all I know."

Lizzy was listening and her face was filled with a warm red glow, she was blushing. "How's Emily?"

Jordan looked at his coffee. "She's up and down to tell you the truth. She just keeps breaking down crying. Then there is the anger and deep rage breaking through her body every time she gets upset."

"I understand that. Maybe, I should talk to her, Mark groomed me too."

"That would be nice. I think she needs to talk to someone who's been through it. Her friend Jane is there around the clock, but it would be nice for them both to hear your story. I'll tell you something for nothing. I'll find out which jail Mark lands in and I'll make sure he gets a good beating every night he's there. I know people in the big house and they are just waiting on him arriving, he's a marked man. Trust me, he'll suffer every night he's there. Men like him are the scum of the earth and inmates are more than happy to fuck them up."

Lizzy shivered and the hairs on the back of her neck started to stand on end. "I just want to get the court date out of the way and try to piece my life back together. Maybe I can go to college and get some qualifications. I always wanted to be an artist, so that might be the path I take."

Jordan smiled. "I can see that; you can do it."

Lizzy swigged on her can of coke. She shot a look at the clock on the wall and picked her bag up. "Thank you so much for meeting me. And thanks for everything you've done for me. I'll never forget it, ever."

Jordan was in a panic. "Whoa, where are you going? You can't just leave like that. I want to see you again. Where are you going to stay anyway?"

She stood up and she was getting ready to move away from the table. "I have a friend who said I can get my head down there until I sort something out."

Jordan urged her to sit back down. "You can stay with me. I'll look after you."

Lizzy chuckled out loudly. "Do you have your own gaff?"

He stuttered. "No, I've had to move back to my mam's but we can stay there for a bit while we start looking for somewhere for both us. No pressure, just as flatmates if you want?" Lizzy sat back down and he looked relieved that he would spend more time with her. "I'll be straight with you. I don't have much to offer you at the moment, but I can promise you that I will take care of you and make sure nobody ever hurts you again."

Her eyes welled up, why was he being so nice to her? He didn't know her from Eve, yet here he was, willing to put his neck on the line for her, to make sure she was safe. She listened some more to him and agreed that she would stay with him for now. If she was being honest, she didn't really have somewhere to stay. She was making it up. The only mates she had were the girls who had been through Alex's house, so it was a blessing in disguise that she was away from them, because who knew what might happen.

★

Tony was in the front room pacing the living room floor. He kept patting his jacket pocket and walking around. Emily walked into the front room and sat next to her mother. "What the hell is up with you Tony? Have you shit yourself or something?"

He smiled and rubbed his hands together. "Where's Jordan? I need him to come in before I tell you my news."

Emily sneered at her mother. Oh my God, did this

man not get tired of telling lies? He'd done this so many times before, none of them believed a word he said. Elsie sighed and dragged her feet up under her bum cheeks on the sofa. "Tony, please, we are not in the mood for your make-believe world tonight. Can we just have a normal night without any drama?"

Tony was up in arms and spoke in a high-pitched voice. "You are so negative. For once, give me a break and shut up for a minute. When Jordan comes in all will be revealed and you can kiss my arse then when you know what I've got up my sleeve. Like I said, Tony Clayton is a man of his word."

Emily closed her eyes and tried to ignore him. She flicked the TV on and started to watch "Hollyoaks" it was one of her favourite TV shows. The front door banged shut and Jordan appeared at the living room door. They all looked at him as he opened the door and edged into the front room. Frank was barking and Tony had to quieten him down. "This is Lizzy, she's coming to stay with me for a while until we get something sorted out. Is that alright with everyone?"

Elsie sat up straight and started to pat her hair down. Her voice changed and she started to talk with a posh tone. Emily and Tony giggled as they listened to her. "Of course it is, come in darling and sit down on the sofa. You're more than welcome here. We don't have a lot, but what we do have, we can share."

Tony burst out laughing. "What the fuck is that voice all about? You never speak like that usually. Turn it in, you sound mental."

Jordan sniggered too, and invited Lizzy to sit down. Elsie snarled over at Tony. "I'm not putting any voice on. Wind your neck in and sit down you muppet."

Tony was still laughing; it was like he had a feather up his arse. Elsie was eager to talk to the new girl. Jordan had hardly ever brought anyone home in years so she must be special, someone he cared about. "So, how did you two meet? Have you known each other long?"

Tony couldn't help himself; he stopped her speaking again. "Fucking hell Columbo, leave the girl alone. She's only just stepped into the place and you're interrogating her. Let her breathe woman." "Will you be quiet. I was only asking a bleeding question."

Lizzy went bright red, what should she say, should she tell them her story, or keep schtum? Jordan jumped into the conversation and saved her bacon. "Lizzy was one of the girls from the house where Emily was. She's got nowhere to stay so I said we will look after her for now."

Elsie wasn't sure about this; she fidgeted about on the sofa and was getting ready to fire some more questions at her. Tony wouldn't stop her this time, nobody would. "You mean they groomed you too?"

Lizzy licked her lips and took time to reply. "Yes, it was Mark who got me involved. I was young and vulnerable, just the same as you Emily."

Emily was listening and her fists started to curl into two tight balls at the side of her legs. "Did he tell you that you were his princess too?"

In her heart Emily hoped he'd never said this to anyone else but as Lizzy answered, she cringed inside for allowing herself to be such a fool. "Yes, he told all the girls he loved them. Each new girl he brought to the house had a similar story to mine. We all thought he was Mr Right, the man who would look after us, but how wrong we all were."

Emily walked over to Lizzy and wrapped her arms around her, squeezing her. "We are the victims here. Don't blame yourself. He took advantage of us, groomed each and every one of us." Lizzy had no tears in her eyes, she'd learned a long time ago that tears would never help her. Emily moved away from her and sat back down on the sofa saying, "Jordan, why don't you make us all a drink?"

Lizzy started to relax; this wasn't a bad place to stay after all. Tony bolted up from his seat, hands up in the air. "Just hang fire. I need to tell you all something first." Elsie let out a laboured breath and plonked back in her chair as her husband began to speak. "Emily, do you remember when you asked me to take you on holiday?"

His daughter nodded, "Yes dad and it never happened."

"Hold your horses, I never said when it would happen, I just told you that I would make it happen, is that correct?"

Emily rolled her eyes. "Yes, it is."

"Well Tony Clayton is a man of his word and I never let anyone down when my reputation is at stake." He dug his hand deep into his jacket pocket and pulled out an envelope. He passed it to his daughter. Emily opened it slowly and started to read the documents. Her head came back up and she wasn't sure if what she had just read was right. She was lost for words and passed the letter over to her mother.

Elsie snatched the documents and started to read them. Every now and then she lifted her head up and looked at Tony. "I hope this isn't one of your daft jokes Tony?" Elsie moaned.

"No, it's bloody well not. We are off to Spain after this trial is over! We could all do with a break and there is nothing more I would like than to see than my daughter smiling again."

It looked like Tony had come up trumps, but where had the money come from? He didn't have a pot to piss in. Emily jumped up and swung around her father's neck. "Dad, this is the best gift you have ever given me. I've never been abroad before. Oh my God, I'm going on a plane for the first time ever."

Elsie was still waiting for the punch-line, come on, where was it? Tony rubbed his hands together and sat proud next to Elsie. "Well, I'm waiting" he said.

"Waiting for what?" she hissed.

"For you to say you're sorry. You said I was full of shit but not this time, nope, not this time. This family is going on holiday to Benidorm for two weeks, all inclusive, so come on, say it Elsie."

Tony was gleeful, it was a first for his wife to be totally speechless, she was in complete shock. Jordan went into the kitchen and flicked the switch for the kettle. He too was in shock. Where had the money come from? Tony came in behind him and his head was in the fridge searching for something to eat. Jordan coughed to clear his throat. "Oi, where did you get the money from? You must have had a decent graft to be able to afford a holiday?"

Tony smiled and walked closer to his son. He didn't

want anyone else hearing. "I got it out of the safe at the house where Emily was. When I went back to get my coat, I saw a safe was open slightly on the wall. I just acted on instinct and grabbed the fucking lot of it. I've not told anyone about it until now. The first thing I wanted to do was to book the holiday and make sure Emily was alright. I got about eight grand, so we have spending money and we can all go to town and buy some new clobber out of it. This holiday will do us all good. We have all been through a lot lately. Look at me, I'm off the shit. Yes, I've had a few times when I've fucked up but I'm getting there. I'm just taking each day as it comes."

Tony was the man of the hour, he could still hear the excitement from his daughter in the next room, she was still in shock. Elsie stood at the door smiling from ear to ear. "Well, credit where credit is due, you done good. I don't know how and I don't really care, but thank you, it's exactly what we all need. Come here you big daft bastard and give me a kiss."

She held her arms out and waited for her other half to come to where she was standing. She puckered up and planted lots of wet sloppy kisses all over his cheek. This was so nice to see; the family was happy for a change. Elsie patted her large stomach with a flat palm. "Fuck me, I better get on a diet, I can't go on holiday looking like this. I need a bikini body in two weeks. How on earth am I going to do that?"

Tony couldn't help himself, he loved winding his wife up. "You're more like a pair of shorts and t-shirts body love; don't you be starving yourself now. I love you just the way you are." She knew he was only jesting with her; she didn't take his comments to heart; it was water off a duck's back. Jordan winked at his father as he walked past him. His secret was safe and he'd never breathe a word of this to anyone. It was official, The Clayton family was set to go on holiday for the first time ever.

CHAPTER THIRTY

Today was the day the Clayton family had been looking forward to, it was day the men would be sentenced who had groomed Emily, Jane and Lizzy. The corridors of the Crown Court were packed and everyone seemed to be rushing about. The trial was coming to an end after a short hearing where the weight of evidence was so overwhelming that the jury had found the men guilty on all charges.

Emily was dressed in black trousers and a white shirt with her hair was tied back. She looked respectable and ready to hear what would become of her attackers. Emily watched as all the men came out and sat in the dock of the crown court. The men had security all around them. There were eight men in total including Jimmy The Chop, Alex, Omar, and Mark. All through the trial, Emily had sat with a stern expression looking over at Mark. She wasn't the one in the wrong here. When she gave her evidence in the stand, she'd broken down a few times crying and the judge had given her a few minutes to get herself together. Mark never flinched as she told the court how he met her on Facebook and arranged to meet her. In fact, all the way through the girls' evidence his expression remained the same. What a heartless bastard he was. Jane had lost the plot when she'd taken the stand. She screamed over at Omar and told him that she hoped he rotted in hell for his crime. He made no attempt to defend himself either, he just growled at her.

Mark had told the courts that Emily had lied to him about her age. This was true but she never admitted it. When Lizzy took the stand there wasn't a dry eye in the house. The extent of her ordeal was horrific. Jordan was always close by to support her when it got too much for her. Lizzy had the biggest story to tell. She had enough information to point the finger at the top dogs in all this. Jimmy The Chop and Alex were going down for a long time. Jimmy's wife was in the court room and when she heard the young girl's story she nearly collapsed. Her temper got the better of her and she stood up in the courtroom screaming at the top of her voice to her husband. "You will never see me or the children again. You're sick in the head. How could you do that to these innocent girls? I thought I knew you. Twenty years we've been married, and you have just thrown it all away. How could you do this, how could you do this to us?" Jimmy's wife was escorted out of court by the usher and a female friend. You could hear her crying even when she was outside. Jimmy just dropped his head and bit down on his bottom lip. In fairness, he was more of a silent partner. It was Alex and Mark who'd arranged all the punters and the parties, Jimmy just provided the muscle.

Jane was shaking from head to toe and her parents were by her side helping her to hold it together. Tina had been the strongest one through the trial and when she gave her evidence each of the criminals knew they would never be walking away from the courtroom. Mark was sat down in the dock and the guard held him down as he banged his clenched fist on the window that was holding him inside. "You bitch Emily. Did you think I could ever love anyone like you?" He pointed his finger at his victims. "You all deserved it. Desperate you are the fucking lot of you." The guard who was at his side pushed him back to his seat but you could see by his eyes that he wanted to kick the living daylights out of this man. Lizzy sat back and closed her eyes as the judge read out how many times she had been raped by her attackers, about how they drugged her and done things to her that were disgusting. How this girl had coped was a mystery, she'd been to hell and back.

Now it was time for the sentencing. The public gallery was full of people who wanted to see these men sent down. The journalists had their pens at the ready and they were eager to write the headlines for tonight's papers. The main court door opened, and Elsie went white as her mouth opened but no words came out. Her parents had come to court. It was inevitable they would have found out; it was all over the news, local radio and the journalist and the police were always hanging about the area. The judge adjourned for a half hour break. He needed some time in his chambers to make sure he got this right. There would be public outrage if he messed this up, so he needed just a bit more time to get his information together. Elsie stood and walked towards her parents, tears bubbling in her eyes. Tony was at her side and he took her hand in his as she met the eyes of her mother and father.

"How did you find out?" Elsie asked, her voice ready to break.

"I heard from one of my friends down the shops. Everyone was talking about it. Why didn't you let us know?"

Tony was the one doing the talking now and he addressed Elsie's father. "Emily wanted to keep it as low key as possible, the less people that found out about this the better. She has to live her life after this, so it was her decision not ours."

Elsie's dad had never had much time for Tony and he was ready to give him a piece of his mind, when his wife shut him up. "Elsie, we understand. This is horrendous and we want you to know that we are here for you and the kids. She's going to need as much love and support as she can get over these next few months and I hope we can all work together to get her through this."

Emily and Jordan came rushing to their grandparent's side. They paused for a few seconds before they flung their arms around them. "Nana, I've missed you so much. I've never forgotten about the time we spent together and all the lovely things you and grandad did for us. I'm so happy we can all be friends now."

Her nana was blubbering, tears flowed from her eyes like a waterfall.

Elsie started to heal the wounds. "We have all made mistakes and things have been said that cannot be taken back, but family is the most important thing in my life – mam and dad, thank you for giving me and Tony a chance. We will prove to you how much we have changed, and you will hopefully be proud of us."

Tony nodded and looked at his father in law. "I know we have never seen eye to eye and you were probably right about me. I've let my family down in the past, but I promise you now that I will be the perfect husband and father to this lot for as long as I live."

Emily snuggled deep into her nana's arms and you could see her inhaling the floral smell from her clothing. The aroma was comforting her, it took her to a place where she felt safe and protected. The family had so many years to catch up on, but for now they all walked from the courtroom together as one.

The men were brought into the dock at Manchester Crown Court. Each of them confirmed their name and date of birth. Elsie and her family were on the edge of their seats ready for the sentencing as Jordan put his arms round Lizzy. Mark stood tall; his cocky expression showed that he had no remorse for his crimes. He received ten years' imprisonment, along with Alex and Jimmy. The rest of the men got five years and eight years. Tony slammed his hand on the brass banister as the judge carried on with his sentencing. He had wanted each of them to get life and now he was screaming over at Mark as he was leaving the courtroom.

"You'll die in jail! I know people who will get to you. I know lots of people who'll make sure every day you spend behind bars is a nightmare. Wherever you land, they'll find you. Don't close your eyes at night because they will be there watching you, waiting for you."

Elsie tried to calm her husband down. Emily stood up and Mark turned his head one last time before he was escorted out of the courtroom. Their eyes met and she scowled at him. Justice was served here today and lessons were learned.

★

Tony held the passports in his hands. He was dressed in bright orange shorts and a white t-shirt. His sunglasses were on the top of his head and he was ready to board the plane. Elsie's parents were there too. They'd arranged to go with the family and try to make up for lost time. Lizzy held Jordan's hand as they started to board the plane. She whispered in a low voice into his ear. "You've saved me in more ways than you will ever know and I know you and me will be part of each other for years to come. I love you."

This was so nice, so endearing to watch. Loud screams were heard from behind them with heels clipping along the corridor as a woman wearing a large straw hat and a long flowing sundress ran along the tarmac. "Wait up will you. Don't you dare think you are leaving me behind." Tina hurried up to the group and sighed as she pulled her boarding pass from her handbag. "Where's the beer? When can we get a drink?" she sniggered.

The family were finally seated on the plane and Tony looked out of the small window to the side of him. For the first time ever he was proud of the mission he'd completed. Fair enough, the money never had come from a graft but still he'd kept his promise and booked the holiday for his family. He turned to his wife and kissed her on the cheek. "I'm a changed man now Elsie, as soon as we are home, I'm going on the straight and narrow. I'll get a job and look after us all like I should have done years ago."

Elsie took what he'd said with a pinch of salt, he'd

always be a bull-shitter in her eyes but for now she let him have his say. Tony stood up from his seat and looked at all the other passengers. It was party time and from the moment the plane took off from the runway he was going to enjoy every single moment of it. He started to sing at the top of his voice, urging the rest of the people there to do the same. "Oh we're off to sunny sunny Spain…" he sang as the rest of the plane joined in.

Emily was looking at her mobile phone. She logged onto Facebook and went to the settings. As she scrolled down, she looked over at Lizzy. "I don't need social media anymore. My life is here right in front of me." She deleted her account there and then and dropped her phone into her new bag. "I love you dad," she shouted over at Tony, "I love you all."

Tony sat back in his seat and closed his eyes. He was bricking it. Elsie reached over and patted his thigh. "You're nothing but a big softy, aren't you?"

Tony smirked and dropped his head onto her shoulder. "I think I've shit my pants love; I've never been so scared in all my life, but keep it on the low, I don't want the kids to know."

Elsie laughed out loud. Some things never changed.

THE END

OTHER NOVELS BY THE AUTHOR

Broken Youth
Black Tears
Northern Girls Love Gravy
Bagheads
Teabags & Tears
The Visitors
Sleepless in Manchester
Covering Up
Riding Solo
Pudding Club
Grow Wars
The Square
Team Handed
The Lane
Bang Up
Whisper My Last Goodbye
Torn
Sins
The Estate

Printed in Great Britain
by Amazon

43265645R00169